NOX WINTERS

And the Midnight Wolf

ALSO BY ROCHELLE HASSAN

The Prince of Nowhere

ROCHELLE HASSAN

NOX WINTERS

And the Midnight Wolf

HARPER

An Imprint of HarperCollinsPublishers

Library of Congress Control Number: 2023944727
ISBN 978-0-06-331457-3

Typography by Molly Fehr
24 25 26 27 28 LBC 5 4 3 2 1

First Edition

For anyone who ever stayed up past their bedtime
to read just one more chapter.

NOX WINTERS

And the Midnight Wolf

1

ON NOX'S FIRST NIGHT IN EVERGREEN, HIS
brother convinced him to jump out the window.

It had taken ten hours, thirty-seven minutes, and three trans-
fers by train and bus to get to middle-of-nowhere Maine, and
he felt a little like a tube of toothpaste that had been squeezed
until it was all crumpled. And like he needed a shower. He
gave his shirt a surreptitious sniff as he followed Noah up the
creaky stairs to the attic, only half listening to his impromptu,
rambling tour of the Day house.

"Here it is!" Noah said, flinging the door open. A pair of
twin beds and a nightstand had been crammed into the narrow room. On the ceiling, a single bare light bulb produced
an oily yellow glow. Opposite the beds was a window with the
blinds drawn up and an old-fashioned wardrobe. Its door hung
slightly ajar, a wrinkled shirtsleeve dangling out at the bottom,
where Noah had probably dumped his clothes in a pile instead
of hanging them. His sneakers had found their way to the corner and under the unmade bed, and he'd tacked up photos and
band posters on his side of the room.

Something in Nox curled unpleasantly, like a buried thing

squirming away from a sudden light. Noah had settled in and made the space his own, which shouldn't have come as any surprise. He'd been here on his own for the last few months. It wasn't like Nox had expected him to sit in an empty room the whole time. It was just that it made it all feel so . . . permanent.

"Hurry up and put your stuff down," Noah said, herding Nox inside and kicking the door shut. "I'm gonna show you something cool."

"Yeah? Like what?" Nox unzipped his suitcase, looked down in dismay at the tangled contents, which he hadn't bothered to fold, and thought longingly of that shower again.

Noah switched off the light.

Nox turned to him and was met with a familiar, devious grin. The two of them were identical twins, had even successfully switched places plenty of times—Nox taking math tests for Noah, Noah covering Nox's detentions—but that smile never looked quite right on Nox's face, no matter how many times he practiced it in the mirror.

"I kind of needed that," Nox said.

"Just trust me." Noah shoved the window open. With the lights off, the moon was bright enough to see by.

"You only say that when you've got a bad idea."

"Please," Noah said, swinging a leg up and perching on the windowsill. "You just had probably the most boring summer of your *life* without me. A bad idea is exactly what you need right now."

Nox grinned back reluctantly. Boredom was Noah's justification for everything: rule breaking, adventure seeking, all his bad ideas—and his best ones. Already, Noah was climbing outside and stepping onto something below the window frame, so that it looked like he was hovering in midair.

"Wait up," Nox said. He kicked the suitcase under the bed and followed him.

So he didn't take much convincing after all.

His feet found a ledge under the window, narrow but sturdy enough. He lowered himself out carefully. They put their backs to the wall and shuffled along the side of the house. The sun had set a couple of hours ago. Below, he could just make out where the edge of the cliff dove away from the house, the northern woods bumping up against the treacherous incline like a whispering sea. Nox had driven through miles of forest earlier, watching the sun travel across the sky through the filter of its canopy and outline star-shaped leaves and prickly pine needles in gold, but now there was only an expanse of cloudy, rustling shadow as far as the eye could see. Light spilled from a downstairs window, but the ground floor was dark. He pressed his palms flat against the wall, feeling the grain of the old wood and the cold seeping in through the back of his shirt.

It was quiet except for Noah's shoes scuffing the ledge next to his, and a hushed *"Here."*

The roof sloped down to meet them. If they went any farther, they'd have to duck under the eaves. Noah twisted around and hauled himself up, swinging a leg over for leverage. Nox did the same. It was a little tricky turning around on the ledge, but once he had a good grip, climbing up was a breeze. And then they were on the roof.

The night was glossy-clear, like a photo in a magazine spread. It felt like he could see each of the millions of stars individually, could've sunk his hand into the night sky and come away with celestial glitter in his fingerprints.

"Wow," he breathed. "You can see everything!"

He scrambled up the slope of the roof until he reached the peak, where its two sides met. Facing the front of the house, he picked out a pale ribbon snaking through the sky.

"Is that the Milky Way?" Noah asked, climbing up next to him.

"Yeah! And over there—" Nox faced the woods again. "That's Polaris. The North Star."

Noah squinted at it, unimpressed. "Isn't it supposed to be the brightest one?"

"Not really."

"So how can you tell which one it is?"

"By looking at the constellations." He traced a W shape in the northeastern sky. "That's Cassiopeia. If you've found Cassiopeia, you've found Polaris." His finger traveled in a line from Cassiopeia's W to the North Star.

In Greek mythology, Cassiopeia was a queen who offended Poseidon and almost got her daughter, Andromeda, eaten by a sea monster. She was the first constellation Mom had taught him about: one of the brightest in the sky, and visible year-round in the northern hemisphere.

A lot had changed over the last few months. But Cassiopeia, at least, was the same as she'd ever been.

Mimicking Nox, Noah traced a line in the sky from Cassiopeia to Polaris. His sleeve sagged a little bit, revealing the spots on his arm where his skin had turned gray, coarse, and bumpy.

Before, he'd only had a few blotches on the inside of his wrist; now the rash went all the way around, like a cuff. Nox grabbed his arm to get a closer look, but Noah pulled away.

"It's getting worse," Nox said, his chest tight with dread. Noah had more of those gray patches on his ankles and his shoulders; Nox wondered if those had spread, too.

"It got worse for a bit, but then it stopped," Noah said. "Aster thinks I've *plateaued*."

"Why didn't anyone tell me?" Nox said, hoping it sounded less accusatory than *Why didn't* you *tell me?* which was what he really meant.

"'Cause you'd have packed a bag and hitchhiked here, and Mom would've had a heart attack."

Noah fixed his sleeve, tugging it down over his knuckles. With his head bowed, Nox could see the raised white spots dotting the back of his neck. Sores, maybe. Those were new. Helpless anger bubbled up inside Nox. Being in Evergreen was supposed to make Noah better, and it hadn't. And this was their last shot, so if it didn't work, then—then Nox didn't know what.

Mom had sent Noah to live with Weston and Aster Day because they were two of the best oncologists in the country. Not that any of the doctors or specialists they talked to were sure an oncologist was what Noah needed. But Weston had assured Mom that he'd get Noah top-notch medical care. He was an old friend of Mom's, apparently, so it was kind of a favor to her.

Noah had left back in May, and Nox hadn't been allowed

to go with him. He and Noah had never been apart; even as babies they'd been born in quick succession, Nox first and Noah following barely a minute later. But despite months of begging, arguing, and shouting matches, Mom refused to let Nox join him in Evergreen.

Then, days into the fall semester, Nox had almost gotten expelled.

Getting pulled out of school and sent to another state should've been a punishment. For Nox, it was an unexpected stroke of luck. Since it took a few weeks for the school transfer paperwork to go through, he was getting a late start to seventh grade, but he didn't care about that. This school would be no different from any other, full of classes he wouldn't care about and people who wouldn't matter to him. Noah wouldn't be there, either, since he was taking his classes online until he recovered. But at least Nox wasn't hundreds of miles away from him anymore.

Even if Noah had been able to come to school with him, their days of switching places were behind them, at least for now. No one would have any trouble telling them apart. Noah went around looking like a last survivor in a disaster movie these days, scavenger-thin, though Nox knew he had plenty to eat; the nutrients just weren't sticking to him like they should. He ran track, or he used to, but his customary tan had faded; he was even paler than Nox now. He'd let his hair grow out. It flopped into his eyes, curled over his ears, and caught in the back of his collar. Mom normally cut it for them. Noah probably hadn't even noticed how long it'd gotten.

"They still don't know what's wrong?" Nox asked. He drew up his knees and wrapped his arms around them.

"Nope. They keep ruling things out, but there's, like, a million diseases. We could be crossing things off the list forever." Noah brightened. "Maybe I have something cool, like an ancient virus that was frozen in a glacier, but global warming melted it and now it's out in the world again and I'm patient zero."

"That would *not* be cool."

Noah picked at a loose thread on his jeans. "They ruled out skin cancer."

"Really?" Nox said hopefully.

"Yeah. But I wish it *was* cancer."

"Don't say that."

"At least then I'd know what I was dealing with." Noah rested his chin on his knee. "And there's treatments for cancer other than 'wait and see.' I hate not knowing."

Before Nox could come up with a response, they were interrupted by the click of the front door opening far below.

Without having to exchange a word, they turned on their stomachs and lay flat on the roof, clinging to the ridge at the peak with their fingertips. They were toward the back of the house, so they probably wouldn't be visible as long as they stayed low.

Weston's and Aster's voices wafted up to them from the front yard, too far away to make out what they were saying. The car beeped as it was unlocked. Its doors slammed. The engine growled, waking up, and a burst of illumination from the headlights threw the roof into deep shadow.

"Where are they going?" Nox whispered.

"Don't know. They're gone almost every night."

"They are?"

"Thea asks them about it sometimes," Noah said. "They tell her they're going back to the hospital for a late shift, but . . ."

"But . . . she doesn't believe them," Nox finished, hearing it in Noah's tone.

Noah shrugged. "I don't think so. She usually gets mad, goes to her room, and slams the door."

Thea was Aster's daughter from a previous marriage; she was about the same age as Nox and Noah. Nox hadn't met her yet. By the time he'd arrived, she had already gone up to bed. *He* was supposed to be in bed, too, resting for his first day at a new school tomorrow.

They sat up as the car's rumble faded, just in time to see the headlights disappearing down the road that led into town. The woods quickly swallowed them, and then it was dark and quiet again.

"When do they come back?" Nox asked.

"I don't know. I'm usually asleep." Noah read the look on his face and rolled his eyes. "They're *doctors*. People don't stop getting sick just because it's nighttime."

"Then why does Thea think it's weird?"

"How am I supposed to know?" Noah laughed. "It's not a big deal. You just think this place is spooky. Admit it."

"You think I'm *scared*?" Nox said. "I'm not a baby. I don't get scared of the woods."

Noah shook his head, grinning. "Whatever." He pointed at

the sky again. "Is there anything over there?"

"Orion," Nox said. He drew a line in the air across the three stars that formed Orion's belt. "He was a legendary hunter who could slay any beast. But then he made Gaia angry—she's basically Mother Earth—so she—"

He broke off when Noah turned away and coughed into his sleeve. As the coughing persisted, Noah pulled a tissue from his pocket and pressed it to his lips. When he caught his breath and pulled it away, it was mottled with reddish-brown stains.

He quickly stuffed the tissue back in his pocket. "Then what happened?"

Nox hesitated. But Noah clearly didn't want to talk about it. "So then," he said, "Gaia sent a scorpion after Orion. . . ."

By the time he got through the story of Orion's death by scorpion sting, Zeus turning him into a constellation, and Odysseus watching him hunt with his bronze club in the Underworld, Noah was nodding off. He shook Noah awake, and they climbed back inside. While Noah went straight to bed, Nox took the most rushed shower of his life and finally passed out sometime after midnight.

Despite his exhaustion, he half woke before dawn, unable to tell if he was dreaming or not. A noise had roused him. Maybe the Days had come back? He listened for the sound of a car door closing or footsteps downstairs. But there was nothing except for Noah's breathing in the bed across from his, and a creak in the walls, like the old house was wheezing in its sleep.

He twisted around in the blankets, too hot; but his skin prickled with goose bumps, as if he'd caught a chill. They'd left the blinds up. The moonlight was so bright it felt fake, like a cascade of silver foil. He closed his eyes for what felt like a long time.

When he opened them again, there was a white face in the window.

It was long, too long to be human, and glossy as ice melting by candlelight—a cool, luminous sheen. The shape of it made him think of some kind of animal skull, a fox maybe, bleached and polished to a shine. And it was looking at Noah.

As Nox watched, it turned to him instead. It had six eyes, each one black as a solar eclipse, and like a solar eclipse, Nox felt he shouldn't be looking directly at them.

Because his mind was running on dream logic, Nox didn't scream or sit up or wonder how a fox—dead or otherwise— had gotten to their third-story window. But he sensed somehow that if he closed his eyes, if he lost this staring contest, the skull would turn its attention back to Noah. And it was vitally important that he did not allow that to happen.

The longer he lay there with his eyes open, the more his mind cleared. He didn't see the fox leave, but by the time he was truly awake, there was nothing outside but black sky and moonlight.

Just a dream, he thought, and went back to sleep.

2

EVERGREEN DIDN'T HAVE A SCHOOL; HE AND
Thea would need to be dropped off in town, where they'd catch
a bus that would take them and a handful of other kids to Grayville. It would make stops in a few minuscule towns along the
way, allowing more passengers to trickle inside until the bus
was full. This meant they had to be up by 5:45 and out the door
by 6:30, which had to be some kind of human rights violation.

Nox had dragged himself through his morning routine,
feeling like he hadn't slept at all. He thought he might have
woken in the night at least once, and his dreams had been restless, though he couldn't remember what they'd been about. But
he always had trouble sleeping in new places. Every time they
moved because their landlord had jacked up their rent or Mom
had gotten a new job, it took Nox's body a few days to adjust. At
least he'd woken up in his own bed and hadn't broken his neck
sleepwalking down the stairs.

He slumped against the counter and stirred his spoon list-
lessly through a bowl of cereal. Weston puttered around the
kitchen, making up plates of eggs, toast, and bacon. Aster was
already at the hospital; they had their shifts set up so that they

could switch off covering breakfast and rides to the bus stop, and it was Weston's turn this morning.

"You sure you don't want any?" Weston said, unbelievably chipper for the hour. "I made plenty!"

Nox mumbled a polite refusal. The greasy smell alone made him a little sick.

Weston was taller than anyone Nox had ever met, and so skinny he almost looked two-dimensional, like if he turned sideways he'd disappear. In a show of either questionable judgment or an enviable lack of concern for other people's opinions, he had paired his crisp white doctor's coat with a fur-lined trapper hat pulled low over his ears.

Nox would never admit it, but he had been relieved when, after Weston had picked him up last night, he'd taken off his hat to reveal a tuft of light brown hair. He'd had a few uncomfortable questions about Mom's "old friend," which he couldn't bring himself to ask her directly but also couldn't get out of his head. It was just *weird* that Mom trusted Weston with Noah's life when they hadn't seen each other in over a decade. She'd never talked about Weston or introduced him to Nox and Noah. But suddenly this guy they'd never even heard of was her best friend? Nox had thought she only had work friends.

So he'd wondered if—

But seeing Weston in person put those worries to rest for good. One of the few things Nox knew about his dad was that he'd had black hair. Nox and Noah had gotten that from him. They had his eyes, too—a gray so dark it was almost black, which made it look like they had no irises, just enormous pupils.

The last thing he'd given Nox was a name; Mom had named Noah, and their father had named Nox. And then he'd walked out on them. Nox thought he should've had his naming privileges revoked after that.

In the corner of his eye, he hazily registered Noah coming down the stairs with Thea Day. She had reddish-brown hair, like autumn leaves after their color faded and they started to disintegrate into the mud, and about a million freckles, from her hairline to her collar, and down her arms from her rolled-up sleeves to her fingertips. He had seen her once or twice in the background when Noah had video-called. She wore boots and a weatherproof jacket—as if she planned to hike to school—and was laughing at something Noah was saying.

Noah waved a hand in front of Nox's face.

"Hey. You in there?"

Nox grunted in a vaguely affirmative sort of way. It was a cosmic injustice that Noah was a morning person. They were twins. They had the same DNA. Noah should be nodding off over the table, too, not bouncing around the kitchen accepting a heaping plate of bacon and eggs from Weston.

"This is Thea," Noah said, dropping into the seat next to Nox. "Say hi."

Thea sat down across from them, her plate by her elbow and a textbook and notepad open in front of her. Her notes were color coded. It looked like she had a test today. Nox's mind wandered back to his blurry, mostly forgotten dreams. Had she been up late studying? Had she felt something strange in the night, like Nox had?

Noah prodded his shoulder.

"Hi," Nox said, far too late.

"Hi!" Thea said brightly. Nox suppressed the urge to groan. *Another* morning person. She and Noah resumed their conversation, Noah taking her notebook and quizzing her. It was only once they'd all piled into the car, Thea in the passenger seat beside her stepdad and Noah in the back with him, that Nox surfaced from his exhausted stupor long enough to realize that something was off.

"Noah?" he said.

"Oh, are you conscious now?" Noah snickered. "Good morning."

Nox squinted at him. "Why are you coming with us?"

The doctors had said that Noah's immune system was messed up, so it was safer for him to take online classes; they didn't want to risk him catching something that would make his mysterious condition worse.

"I'm going to the hospital with Weston after we drop you off," Noah said, unconcerned. "They're going to take my temperature and stick me with needles."

"It's just a checkup. We're trying a new course of medication," Weston said, glancing at them in the rearview mirror. "He's shown great progress already. We're hoping to build on that."

Nox's eyes strayed down to Noah's sleeve, which hid the spreading rash. They were trying something new because what they'd tried before hadn't worked. And Noah had said he'd *plateaued*, which meant he'd stopped getting worse, but he also wasn't getting better.

14

If his condition worsened again, how bad would it have to get before he'd tell Nox?

The Day house perched on an outcropping of land that hung over the woods, curving like a crooked finger. From the front of the house down the long driveway to the gate, the ground was covered in prickly bluegrass and spear-like foxtails. The gate itself was a heavy cast-iron structure; it was open now, but when they'd come in last night, it had been chained shut. Weston had stopped the car to undo the chains and heave the gate open. Then he got back in the car, drove them through, and stopped once more so that he could get back out and chain the gate shut again. Nox had watched this whole production in silence.

"What're you trying to keep out?" he'd asked.

"Haven't you ever heard of the *highwaymen*? They're outlaws who roam the wilds, preying on unsuspecting travelers." Weston beamed. "No need to worry, of course! They won't be giving us any trouble."

Fine, Nox had thought. *Don't tell me, then.*

But Weston left the gate open this time, and they drove away on the one-lane dirt road that would take them through the forest, down a steep incline, and into the outskirts of town. The trees pressed in so close it seemed a miracle that they weren't raking the sides of Weston's car—a battered white Civic, all dented and scratched like it'd gone a few rounds with a hellhound. Sunlight trickled over the windshield. Evergreen's scant rooftops appeared and disappeared between the trees. Nox watched through the window as they passed by, since it had been too dark to get a good look last night, but there wasn't much to see even by daylight; they didn't go through the center of town, just veered around the edge of it. The bus stop stood alone a short ways down the main road that led toward Grayville.

They pulled up next to it, and Nox and Thea climbed out.

"Look out for Nox, all right?" Weston told Thea.

Noah leaned out the window. "See if you can get through a day without ending up in detention."

"Sure, whatever. I'll be good."

"That sounds like a threat when you say it."

Nox put his hand flat on Noah's face and pushed him backward, the way you might press down the lid of an overflowing garbage can to make its contents fit. Laughing, Noah allowed himself to be crammed back inside the car.

Weston drove off. Nox watched until the car went around a bend and disappeared.

"Are you worried?" Thea said.

Nox jumped. He'd almost forgotten she was there.

"No," he replied instinctively, and then didn't know why he'd said that. Obviously, he was worried. What kind of question was that?

"He's going to be fine," Thea said, as if she'd heard the real answer underneath the false one Nox had given.

Nox glared at her, unaccountably annoyed. "How do you know that?"

"I guess I don't, but my parents are sure he'll be okay. I believe them."

"Must be nice. Do your parents always tell you everything?"

Nox said, and felt a rush of petty satisfaction when she faltered and looked away. He was using what Noah had told him against her—that she'd been fighting with her parents—which was something Nox shouldn't even know about. It wasn't fair of him, but he didn't really care.

They waited in strained silence until the bus came. Although it was almost empty, they picked seats on opposite sides of the aisle. Nox zoned out until they were dropped off at school a little over an hour later. He stood on the sidewalk in front of Grayville Middle as people streamed past him, looking down at his schedule.

"Let me see that," Thea said, holding out her hand. He was surprised to see her there; he'd lost track of her in the throng and had expected she'd already be inside. "I'll help you find your first class."

"I got it, thanks."

He walked away before she could reply.

School was actually kind of a reprieve. It was routine, normal. He kept his head down, did his work, and didn't bother talking to anyone.

He was swapping out books at his locker around midday when someone reached over his shoulder and slammed the door shut. Nox jerked back just in time to avoid getting his hand crushed. The *bang* made the people around them jump. Heads swiveled in the hall to see what was happening; there was snickering from some of the onlookers.

Nox gritted his teeth, turned around, and looked up. And then up some more. The kid looming over him towered head and shoulders above most everyone else. He stood unnecessarily close, which was probably meant to be intimidating or something, except he had an unfortunate buzz cut that made him look like a used eraser, all pink and lumpy with a smattering of coarse blond shavings clinging to his head. Didn't exactly strike fear into Nox's heart.

"Oops. My bad," the boy said, grinning widely.

Nox's hands curled into fists, but he kept them down at his sides. "Don't worry about it."

"I won't." With a laugh, the other boy planted a hand on Nox's chest and shoved hard, slamming him against his locker with an impact that made Nox's teeth ache. "You new here?"

"Do I look new?" Nox said.

"Never seen you before."

"Wow. Look at you, putting the pieces together all by yourself," Nox said, in his snottiest, most patronizing tone of voice. "Nice job. Want a treat?"

He probably didn't need to be that snarky, but when someone came to Nox looking for a problem, it was Nox's policy to provide them with one.

Then he was being pinned by a forearm braced across his chest with crushing strength, the other boy leaning in close enough that Nox got a whiff of Cheetos-breath and had to wrinkle his nose.

"I don't know how it was at your old school. At this one, you don't talk back. Got it?"

Any other time, Nox would've said, *What happens if I do?* and shoved him away twice as hard. But Nox couldn't do that now. He couldn't keep escalating things. That was one of Mom's favorite words, *escalate*, which was when someone was kind of annoying and Nox retaliated instead of taking the high road and letting things blow over. So he gritted his teeth and didn't say anything. The boy seemed to take his silence as some kind of concession, because he gave Nox a final jarring push into the lockers, making the door and Nox's skull rattle, before letting him go and strolling away, laughing.

Taking the high road felt like crap. No wonder no one ever wanted to do it.

"Nox!"

He jumped. But it was only Thea, scurrying toward him.

"What?" he said curtly.

"I just saw Zack Millard leave. Did he say something to you?" she asked. "He's a jerk to everyone. Just ignore him."

"I'm fine," Nox bit out. "He didn't do anything."

Thea's concern for him was more embarrassing than getting slammed against the lockers like a punk. Did she really think he needed to be coddled because some oversized blond rat had been a little mean to him? Nox could've knocked that guy out. He could take care of himself.

He inhaled deeply, trying to count to ten like Mom was always telling him to do when he wanted to get his temper under control. It had never worked for him, but maybe a miracle would happen.

"You've got lunch next, right?" Thea said, oblivious to his darkening mood. "You can come and sit with me and my friends."

"Save it," he snapped. "I know your dad told you to be my

chaperone or whatever, but I don't need pity friends."

He almost felt bad about that one. Thea hadn't done anything wrong. She'd been trying to be nice to him all day. The anger he couldn't direct at Zack Millard just had to go somewhere, so here he was, lashing out at someone who didn't even deserve it. Nothing that Thea could have said or done in that moment would've been the right thing.

Thea's face turned such a brilliant shade of red that it clashed with her hair. "Right, because you're *great* at making friends on your own."

"Sure, when I want to be," Nox said. "Take a hint."

"Whatever. Offer's open. See you later."

She stormed away.

Nox glared at her back. Typical busybody, offering him help he didn't even ask for and then getting annoyed when he turned it down.

He found a quiet place to eat outside by himself, but he didn't truly relax until he'd made it to the end of the day without seeing Zack again.

He had to control his temper. Getting into any more fights would ruin a lot more than just his permanent record.

Last month had been the first time he'd ever started school without Noah, and it had been a disaster even by Nox's lofty standards.

It was just that Nox was *mad*. Mad all the time. Especially since Noah had gotten sick.

He'd always been more quick-tempered than Noah, so it

wasn't new, exactly. When they were younger, they used to get picked on. If you grew up poor, with secondhand clothes and haircuts done by your mom in front of the cracked mirror of your tiny bathroom, and you were skinny and short and quiet on top of that, you went around looking like an easy target. And Mom had never known what to do when they got picked on. She had them so young—the closer he came to being a teenager himself, the more he started to understand *how* young. She'd been the same age as the girl who stocked the shelves in the corner store and stuttered when you talked to her. The same age as the cheerleaders at the high school down the road who had glittery cell phone cases and smoked on the bleachers after practice when the coach had left. He bet *they* wouldn't know what to do, either. The best Mom could do was call the school and get brushed off by overworked administrators. So he and Noah stopped telling her when something happened and learned to deal with it themselves.

The way Noah dealt with it was, he learned how to be nice and charming and funny. He made friends with everyone. He got into track and helped build sets for the drama club. No one bothered him because too many people liked him, and anyone who messed with him just came off looking like the bad guy. But that was a long-term solution. Nox liked immediate solutions for immediate problems. He'd learned to fight. And he'd gotten pretty good at it.

Nowadays, most people knew to leave him alone. But there was always *someone* who didn't know how to stand up for themselves, some kid with clothes that didn't fit or bad acne or a lisp.

Telling people to lay off wasn't enough. You had to *make them*. The last time, though, he'd gone too far. The jerk he'd picked a fight with was the principal's son, and it didn't matter that he'd made a sixth grader cry *or* that he'd hit Nox back. Nox had thrown the first punch, so Nox was at fault.

Mom had only managed to save Nox from expulsion by promising to transfer him to another school. Immediately.

She'd sat Nox down that night, pressing an ice pack to his swollen cheek and looking so disappointed Nox hadn't been able to meet her eyes. He'd glared down at his bruised knuckles, jaw clenched so hard his teeth hurt, and waited.

"I should have known this would happen," she'd said.

Nox had flinched away from her touch. Usually, this was the part where Mom would begin her lecture about how violence wasn't the answer and how she knew he was better than this. He hadn't known, until just that moment, that her believing he was better mattered to him.

"Don't move," she said gently, pressing the ice pack to his face again. "Listen. I should have expected this. I know you're having a hard time without your brother. You've been so angry, and—and just miserable. I don't think I've seen you laugh once since he left. It breaks my heart."

Nox shook her off, took the ice pack, and held it up himself. "Am I grounded?"

"I should ground you. But we need to talk about what happens next," she said. "Now, this is *not* a reward. I don't want you to think just because you're getting what you want here that you did the right thing."

"What?" Nox said, not understanding. He finally glanced up.

Mom had pinned back her light red hair, a few wisps of it escaping the clip to frame her round cheeks and blue eyes. She straightened it for work, but it always frizzed to softness by the end of the day. Nox and Noah were pretty much the opposite of her, skinny with sharp angles, and already about her height.

"You need your brother. He keeps asking for you, too. Every time I talk to him without you. He's been begging for me to send you to Evergreen," she said. Nox blinked at her. He hadn't known that. Noah always acted like nothing was wrong when they spoke. "I talked to Weston and Aster, and they said they have room for you. So you're going to stay with them for a while."

"Are you serious?" Nox said, sitting bolt upright, the hand holding the ice pack falling limp to his side.

"You're still in trouble," she reminded him in her sternest voice. "And if you get in any fights over there? You're coming straight back here. I don't care if you get kicked out of every school in the county and I have to scrounge up the cash to send you to some fancy private academy for rich snobs. Got it?"

Nox nodded in numb silence, barely hearing her.

Mom must have sensed his distraction, because she put her hands gently on his bruised face, turning him to look at her again. Her blue eyes were soft and sad.

"You *have* to learn to control your temper, Nox," she said. "I don't want you to get hurt. I know you can defend yourself, but what happens if the other guy pulls out a gun? You never know, these days."

"I won't fight anyone with a gun," Nox said tonelessly.

"It's not funny," she said, sounding so upset that Nox instantly regretted opening his mouth. "And if you really hurt someone—hurt them badly—you'd regret it forever."

When Nox picked fights, he always went for the bullies. But he wasn't standing up for anyone, not really. When the shy, awkward kids he rescued wanted to thank him, he always snapped at them to leave him alone, making sure they understood that this didn't mean they were friends. Like he needed some lost cause with even worse problems than him hanging around. Sometimes his anger was like a living thing trapped in his chest, pressing on his skin from the inside, until he thought it would rip him open if he didn't find a way to let it out. Bullies just gave him an excuse. They stuck the bull's-eye on their own backs.

If he really hurt someone, would he regret it?

He honestly didn't know.

3

WESTON EITHER IGNORED OR FAILED TO NOTICE
the frosty silence between Nox and Thea as he chattered away
during the drive home. The gravel on the driveway had barely
settled before Thea flung the car door open and stomped up to
the house. Nox trailed after her slowly, hoping to slink up to the
attic and not speak to anyone but Noah until dinner.

But Aster was waiting to pull Nox aside the moment he
came in. She looked a lot like Thea, with her dark red hair and
freckles, but she didn't have the kind of face that Nox could
imagine scowling like Thea had at him, or laughing the way
she had with Noah. Aster was calm, poised, and professional,
and probably a really good doctor, not that it made Nox feel any
better about what she had to say.

"Noah might be asleep," she told him. "The trip to the hospital took a lot out of him."

She said it so casually, like nothing was amiss—like Noah
didn't use to be the fastest runner on the track team, and now
he needed a whole day in bed to recover from a car ride to the
doctor. Nox's throat closed; he felt like he'd been hit in the gut
and couldn't do anything but move with the blow so that it

wouldn't knock him to the ground.

He nodded stiffly, not responding, and went upstairs. He was careful on the steps to the attic door, putting his weight down gingerly, as if that would stop them from creaking. Clutching the strap of his backpack with one hand, he eased the door open and peeked inside.

At first, he thought Noah really was asleep. He was curled up on his side under the covers, a mess of black hair splayed over his pillow. But before Nox could withdraw, the lump under the blankets stirred. Noah pushed himself up on his elbow, wincing, as if moving even that much had taken all his strength.

"Nox?" he said hoarsely.

"Yeah." Nox dropped his backpack on the floor and climbed onto the end of Noah's bed. "What happened?"

"Don't know," Noah said, flopping on his back. "I started feeling kind of bad as soon as we started driving, but I thought I was just tired. By the time we got to the hospital, everything hurt. Like . . . I was sore after a long run or something. And stiff. It was kind of hard to move."

"Does it still hurt?" Nox asked.

"Not anymore. I started feeling better once we got back here. Now I'm just moping." Noah smiled shakily. "First time I get to go anywhere in weeks, and this happens. I know I'm lucky Weston and Aster can give me most of my treatments at home, but it sucks."

"I know," Nox said uselessly. He tried to come up with something better to say, but Noah was breezing past it already, evidently done with the whole subject.

"How was your first day?" he asked, tilting his head on the pillow to look up at Nox. "Did you hang out with Thea? Do you have a ton of homework?"

"Not a ton," Nox said, choosing to ignore his other questions. He gave Noah's foot under the blanket a light kick. "Maybe I'll take a nap, too."

"Ugh." Noah made a face. "Can we watch something?"

They ended up downloading some horror movies onto the laptop Noah used for his online classes. Spending the afternoon crammed together on Noah's twin bed with the laptop between them was the most normal Nox had felt in months. But Noah leaned heavily on his shoulder, and every now and then, he rubbed at his wrist over his sleeve. Most of Nox's attention was on the movie, but part of it was focused on Noah, hyperaware of every change in his breathing and every restless fidget.

Noah was feeling better by dinnertime, so they went downstairs together. The Days and Noah carried the conversation. Thea chimed in every now and then, but Nox didn't talk unless someone spoke to him directly—usually Noah, the only one who knew how to get anything other than one-word answers out of him. Nox and Thea were on dish duty after. They managed to do all the cleaning up side by side at the sink almost close enough for their shoulders to touch without saying a single word to each other, talking only to Noah, who sat beside them on the counter.

"Come upstairs with us," Noah said to Thea, hopping down once they'd finished. "We're doing a *Conjuring* marathon. *Annabelle*'s next."

Thea hesitated, glancing briefly at Nox.

"Sorry," she said. "I've got an essay due tomorrow. Next time?"

"Sure!" Noah said. But as soon as she was gone, he rounded on Nox. "What did you say to her?"

"Nothing," Nox said indignantly.

Noah crossed his arms, not buying it.

"I just told her to leave me alone. She's kind of annoying, that's all," Nox said. "So what? She doesn't like me, either."

"Thea's cool," Noah said. "And you're both nerds, so you'd probably get along."

"Shut up," Nox grumbled. Nox wasn't a nerd the same way Thea was, based on what little Nox knew about her from Noah's calls. She liked going to school and studying, and it was safe to assume she really was working diligently away at that essay right now, not slacking off like the two of them. Nox didn't have a hard time in class, but he didn't care about it, either. He had a good memory for mythology because old stories about guys with swords killing monsters were kind of cool. And he knew a lot about the stars because, when Nox and Noah were little and they couldn't sleep, Mom would take them up to the roof of their apartment building. Though the light pollution made it impossible to see anything but a flat navy sky, she'd pull up a star map on her phone and point to where all the constellations were.

Even when you can't see them, they're there, she'd said, a little wistfully, like she was thinking of something else. *Nothing lasts forever, but the stars come pretty close.*

Noah used to fall asleep in Mom's lap almost immediately, but Nox would stay up as late as she'd allow before she took them both back downstairs, Noah cradled against her shoulder and Nox clinging to her hand. When he got older, he'd study the same star maps by himself; and when memorizing the positions of the stars wasn't enough, he'd read astronomy books so that he'd understand what he was looking at. He liked most things better when they made sense to him. A star was basically a core of hydrogen atoms reacting to make helium, giving off energy in the process, and emitting heat and light. A lot of the mystery went away once you understood that. Noah said the mystery was half the appeal of the stars. Nox didn't agree.

"Thea's the one who showed me how to get onto the roof," Noah said now. "She could tell I was homesick, so she kept me company even when it meant blowing off her other friends. She wants to work in wildlife conservation, so she knows, like, everything about the plants and animals around here, which you have to admit is a *little* cool—"

"I get it, you're friends," Nox said. "That doesn't mean I have to be friends with her."

"If she's avoiding you, that means she'll have to avoid *me*, too!" Noah said. "At least try and be nice? Please?"

Noah had always had a lot of friends, orbiting him like planets in his own personal solar system. But Nox had never needed or wanted that many people around him. He had Mom and Noah, and that was enough; most other people were a hassle.

Noah's friends didn't usually bother him. Rarely did people make the mistake of treating them like the same person, not after they'd spent more than five minutes around them. And no matter how many friends Noah had, Nox was his only brother. So why was Thea different? In the privacy of his own mind, he could admit that it had taken very little for Thea to get under his skin.

He decided he'd really prefer not to think about it.

"All right," he said. "I'll try, okay?"

This underwhelming promise was enough to satisfy Noah for now, and they went back upstairs. By the time they got to the end of *Conjuring 2*, Noah was nodding off against Nox's shoulder. Nox hit pause and slowly closed the laptop. Before he could figure out how to get back to his own bed without waking him up, Noah stirred.

"Hey, Nox?" he mumbled, struggling to keep his eyes open.

"Yeah?" Nox said.

"Don't tell Mom, but . . ."

"What?"

"I'm, uh. I'm kind of scared."

He wasn't talking about the movie.

Nox swallowed hard. "Me too," he admitted after a long moment.

They were good at switching places. Nox would have given *anything* to be able to switch with him now.

There was no response; Noah was already asleep.

Nox, for his part, got very little sleep that night.

He quickly came to view the Day house as an enemy. It was too big, too creaky, too isolated.

The north side of the house bordered a sheer drop. When Nox paused at one of the north-facing windows in the second-floor hall on his way to the attic stairs, the woods went on forever. The forest canopy was impenetrable. Even now, in the fall, when the leaves had gone a delicate papery yellow and some of the branches were already bare, there was no telling what lay underneath. The only distinct shapes were the needle-tipped branches scratching at each other, like claws reaching up from the earth to dig up the house's foundations and pull it down.

Nox didn't like the north windows. Even more than that, he didn't like the sounds he heard at night. The raucous calls of the coyotes were always too close for comfort. The old grandfather clock in the hallway chimed every fifteen minutes with a hollow toll like a church bell. Sometimes birds landed on the roof or squirrels made daredevil ascents up the drainpipe, and you could hear their footsteps no matter where you were. The crickets sang incessantly. On that subject, Thea had this to say: "They lay their eggs this time of year. In the soil. Then they don't hatch till spring."

Nox wrinkled his nose. "Gross."

"It's not *gross*," she said, rolling her eyes, like talking about cricket eggs at the dinner table was totally normal.

"Know-it-all."

"Jerk."

Noah kicked him under the table, and Nox bit back the response he would have made. Aster shot Thea a narrow-eyed look of warning. "Never mind, Antheia."

"It's *Thea*."

"Mm-hmm. Of course."

Thea sighed. The subject was changed.

If the coyotes and crickets weren't bad enough, the house recited a litany of complaints each night. It groaned from its foundations to its rafters. The ancient pipes banged whenever the heat came on. The bluff cut the wind in half so that it sheathed the house like a blade, its moans and howls coming as if from every direction.

The only sounds he couldn't explain were the wingbeats.

They began late in the night, their soft and steady rhythm washing over him just before he finally dropped off. Whatever was making that noise, it had to be huge. Like a bird of prey circling the house on its way to roost in the distant mountains. He found himself checking the ground for stray feathers in the morning, but he never saw any.

You'd think he would've enjoyed living in a real house after growing up in an apartment the size of a postage stamp. It had a laundry room with a washer and dryer—no weekly pilgrimage to the laundromat needed. It had a whole bookcase in the living room full of books the Days owned. It was always stocked with Kleenex boxes (the Days never used toilet paper to blow their noses) and Ziploc bags (which the Days threw away after one use instead of washing and reusing until they got cloudy). There were always fresh fruit and vegetables in the fridge; they never bothered with the canned stuff.

But it was so much bigger than what five people—let alone three—really needed. They clattered around in all that space like coins in a glass jar. It had occurred to Nox that if anyone or anything other than Weston and Aster approached the house in the night, they'd be in pretty bad shape. No car to escape in. No neighbors to go to for help. Nowhere to run, up on a cliff with dense woods surrounding them on three sides and a chained-up gate on the fourth. Trapped.

All in all, he was lucky to get even a few hours of sleep every night, when everything about this house made him feel so uneasy. In the mornings, he stumbled down the stairs and leaned against the wall by the bathroom, waiting for Thea to get out. Sometimes he'd nod off right there, standing up, until the sound of the bathroom door opening startled him back into wakefulness.

Thea left her bedroom door cracked open one of those mornings. It was across the hall from the bathroom, so Nox caught a glimpse inside. Her room was a riot of sunlight and greenery, like a portal into a tropical rainforest. Curious, he stepped closer. Nearly every surface of Thea's room was covered in plants: leafy fan-shaped ones on the desk and windowsill, viny dangling ones tucked into pots that hung from the ceiling, succulents in glass terrariums. And then there were the insects. Beetles, butterflies, spiders, praying mantises, all lovingly preserved in glass cases, their shiny scales and exoskeletons gleaming in the sunlight. Nox's stomach turned over. He'd never seen so many creepy little legs and antennae in one place.

"Get *out*," Thea said. He jumped.

"I wasn't *in*," he said, irritated. He hadn't even touched the door.

"Just mind your own business." She stepped around him.

"Doesn't that stuff freak you out?" he blurted.

"What? The bugs?"

"No, the curtains. Obviously the bugs."

She stared at him, forehead creased as if she was puzzled. As if this was the first time anyone had said anything like that to her, which Nox felt certain couldn't be true.

"I think they're beautiful," she said.

He gave a harsh laugh. He just couldn't help it.

"You're so weird."

"And you're immature."

"Whatever." He turned away and shuffled into the bathroom, which meant he couldn't *see* her roll her eyes, but he knew she did.

He washed his face and hands thoroughly, scrubbing at his skin, unable to shake the phantom sensation of tiny bodies crawling over him. When he closed his eyes, he saw all those skittering, winged, many-legged things waking up in the night, moving in the dark against their glass chambers. Maybe those were the sounds he kept mistaking for wingbeats. Maybe that was why he couldn't sleep.

Nox didn't like the house and its windows. He didn't like the sounds at night.

And he didn't like Thea.

He never mentioned any of that to Mom when she called to check on him and Noah, though. Mom had a lot of bad memories from Evergreen. It had been hard for her to send them here, especially since she couldn't get time off work to go with them.

She was born and raised in Evergreen. But then she got pregnant with him and Noah when she was a teenager, and her dad had been furious. He told her she could give up the baby—she hadn't even known she was having twins yet—or she could get out of his house. So she'd packed up and left. She chose Nox and Noah over everything and everyone else.

Weston's parents had offered to take her in. She and Weston had been best friends since preschool or something, and she used to spend so much time at the Day house she practically lived with them anyway. Thea and her mom weren't around then—Weston had only met his wife a few years ago—so they had the space. But Mom went off on her own instead.

Grandpa Winters died years ago. Good riddance. But Mom never came back to Evergreen, and she'd almost changed her mind at the last minute about letting Nox go. He'd seen it on her face as she'd dropped him off at the train station. She hadn't smiled. Her *goodbye* was strangled and faint. Then, clearing her throat, she'd said, "Nox, I don't know . . ."

Instead of comforting her, he'd replied: "I'm gonna be late."

He'd been so desperate to avoid another argument he'd turned tail and fled through the gates to the platform without even waiting for her usual goodbye hug. He felt bad about it, but she never should've separated them in the first place. Especially when Noah was sick. Because what if he got even worse? What if . . . And Nox wouldn't have been there if something happened. Noah would've been alone in this big, creaky house, locked behind a gate, while Weston and Aster disappeared until dawn almost every night.

Nox *had* to be here. And no creepy noises, iron gates, or obnoxious redheaded housemates would change that.

After a week in Evergreen, Nox had mostly gotten used to the sounds of an old house in the middle of nowhere. That night, he fell asleep before the hour when the wingbeats usually started.

When he woke up—for what turned out to be the first time—moonlight shone through the blinds, a silver ladder to nowhere. His chest felt heavy, the sheets tacky with sweat. He shifted sluggishly, registering Noah's outline in the corner of his eye. Then sleep pulled him under once more.

When he woke the second time, the window was black and the moonlight was coming from somewhere *inside* the room. Its cold white illumination washed over the old wardrobe and the slanted ceiling, tossing splintered shadows into the corners.

Nox blinked, forcing his eyes open when all they wanted was to seal themselves shut. He rolled over and squinted through the darkness at Noah's bed—

That was where the light was coming from. But it wasn't moonlight.

It was something alive, prowling over Noah's sleeping body, its pale fur shining so brightly that Nox's tired eyes burned. Through the spots in his vision, he made out the lines of a sleek, muscular frame, its tail like a cloud drifting after it, puffy and swaying a little where it was held upright. Noah's mattress dipped under its weight.

Was Nox dreaming again?

The creature lifted a paw over Noah's chest, claws extended, as if to rip him open.

Nox made a choked noise in his throat—a half-formed protest, the beginnings of a scream—

The creature whirled around and looked directly at Nox. It had a narrow snout, its lips pulled back to reveal deadly fangs, and triangular ears like a wolf's—except wolves didn't have six eyes, a row of three on either side and all of them huge and round and black like empty craters. It was arresting; he *knew* that stare, but how, he couldn't have said.

His breath lodged in his throat like a golf ball. Every ounce of warmth in the room fled, and he was cold, paralyzed down to his fingertips with fear.

The creature leapt down from Noah's bed. Nox shrank away, but it didn't come any nearer. It bounded to the window and passed noiselessly through the blinds.

Without its glow, the room was pitch-black.

His body did a system reboot, his lungs taking in a gasp of air and his heart kicking into a gallop. He sat up without consciously thinking about it. The moonlight came back through the window, as if a cloud had drifted out of the way. As soon as his eyes adjusted, he looked at Noah.

Still asleep. He hadn't moved an inch.

If Nox hadn't woken up . . . what would have happened?

He climbed shakily out of bed and stumbled to the window, practically falling against it, hands splayed over the sill. With trembling fingers, he lifted one of the slats in the blinds and peered outside, cold with the prospect that the glow of moonlight might not be moonlight at all—that it was the wolf, crouching on the ledge under the window, and he was about to see those black eyes again, looking back at him.

But there was nothing. Below, the woods shifted with the rhythm of night breezes. When he listened carefully, he thought he could pick up the dry rasp of its leaves, a sound like falling sand in an hourglass. He was all but plastered to the window; the glass was so cold that his skin caught its chill without him having to touch it.

Something caught his eye. *There*, moving through the woods, a flash of pale brilliance visible briefly through the lattice of branches. Something the color of moonlight. He pushed up on the blinds, widening the gap and trying to follow the movement. Was that it? Was that the thing that had been in the room with them just now?

Another flash of light off to the side made him jump. It was brighter, harsh, and his heart rate ratcheted up until he recognized it: headlights, coming from the direction of the road. The Days were back. The light vanished just as quickly as it had appeared as their car pulled up to the house. But whatever he'd seen in the woods was gone, too; there was no silver gleam down there anymore, just restless darkness.

He picked his way over the clothes on the floor and got his phone off the nightstand. It was a little past four in the morning. He hesitated, glancing at Noah again.

Had he imagined the whole thing? Minutes ago, it had felt so real, but now that he was fully awake, the memory of what had happened felt like a dream. He thought of those piercing, oddly familiar black eyes again, and shuddered.

Downstairs, the front door opened and closed.

Without giving himself time to second-guess, he slipped out of the attic and padded down the steps. Quickly, he ducked into the bathroom, leaving the door cracked open and the lights off. The bathroom door stood across from Thea's room and next to the stairs that led to the first floor. The Days' bedroom was at the far end of the hall, past the attic. He could just hear the murmur of their voices down in the kitchen.

A muttered, pained curse—that was Weston. His wife shushed him.

"Hold still," she said. "I'm almost done."

"I can't believe this. I wasn't this clumsy when I was a kid."

Aster gave a quiet laugh. "I guess you're not as spry as you used to be, old man."

This was probably supposed to be funny on account of Aster being the older one in the couple. Nox wasn't sure how much older, but old enough that when she'd had Thea, she hadn't been a teenager and probably hadn't been forced to flee her hometown over it.

Footsteps on the stairs. Nox stiffened, backing away from the door. Were the voices coming closer?

No—the footsteps were going *down*, not coming up.

"Mom?" Thea said, around a yawn. "Dad?"

"Hey, sweetie. What are you doing up?" Aster said.

"I heard a noise. Did you just get back?"

Thea was lying, Nox realized. She was acting like she'd just woken up, but she had been on the stairs, waiting for them to come in so that she could catch them. That was why Nox hadn't heard her come out of her room.

"We're sorry we woke you. Go back to bed," Aster said. "You have school tomorrow."

"What happened to Dad?"

"Just a scraped knee! Nothing to worry about," Weston assured her.

"Wow. That's impressive," Thea said nonchalantly. "Must be hard to scrape a knee on hospital tiles. How'd you pull that one off? I didn't think muddy boots went with scrubs, either."

Nox covered his mouth to stifle a laugh. He knew that tone of voice. That wasn't Thea the model student. That was the Thea who had bluntly accused him of being incapable of making friends.

Aster must have been familiar with that voice, too, because she said, tiredly, "Not now, Thea. Go to sleep. We can talk about this later."

"Can we? Because you never tell me anything anymore," Thea snapped.

Aster shushed her—Nox couldn't hear what she said exactly. A whispered exchange followed. Then Thea's voice rose again.

"You haven't been anywhere near the hospital. You look like you've been out for a hike," she accused. "In the middle of the night? When you always tell me how dangerous it is to wander around after dark? You won't even let me take the trails after sunset—"

"Thea. Enough."

Nox had never heard Aster sound so sharp. Thea fell silent.

After a pause, Aster continued. "I know a lot of things have been confusing lately. But this will all be over soon."

He shivered. Why did that sound so . . . ominous?

"What does that mean?" Thea demanded.

"Go to bed. *Now*."

Thea did as she was told and went upstairs. Nox shrank back into the shadows, paranoid she'd somehow sense him there, and didn't relax until he'd heard her door open and close again.

Weston murmured something comforting to his wife. Not too long after that, they came up the stairs together and went to their room, closing the door. Nox counted the seconds until a full minute had passed. When he was sure it was safe, he crept out of the bathroom and tiptoed back to the attic stairs.

Thea's door opened behind him. Light spilled into the hall.

He froze and turned back as Thea emerged, squinting in his direction; he stood just beyond where the light reached. It framed her in gold and highlighted the shades of autumn in her hair but left her face mostly in shadow.

"Noah?" she said.

He made a split-second decision. If Thea realized that Nox had been eavesdropping on her, she would be furious, and he had promised Noah that he'd try to keep the peace between them. And Nox was no good at playing innocent. But Noah was.

So he let his shoulders relax and smiled warmly at her. "Hey. You all right? What are you doing up?"

She wiped her eyes roughly on her sleeve. They were red and puffy, as if she'd been crying.

"Nothing. Just couldn't sleep. You?"

"Bathroom. I was worried I woke you up."

"Nah. I was already . . ." She rubbed at her eyes again and laughed under her breath. "I was spying on my parents. Can't believe I did that."

Despite himself, Nox was starting to feel bad for her.

"You were just worried about them," he said, because it was what Noah would say.

"Mom and I used to tell each other everything," she said, her voice so quiet that Nox, unwisely, inched closer to hear her better. "But there are things she won't tell me about Evergreen. I thought she just didn't know, but she does. They both do."

"Didn't know what?" Nox said, coaxingly, hoping his urgency wasn't too obvious.

"Why people disappear from there."

Nox's skin prickled with goose bumps. Words failed him; for a moment, only the creak of the house and the hoot of an owl broke the silence.

She sniffled and turned her face away, as if embarrassed. "Sorry. You should go back to sleep."

"Are you going to be okay?" Nox asked, because as much as he desperately wanted to wring every bit of information he could out of her, Noah would back off.

"Fine. Just remind me next time I decide to play secret agent that I'm *really* bad at it."

"You could get better at it. I mean," he said, still using his Noah voice, "if your parents didn't want you to spy on them, then they should've just told you the truth, right?"

Thea's brow furrowed. "No, that's not . . . Wait." She took a few tentative steps forward. "Nox?"

He hesitated. "Yeah," he said, dropping the act.

She stared at him in disbelief, an angry flush rising over her face.

"Why'd you pretend to be Noah?" she hissed. "Did you think it was funny to trick me?"

He didn't know how to explain that he'd been trying *not* to upset her. He shrugged. "Habit, I guess."

Without another word, she turned and vanished into her room, and the light disappeared with her.

Nox trudged back upstairs. The room was still undisturbed, the closed blinds allowing only the faintest trace of moonlight to seep inside. Noah slept on peacefully. Had there really been something in here with them less than an hour ago? His mind swirled with visions of the Days wandering the woods in the middle of the night, and the luminous, wolflike creature that had very likely come out of those woods. Come into this house when the Days had deliberately left them alone.

It had been real. He was sure of it.

And Weston and Aster knew something.

4

IN THE MORNING, THEA DIDN'T LOOK AT NOX or acknowledge his existence in any way. Aster was the one driving them to the bus stop today; Thea ignored her, too.

"Good morning, Nox," Aster said, paying no heed to the palpable tension. "Did you sleep well?"

"Um . . . ," Nox said. "Yeah."

He snuck glances at Aster's face in the rearview mirror as she started the car, searching for signs of exhaustion. How did she manage to stay out that late most of the week and still function?

But this was the least of Nox's concerns. As he had lain awake for the past couple of hours, he had replayed what Thea had told him: *People disappear from there.* What did *disappear* mean? Like kidnapping? Like walking into the woods and never being seen again? It was the first he'd heard of vanishings in Evergreen. Whatever was going on there, did it have something to do with what he'd seen last night? Thea had been worried about what her mom did or didn't know, but Nox thought if anyone was keeping secrets, it was her stepdad. Weston had grown up in this house, after all, with the woods on his doorstep. Chances were, he knew better than anyone else what lurked there.

The last thing Nox wanted was to go to school right now, not when it meant leaving Noah behind. Noah was still out cold and happily oblivious. He had never been such a heavy sleeper before he'd gotten sick; the two of them had always had trouble sleeping through the night. When they were younger, they'd had a sleepwalking phase. Mom used to be terrified one of them would fall down the stairs or wander out onto the street.

But Noah needed his rest, so Nox hadn't wanted to wake him up, even to tell him what had happened. It would have to wait until after school.

He endured his classes in a state of complete distraction. At lunch, he went outside and found a quiet spot against the wall by the parking lot. The front doors around the corner squeaked every time they opened, so he'd hear anyone coming. The cars he could see from where he sat were deserted. This was the only chance he'd have to be alone today, since he shared a room with Noah and at least one of the Days was always home after school.

Before he could overthink it, he took out his phone and called Mom. It rang for so long he almost hung up before she answered, but she did, at the last second, and the first thing she said was, "Nox? What's wrong?"

"Nothing," he said quickly. "I just wanted to call you. Are you at work?"

Mom was a receptionist at an advertising company while she worked on getting an online degree in graphic design. It was taking her forever because of how busy she was. Maybe now that he and Noah were both gone, she'd have more time for her courses.

"I stepped out." She was quiet for a second. Nox heard traffic and the gusty roar of wind on her end of the line. "How's school?"

He grimaced. He had an essay due next week for a book he had no intention of reading, an algebra exam he didn't plan to study for, and the ever-present attention of Zack Millard, who shoulder-checked him hard enough to almost knock him over anytime they passed each other in the hall.

"Fine," Nox said. "I wanted to ask you something."

He had been thinking about it all day. Something he'd heard Weston say last night had stuck out to him.

I wasn't this clumsy when I was a kid.

If Thea had been right about her parents spending their nights out in the woods, what were they doing there? And why had it brought back memories from his childhood? Mom said that she and Weston had been inseparable growing up. So whatever Thea's parents were involved in—did that mean Mom was in it, too?

But even if she knew that there were dangerous, unnatural things in the woods near Evergreen, she must have believed they'd be safe in the Day house.

"How come you never came back to Evergreen after Grandpa died?" he asked finally.

There was a sharp inhale on the other end of the line.

"It just wasn't home for me anymore, baby," she said.

"But you never even visited."

The wind crackled over the line again, a sound like paper

tearing. It took so long for her to respond that he checked the screen to make sure the call hadn't dropped.

Finally, she said, "I know. Weston and I always imagined we'd raise our kids together. It's my fault that didn't happen. And we don't have any relatives, either. I'm sorry. I never meant for us to be so alone."

"No, that's not—" He wasn't trying to make her feel like she'd failed them somehow. He didn't care if they'd never visited someone she'd been friends with a decade ago, who lived in a creepy old house in a town where she'd been miserable. "Is there some other reason you avoided this place?"

"Nox, what's wrong? What is this really about? Talk to me."

There were so many things wrong he didn't even know how to begin.

"Noah says he's not getting better," he said in a rush. "Can't we—try something else?"

"I know you're worried about him," Mom said. "Trust me, I am, too. And it's hard to watch someone you love suffer and . . . and not be able to do anything to—"

Her voice broke.

"Why can't we get a second opinion?" Nox insisted.

"We tried that. We had . . . god, a third and fourth and fifth opinion before I went to Weston. Is this because you want to leave? It's okay if you do. Your brother wouldn't blame you."

"No! That's not it."

"Okay. But you know you can always come home."

He struggled to find the thread of his argument again and failed.

"Okay," he said at last. "I mean, no. I'm fine. I'm staying."

"If that's what you want, then all right." She paused as if waiting for a response, but he said nothing. "I have to go back in now. You sure you're fine?"

"Yeah. Bye, Mom."

"Bye, love."

She hung up. He sat with the phone pressed against his ear for a long time, staring at nothing, until the bell rang for next period. On his way back inside, a hard shove almost sent him flying into the lockers.

He whirled around, the blood pounding in his ears. It was Zack again, smirking over his shoulder as he walked away.

Something in Nox lit up, igniting like a fuse. It made his hands jittery, so he had to clench his fists to stop them from shaking, and his vision go dark around the edges, like it was homing in on a target.

"HEY!" Nox hollered. Zack stopped. His height made him impossible to miss; he stuck out of the passing period throng like a big blond ostrich. "Don't touch me again. *Ever.*"

"What did you just say?" People cleared a path for him almost before he even moved, and then he was looming over Nox.

And maybe Zack saw the look on Nox's face and faltered. Just for a second. Like somewhere in his tiny brain, a self-preservation instinct he'd never needed had woken up for the first time, blaring out warning signals he was too slow to understand.

No way, Nox thought. *You're not getting away this time.*

"Are you just playing dumb, or is it genuine?" Nox said. "I said, *don't touch me.*"

Zack's ruddy, marshmallow-soft features stretched into a smug smile. "Yeah? And what happens if I do?"

He reached out and gave Nox's shoulder a firm push.

Nox took a half step back for balance, drew up his fist, and swung.

The fight couldn't have lasted more than fifteen seconds. In the background like ambient music were shouts, footsteps, the bell ringing to signal the start of the next period, the crowd swarming around them, and finally, a pair of strong hands grabbing Nox by the upper arms and bodily lifting him off of Zack.

As the crowd dispersed and Nox was led to the principal's office, he glanced back over his shoulder. Zack leaned heavily on another teacher for support. Blood ran down his face from where Nox's knuckles had split his eyebrow open, and his lip had inflated to twice its size. He'd managed to get a few blows of his own in, but those might as well have been mosquito bites for all Nox felt it. Actually, Nox felt *great*.

When he met Nox's gaze, blinking with the one eye that wasn't swollen shut, Nox gave him his widest grin.

He wouldn't be bothering Nox anymore, that was for sure.

If only his other problems were that easy to solve.

One-week suspension, for both him and Zack, and they had to write each other apology letters. All things considered, he'd gotten lucky.

Weston turned up at some point. Nox tuned out the apologies he made to the principal on his behalf. He was already mentally preparing himself for the inevitable argument with Mom.

Nox used to be a lot better at not getting caught. That way Mom didn't have to worry about him, except on the rare occasion that someone snitched or Nox came home with a bruise he couldn't hide. Or the even rarer occasion that Nox was careless enough to fight the principal's son, and then, barely a month after promising to take up a life of pacifism, brawl in front of a crowd of witnesses.

Yeah. Not the smartest decision he'd ever made.

He followed Weston to the car. His one-week suspension started now.

"I heard from Celia before I came to get you," Weston said. "She wants you to call her right away."

Nox considered waiting until they got to the house, but that would mean having this conversation in front of Noah. There was no winning either way. He pulled out his phone and dialed. This time, Mom picked up on the first ring.

"Nox," she said, her voice deadly calm.

"Uh. Hi." He picked at a loose thread on his shirt. "Weston said I should call."

"Are you hurt?"

He shrugged, as if she could see. "No. I mean, a little, but it's nothing."

She sighed deeply. "Okay. Do you remember what we agreed on? Before I let you come to Evergreen?"

Nox didn't say anything.

"Nox, you made a promise," Mom said quietly. "And I made

you a promise, too. We agreed that if this happened again, you would have to come back home."

"We . . . we also agreed that Noah needs me here," he managed.

And, he left unspoken, that he needed Noah.

"Sometimes, there are good reasons to break rules," Mom said. "But breaking a promise isn't something I take lightly. I can't let you keep going down this path, Nox. It's self-destructive. One day, you'll walk away from a fight with a lot worse than a few bruises. Or maybe you won't walk away at all. And it'll be my fault for not doing more."

Nox opened his mouth again, but the words wouldn't come. He didn't know how to make her understand how important it was for him to stay here. Or how the idea of leaving Noah alone made him feel like he was drowning. When you inhaled water and your whole chest burned. At the very least, he tried to make himself apologize. But he wasn't sorry. And he was pretty sure Mom knew that already.

"Can you put her on speaker?" Weston said.

Nox looked up at him numbly but did as he was asked.

"Weston? What is it?" Mom said.

"I was talking to the principal just now, and it's all straightened out," he said cheerfully. "Apparently the other boy is a long-time disciplinary problem, and he's been provoking Nox all week. Plenty of their classmates saw him start their little scuffle today. He didn't know he was biting off more than he could chew with our Nox, though, did he?"

Nox stared at him in total bewilderment. After what Nox

had done, Weston was . . . sticking up for him?

"In light of all that," Weston said, "maybe we can just . . . let this one slide? I'm sorry if I'm overstepping, but—"

"No, no," Mom said. Nox looked at the phone as if it had grown legs and tried to wriggle out of his hand. "You know I trust your opinion more than just about anyone's, Wes. I guess . . . if you believe this was a fluke, and that the other boy was at fault . . ."

"I do. And I'm sure it won't happen again." He looked at Nox. "It won't, will it?"

"No?" Nox said cautiously.

"Great!" Weston said.

Just like that, Nox was basically off the hook. Mom said goodbye, and they headed home.

"Why did you do that?" Nox said after they had driven in silence for several minutes.

"I was just making sure Celia had all the facts," Weston said. He looked at Nox thoughtfully over the rim of his glasses. "You're really not used to having anyone but Noah in your corner, are you?"

Nox didn't have a response to that.

5

"YOU DIDN'T EVEN MAKE IT TWO WEEKS WITH-
out punching someone in the face. That's a new record," Noah
said.

"Can we focus on the thing I saw?" Nox said impatiently.
"You believe me, right?"

"I don't *not* believe you."

"Come on."

"I believe you saw *something*. I'm just not sure what it was."

"Yeah, well, great, 'cause that makes both of us."

It was the day after Nox had been suspended. They had the
house to themselves, but they mostly kept to the attic room.
Noah worked on his online classes, and Nox lay on his back
with his head dangling upside down over the edge of the bed,
the notebook with his half-written apology abandoned at his
side.

"*If* it was real," Noah said, "then what are we going to do?"

"We need more information," Nox said. He'd been thinking
it over as he stayed up all night, staring at the window until his
eyes burned. The wolf hadn't come back.

Maybe it had known he was awake. Somehow.

He sat up, blinking the spots out of his vision.

"Like what information?" Noah said, tapping away at the keyboard. His too-long bangs hid his eyes. He kept coughing discreetly into a tissue wadded up in his hand. Maybe Nox was imagining it, but Noah seemed to get a shade paler every day. The blue lines of his veins stood out like highlighter marks on his neck and cheek. If he faded any more, he'd disappear.

People disappear from there, Thea's voice whispered in his memory. He ignored it.

"Like, where are Weston and Aster going every night?" Nox said. "Do they know about the wolf? What did it want from you?"

The tapping paused. Noah glanced up, brow furrowed. "You can't be sure it wanted anything from me. Maybe I was just a random victim."

The alarm on Noah's phone went off, and he grabbed the pill bottle off the nightstand. He quickly downed a couple of capsules, washing them down with water.

"Then that's the first thing I need to find out," Nox said, looking away. "If anything like it has ever turned up in Evergreen before."

He flopped down on his pillow. At first, he'd thought getting suspended was the best thing that could've happened to him. It gave him time to investigate. But he'd quickly figured out that there was little to no useful information on Evergreen to be found online, and not a single mention of people going missing in the area. All the places where he could've checked public records and old newspapers—the courthouse, the county clerk's office, the library—were in Grayville. He'd have to wait until he was back at school next week, sneak out during lunch, and see how much research he could cram into an hour.

Or you could go to the woods, a sly voice in his thoughts said. It was the same voice that liked picking fights with guys twice his size. *That's where the wolf probably came from. That's where it has to be hiding.*

He scowled at the ceiling. Yeah, right.

On the weekends, Thea and Aster usually went hiking, Thea's backpack loaded up with jars to collect interesting plants and bugs. Nox had no idea where she found space to put them. Her room was mostly jungle already. Aster had told Nox he was welcome to come along with them anytime, but he wasn't eager to go walking into the woods when he didn't know what else might be hiding there.

Besides, more time with Thea Day was the last thing he needed right now.

"You could always go down to Evergreen," Noah said. "I think it's like a half-hour hike. You'd have to hop the gate, but . . ."

Nox propped himself up on his elbow. "Why? What's in Evergreen?"

"I don't know. Maybe you can learn something. If there really *is* a giant mutant wolf terrorizing people, you can't be the only one who's seen it."

"You're right," he said, sliding off the bed. He had a feeling Noah was just trying to distract him, or maybe tire him out so he'd actually get some sleep tonight. But he did have a point.

He was more likely to learn something useful in Evergreen than he was sitting around in their room worrying all day. Or trying to figure out how many insults about someone's intelligence, his looks, and his mother you could sneak into an apology letter.

"You're gonna text Weston that you're going, right?" Noah said.

"Yeah, sure I will."

"Nox."

He stopped in the doorway and looked back at Noah. Against his will, his eyes traveled again to the pill bottle next to him. It was the new medication they'd started him on last week. No telling if it was working yet. At this point it was like they were throwing darts at a board with their eyes shut. Just trying and hoping for the best.

"What?" he said, a beat too slowly.

"Weston and Aster are helping me," Noah said firmly. "Whatever you saw—I don't think they have anything to do with it."

"What makes you so sure?"

"I don't know. I just am."

Nox would have liked to believe that Weston Day was exactly what he appeared to be: a nice guy who just wanted to help out an old friend and her kids. The way he'd talked Mom down yesterday when she had been on the verge of putting Nox on a bus straight back home was nothing short of astonishing. But he had too many questions he couldn't ignore. Even Thea—who loved her mom and stepdad—was so freaked out about whatever they were hiding that she was willing to sneak around looking for answers.

"So you really don't think there's anything off about them or the house?" Nox said. He and Noah were usually on the same page. Now they were out of sync, and he hated it. "Everything here feels normal to you? Because I felt like there was something wrong before I ever saw the wolf."

"Of course I don't feel normal, but that's the whole deal with being sick, isn't it?" Noah said. "Like, how can I feel normal when I'm dying?"

"You're not dying."

"Hopefully."

He said it like a joke. Like there was anything remotely funny about what was happening to him. Maybe it was easier for him to pretend that he hadn't confessed to Nox how scared he was. But Nox couldn't pretend, not now.

"You don't think they're lying to us?" Nox pressed, feeling himself get more and more wound up, but not knowing how to stop it. "That Mom's hiding something, that your symptoms—You're not getting better! Why aren't you getting any better?"

"This isn't *The X-Files*," Noah said. He gave Nox a serious look, no more joking around. "I'm just sick. Mom's just worried about me. Weston and Aster are weird, but not *that* weird. And no one is lying to us."

No one is lying to us. Maybe that was the most basic core belief that Noah had and Nox didn't. A lot of people lied to them. Teachers, politicians, people on the news. Mom lied, too, usually about money and her job so they wouldn't worry. Kids at school lied to protect themselves or to impress someone or to save face. And some people lied without even meaning to, when they said things like, *It's going to be okay.* Even Nox lied sometimes, for no reason at all, just because he felt like it. He lied to end conversations and he lied so people wouldn't think less of Mom, and he lied when it was convenient or when he had nothing better to say.

It wasn't that Noah was too naive to realize that people weren't always 100 percent honest. He just believed that people—even dishonest people—generally had good intentions. Nox didn't.

Noah thought no one was lying to them.

Nox knew *everyone* was lying to them.

It was a straight shot from the gate to town, walking on the side of the road they took to the bus stop every morning. The early October air smelled of pine and damp earth. His footsteps were underscored by the crinkling of brittle leaves disintegrating beneath his shoes. A screen of clouds halfway obscured the sun, giving the day a muted gray cast. The only wingbeats he heard were accompanied by the trills of the cardinals flitting about overhead.

If he didn't know better, he'd think it was kind of peaceful.

He turned off the one-lane road and found the main street that looped through town. Evergreen had an unformed quality, like someone had gotten part of the way through assembling it, got bored, and gave up. The buildings were sparse, yielding to the stately old pines and oaks that jostled against them as if asserting dominance. The edges of town tapered off till the encroaching forest ate them up like a flood making a riverbank disappear.

The road took him to a tidy square at what he figured was the town center. After his solitary hike, the bustle of people coming in and out of the small shops set him at ease. A modest white chapel staked down the corner. And in the middle of the square stood a statue. A monument, even. Not to some dead politician, or a Founding Father, or a soldier. The statue was winged, fanged, and ghoulish as a movie monster.

A group of tourists was parked in front of it taking pictures. Nox inched closer for a better look. It had curved horns and hooves, batlike wings, and a snout with fangs bared in a frozen growl. The rest of it was mostly human. The plaque on its pedestal read: THE EVERGREEN DEVIL.

Unbidden, the memory of wingbeats in the night came to him.

Then he thought about what Noah would say if he could see Nox getting spooked by a misplaced Halloween prop and wanted to laugh at himself.

He walked along the square and passed a small grocer with baskets of produce lined up outside under an awning, a diner that puffed out maple syrup–scented air, a post office with a community bulletin board by the door. A rack of postcards caught his eye. WANTED: EVERGREEN DEVIL and EVERGREEN, MAINE: DEVIL TERRITORY, they proclaimed, over illustrations of the winged creature from the statue, aerial photos of the surrounding forest, and black-and-white night-vision shots of something big and blurry roaming the woods.

Impulsively, he picked one of the postcards at random and took it inside. As the bored clerk rang him up, Nox said, "What is this? Some kind of Jersey Devil rip-off?"

The clerk shrugged. He must've been just out of high school, gangly and with bad acne, and looking like he wanted to be anywhere but behind that counter. "*Pre*tty much," he drawled. "But don't say that in front of the locals unless you're ready to hear all about how Jersey copied us and not the other way around."

"Is that . . . true?"

"Eh." He waved a hand dismissively. "Doesn't really matter."

Nox handed over a dollar and change. When Mom had given him a bit of emergency cash for the road, she probably hadn't pictured him using it like this. But he was pretty sure this situation counted as an emergency.

"So people really come all the way up here to see . . . that thing?" he asked.

"We get a lot of the runoff from the International Cryptozoology Museum in Portland." He propped his elbow on the counter. There was an old coffee stain on the cuff of his sleeve. "People go there, get hooked, then come here looking for more of the same. Anyway, it's just a legend. We like to play it up. Brings some cash into town."

"Oh," Nox said. So this had nothing to do with monsters, then. Just money. That, at least, was the kind of lie that made sense to him.

The clerk drooped a little more, resting his chin on his hand. "If you're curious, you can head to the museum down the road."

"There's a whole museum about this?"

"And a gift shop, a themed restaurant, a B and B . . . they don't do things halfway around here. Need your receipt?"

"Uh, no thanks," Nox said. If he made the clerk talk any longer, he figured he'd be face down on the desk before long. He took his postcard and headed for the door. At the threshold, he paused, hesitating. "There isn't anything else here, is there?"

"Anything else?" the clerk repeated in a monotone.

"Other, uh, cryptids," Nox hurried to explain. "Maybe something that looks like a . . . wolf?"

The clerk rolled his eyes. "Don't worry. You're a little too far north for a run-in with the Chupacabra."

"Right, okay," Nox said. He didn't know what he'd expected. "Thanks."

The clerk was right: not far from the post office, he found the Evergreen Devil Discovery Center, a log building with enormous plaster bat wings sprouting from the roof. The entry fee was twenty dollars, and Nox wasn't curious enough to pay that much for an obvious scam. A flyer on the window advertised guided tours: for the low, low price of forty-nine dollars, you could spend two hours tramping through the woods in the cold with a bunch of strangers in search of a fictional bat monster. Next door was a gift shop stocked with T-shirts, mugs, hats with miniature horns sticking out of them, and ice cream pops with chocolate wings; it came equipped with a "life-sized" cardboard cutout of the Devil himself out front for people to take selfies with. It took a real force of will for Nox to resist a once-in-a-lifetime opportunity like that, but he managed.

He did stop to study the freestanding sign outside, though. It was a giant map of "sightings" in the area, most of which were conveniently located along hiking routes or near campsites. The back of the sign had a timeline—not of Devil sightings, but of missing people. REMEMBERING THE VICTIMS OF THE EVERGREEN DEVIL, the heading at the top said. Nox scanned the grainy portraits. *Sarah Parker, age 32. Tom Bradley, age 19. Eliza Turner, age 54. Tanya Ford, age 9.* There were dozens. The captions detailed when and where they'd disappeared, all of them under mysterious circumstances.

On a hike, he rounded a bend in the trail ahead of his companions; the others caught up moments later, but he was nowhere to be seen, one read.

She returned to the car to take a nap while her parents packed up the campsite in view of their vehicle, making frequent trips to and from as they loaded the trunk; when they returned the last time, the car was empty, another said.

Ten minutes away from the bus stop, she called her husband to come pick her up. He was there when the bus arrived, but his wife wasn't on it, and the driver had no recollection of seeing her, claimed yet another.

It went on like that: *Taken from bed. Vanished while walking home after school. Tent found abandoned.*

The first few stories were more than a century old; the date on the newest was only a few years ago. Was *this* what Thea had meant about disappearances? She didn't buy into this Devil stuff, did she? There was no way.

"A lot of missing people for such a small town," a woman nearby murmured to her husband. Her arm was wrapped around a little boy's shoulders. He was eating one of the chocolate bat

Popsicles and not paying the slightest bit of attention to the sightings and disappearances sign, which in Nox's book made him the smartest person around.

His dad scoffed. "None of those stories are real. Guaranteed."

Privately, Nox agreed with him.

"They're as real as I am!" croaked an old man hobbling past them with a cane. "That one right there is my big sister, taken when I was your little one's age."

He was pointing at *Tanya, age 9.*

The woman smiled thinly, her arm tightening on her son's shoulders. "I'm very sorry for your loss."

No, she wasn't. Why would she be sorry? She didn't know the old man *or* poor Tanya.

The old man scoffed. "Humph. Don't be. We brought it on ourselves."

"I'm . . . sorry?" she said again. Not offering condolences this time. Just confused.

"All this, these woods, this town, it's the Evergreen Devil's territory," he said darkly. "He collects a tithe of souls from those who make their home here. One soul for every few years of peace and prosperity."

He volunteered all that like he went around spouting unnerving nonsense at total strangers on a regular basis. Maybe he did. He could be on the discovery center's payroll, for all Nox knew.

"But," he added, "there are worse devils than ours."

"All right, that's enough history," the woman's husband said, and he steered his family back inside the gift shop.

The old man made eye contact with Nox and started to speak again.

Nope, Nox thought, and walked away. But he'd be lying if he said the words *tithe of souls* weren't still reverberating through his head.

So . . . this was his hometown. Kind of. He *had* been born here, even if he couldn't remember it. Maybe seeing things that didn't exist was in his blood.

The clouds started to clot together overhead, so Nox headed back. He didn't want to be stuck in Evergreen during a storm. He passed a shack emblazoned with the words *Evergreen Adventure Outfitters*, which sold camping gear. It was stationed on the edge of town, where many of the hiking trails began. Inside on the counter was a stack of brochures with a map of the area, including a copy of the "sightings" guide from the discovery center. Nox stuck that in his pocket along with the postcard. Noah would get a laugh out of it.

The sky cracked open a few minutes before he made it back to the house. He ran over the dirt road as it softened like dough, holding the hood of his jacket down over his head. He managed to climb the gate, half slid down the other side, sprinted up the driveway, and was splattered in mud by the time he let himself back into the house. The sound of rain battering the walls and the howl of the wind seemed magnified, as if there was an echo. Nox locked the door behind him and looked around the drafty front hall, wiping his wet face off on his shirt, listening to the storm and his own breathing.

Despite the ridiculous Devil thing, Evergreen was kind of

welcoming, in a way that made him think of log cabins and marshmallows and campfires. It was probably designed that way, for the tourists, but it worked.

But the Day house—even though it was technically part of Evergreen—wasn't any of that. It was just cold and lonely.

6

EVERY NIGHT, WITHOUT FAIL, NOX STAYED UP
and waited. He heard the Days leave. He heard the house creak
and moan, heard the wingbeats, heard the wind.

Every night, he fell asleep before dawn, and the wolf did not
return.

Nox was slowly losing it. If he didn't know why the beast
had come in the first place, then he couldn't predict if or when
it would come back. He just had to be awake when it did. But
even Nox, a lifelong insomniac, was starting to feel the lack of
rest. His eyes wouldn't focus. Thoughts would slide away from
him. When he slept without meaning to, he'd wake less than
an hour later in a heart-pounding, chest-crushing panic. Noah
watched him like he expected Nox to drop dead any second,
which was hilarious considering only one of them was (1) wolf
bait, and (2) sick with the plague, and it wasn't Nox.

His suspension passed, and he went back to school, depos-
iting his totally sincere, definitely-not-copied-and-pasted
apology letter in the principal's office. School meant access to
the campus library, as well as the public library a few blocks
away. He scoured the internet and local newspaper archives for

anything that sounded even remotely like what he'd seen, or for something other than anonymous posts in sketchy forums to back up the stories about disappearances in Evergreen. In class, he sat in the back and dozed off. If this lasted any longer, his grades were doomed to die a slow, brutal death.

By Friday afternoon, Nox felt like a walking skeleton. He barely remembered the bus ride back to Evergreen. Somehow he ended up in Weston's car, where it took all his willpower not to drift off in the passenger seat. His mind wandered. It felt like only an instant had passed before they were pulling up to the house. Weston held up his hand before Nox and Thea could get out.

"Nox," he said. "Would you mind staying for a minute?"

Nox shrugged. "What's up?" he said, once Thea left.

"I think you know." Weston peered over at Nox. "Your mom is pretty worried."

Since Nox didn't make a habit of incriminating himself, he stayed quiet.

"She sent you here because she thought being together would do you both good," Weston said. "But it hasn't been good for you, has it?"

Nox scowled at the dashboard. "Sure it has."

"Really? Then how come you're always skipping class, or sleeping through it?"

Nox wavered. He could pretend he was having nightmares—normal, run-of-the-mill nightmares—and that was why he couldn't make it through an hour of geometry without nodding off. But wouldn't that be a pretty good reason to send him home anyway? If he could just think through the fog—

"Your brother's worried, too. Stress is the last thing he needs right now, when he's trying to heal—"

More than anything else Weston could've said, that was the one that stung the most.

"You think being around me is going to make Noah *worse*?"

"I didn't say that."

"You implied it!"

Weston sighed gustily, taking off his glasses to rub at the bridge of his nose. "See, Nox, it's that—hostility. What's going on? What aren't you telling us?"

Nox couldn't come up with an answer. Weston replaced his glasses and turned in his seat. "Come on. You can talk to me," he said.

Nox studied him warily. Could he trust him?

Weston had stood up for Nox when he got in trouble for fighting. He'd talked to Mom so that Nox wouldn't have to go home. He didn't have to do that; he could've just sent Nox away and saved himself the headache. Maybe Noah was right. Maybe Nox was being paranoid and unfair, thinking the worst of people who were only trying to help.

Haltingly, he told Weston the truth. All of it. Weston listened intently. And then, when Nox was done speaking, he said: "Sounds like a pretty scary nightmare."

Nox's heart sank. His face went hot with embarrassment.

"You think I'm delusional," he said. "Like I can't tell the difference between dreams and reality."

"Not at all. You're just scared for your brother."

"I'm *not* scared."

"It's hard to see someone you love like this. You've been through everything together, and now there's this one thing that—that he has to go through without you."

Weston's voice was so kind Nox wanted to twist it around his neck like a rope and strangle him with it. He stared at his fists, which were clenched tight in his lap.

"You think I'm making things up."

"No. I think you believe everything you told me," Weston said. "But . . . monsters are so simple, aren't they? They're big and scary and you can fight them. You can win. Diseases aren't simple like that. There's nothing to fight. The thing hurting your brother is inside him."

Nox was so mad he thought he'd explode. But cold clarity cut through the red haze of his anger. Yelling and arguing wouldn't get him anywhere. Either Weston knew the truth and was deliberately hiding it from Nox, or he didn't know and would never believe him. There was no getting through to him either way.

He didn't need Weston on his side. He didn't need *anyone* on his side. He just needed to get him off his case so that Nox could figure this out on his own.

"You're right," Nox said. "Sorry. It must have been a nightmare."

"It's okay, buddy. Are you going to try to do better in school?"

"Yeah."

"That's great." Weston patted Nox on the shoulder. "If not, well . . . I'm not sure anything I say will change Celia's mind about bringing you back home this time. Don't worry about that, though. I'm sure you'll work hard and make your mom proud."

Nox knew a threat when he heard one. *Do what you're told and don't ask questions, or else.*

"I will," Nox said.

"I believe you. All right, let's go see what I can scrounge up for dinner."

Nox followed him tamely. If pretending was the only way to stay here, with Noah, then that was what he'd do.

Nox was on his best behavior during dinner. He didn't really know what *best behavior* was supposed to look like, but he made a decent stab at it. He thought so, anyway. He didn't speak unless spoken to, didn't argue with Thea, and didn't scowl at anyone. The Days were unusually quiet, and Noah kept shooting him worried glances.

Afterward, Thea paid her first visit to the attic room.

The sound of hiking boots stomping up the stairs was his only warning before a freckled hand flung the door open, and Thea stormed in. Noah was downstairs in the shower. Nox had been flipping through the notebook he was using to compile the research he'd gathered on Evergreen; at her dramatic entrance, he hurriedly shoved it under the pile of clothes at the foot of his bed.

"Why did you act like such a jerk at dinner?" she said.

"*Huh?* I didn't even do anything!"

Nox had been in trouble plenty, but not when he was *trying* to be good. It was a little insulting.

Thea looked like she was ten seconds away from floating off the ground with her head spinning like a top. Her face was so red her freckles had disappeared. He hadn't realized she was capable of that kind of anger, and he observed it with detached interest.

"You looked like you were plotting murder," she told him.

"Back *off.*"

"*You* back off. Ever since you got here, all you've done is be moody and judgmental—"

"Why don't you mind your own business?" he snapped.

Thea's fists clenched and unclenched at her sides, as if they were catching and releasing her anger bit by bit. She shut her eyes and half turned away from him, and he thought she was going to leave—but she didn't.

"You figured something out, didn't you?" she said.

His back stiffened. "What do you mean?"

"I know this place is . . . weird. And I think you do, too."

"Please tell me you're not talking about the Devil thing," he said derisively. "There's no way you believe that."

"No, but there's obviously something happening here that—"

"What do you mean, obviously? Everyone acts like nothing's wrong—"

He cut himself off. He was tired of trying to put into words the deeply unsettled feeling he'd had since the first day he'd set foot in Evergreen. He couldn't even explain it to Mom and Noah. But maybe this was his chance to learn something he couldn't find out for himself. If he could get Thea to keep talking.

"Most people live here because it's where they were born," she said. "They've never left. They're never going to leave. To them, this is normal."

"But not to you."

"My mom and I only moved here a few years ago," she said. "And I'm not staying. I'm going to travel around the world and never come back."

She glared as if daring him to contradict her. Nox was still thinking about what she'd said before. *This place is weird.*

That was one way of putting it.

"Weird how?" he said. "What's that mean?"

"I mean . . . You know . . ."

"Maybe. Pretend I don't."

They scowled at each other.

"Fine," Thea said. "Some people think Evergreen is haunted."

Nox mulled it over. The wolf had jumped through solid glass. Like a ghost. And part of him *wanted* it to be a ghost—wanted to put a tidy, five-letter label on what he'd experienced and know that there were others out there who might understand. "That could explain the sounds I keep hearing."

"You hear it, too?"

"The wingbeats?"

"Yeah. And the scratching."

Nox blinked at her. "Scratching?"

Thea's shoulders slumped. "Guess not."

"What scratching?"

"It sounds like twigs scraping the outside of my window," she said. "Just sometimes. It's been happening ever since I moved here. Your mom never said anything about that?"

"Why would she?" Nox said, baffled.

"My room used to be a guest room. Dad says she stayed over a lot when they were kids, so that's where she would've slept."

"Oh." Nox looked at his hands. "No. She doesn't talk about this place, like, ever."

"But we've both heard the wingbeats."

"Yeah. So that's your theory? Ghosts?"

He could sort of see where she was coming from. Hauntings and mysterious, creepy noises went hand in hand. According to the movies, anyway. And he didn't really have a better frame of reference.

But she said, "No. Of *course* not. Ghosts aren't real."

This was the longest conversation he had had with Thea, and he was already regretting it. "Then *what*?" he said impatiently.

"I don't know yet! But there has to be a reason why people go missing."

"The people from the stories about the Evergreen Devil?"

"Yeah, only it's for real," Thea said. "We lose someone every few years. People just accept it, and Evergreen's not important enough to make national news. This isn't the only place where people just . . . stop existing and the rest of the world doesn't notice. But I don't think it's, like, human trafficking. Or an imaginary devil. I think it's something else."

Could a ghost make people vanish?

"A haunting wouldn't explain what your parents are up to," he said. "And it wouldn't explain—"

It wouldn't explain why the wolf had come for Noah. Why him? Why not someone else?

Thea stared at him with something that almost looked like concern. "What?"

For a moment, he considered telling her the truth. She was Noah's friend. She wouldn't want him to get hurt.

Nox didn't like Thea. But he could admit to himself that his animosity toward her had very little to do with anything she'd done, and much more to do with everything and everyone else. Thea had been with Noah when Nox wasn't allowed to be. She would still be here if Nox got sent away. She was the one who wasn't surprised when Noah got in the car with them in the morning because she already knew he had a checkup, and the one who'd sat with him on his bad days when Nox wasn't even aware Noah was having days that bad. If Nox had been told that Noah was getting worse when he still wasn't allowed to come and see him, it would have been a form of torture. But that didn't make it any easier to accept. And now, after he'd just gotten Noah back, he could lose him again—maybe for good this time. Because of the wolf or because he was sick, or because of any of the strange secret things about Evergreen or the Day house, things Nox didn't even know enough about to be afraid of yet.

He could tell Thea what he'd seen. Even if she didn't believe him, she was at least willing to investigate. She wanted to know what was going on as badly as he did. Maybe they could help each other.

But he had messed up when he'd confided in Weston earlier.

74

He wasn't going to make the same mistake again.

"Nothing," Nox said. "Can you leave me alone now? I'm tired."

"Ugh. Whatever, Nox." Thea turned on her heel and flounced away, as much as anyone could flounce in a pair of boots. Nox almost felt bad about shutting her down. *Almost.*

But he couldn't deal with another person telling him he hadn't seen what he'd seen. Not tonight.

7

NOAH ROLLED OVER ONTO HIS SIDE, FACING Nox. The attic was dimly moonlit, and Nox was so tired he was seeing stars. He sat against the headboard, clutching a can of Red Bull in one hand; his other rested on the baseball bat next to him.

The creature hadn't come back yet. But when it did, he'd be ready.

Noah yawned loudly, stretching out his arms and flopping over onto his back. "I'm *soooo sleepy*," he said.

"So go to sleep."

"Yup. About to do that. In my extremely comfortable—"

Nox snorted.

"*Luxurious*, soft, warm bed . . ."

"I'm very happy for you. Good night."

Nox glared at the window. He had a row of extra Red Bulls on the nightstand between their beds, and he was fully dressed, still wearing his shoes and jacket and everything. It would be easier to stay up that way.

"When are *you* going to sleep?" Noah said, propping himself up on one elbow.

"I took a nap earlier."

"And if it comes back," Noah said, "you think a baseball bat's going to stop it?"

"It's better than nothing."

"Practice your swing lately? I've seen you in PE. You're about as likely to miss and take out the lamp as you are to hit the thing."

That one stung a little.

"Someone's in a bad mood," Nox said, biting back the angry response he could've given. "I thought you said you were tired."

Noah sat up. "I'm sick, but I'm not *helpless*. You don't have to protect me."

"I know you're not!" Nox said, taken aback.

"You're killing yourself because you think you have to defend me from some monster. I don't *want* that."

"I know you don't believe me—"

"I do believe you! I just don't care! Let it come and get me. That's better than—"

He cut himself off with a frustrated noise, twisting the edge of the blanket in his hands.

"Stop," Nox said, knowing how that sentence would've ended. "You're not dying."

"Then how come I'm getting worse again?" Noah said, voice breaking.

"What?" Nox reached over and flicked on the lamp. "What are you talking about?"

Noah rolled up his sleeves. The deadened gray skin on his wrists had spread in patches over his forearms. The raised white and yellow spots on the back of his neck had shown up all over his knuckles, which were swollen and red. He moved his hands stiffly, but Nox couldn't tell if it was because they hurt or if those awful sores made it hard to bend the joints.

"And earlier today, I spat out . . . this." He pulled a folded paper towel out from under his pillow. Inside, covered in the sticky red-brown substance Noah kept coughing up, was a motionless cone-shaped lump that Nox mistook for an insect at first. But it wasn't. It was a catkin, like off a tree, its downy surface glued flat.

Nox stared down at it, nauseated.

"Did you show that to Weston?" he asked, staying calm for Noah's sake. They couldn't both freak out.

"No! Because it means you were right. This isn't just some skin disease," Noah hissed. "They've been giving me all these pills and injections, but none of it helped. I didn't get any side effects, either. I think they were fakes. And if Weston's been using fake treatments on me, then . . . I don't know what it means. I don't know what to do."

He sounded terrified.

"We'll call Mom tomorrow," Nox said. "We'll get out of Evergreen."

"But she's the one who sent us here in the first place."

"Maybe she didn't know," he said staunchly. Even if Mom was hiding something, he was certain at least that she wanted Noah alive. "And if she doesn't believe us, then we'll leave anyway. Go to Portland and find a hospital there. They'll have to help you once they see this."

First thing in the morning, if Mom didn't say she was coming to get them, then he was stealing Aster's credit card and getting the two of them on the first bus out of here.

"Last time I left the house, I got—really, really sick," Noah said in a hoarse whisper. "What if I can't get away?"

"I'll carry you if I have to," Nox said. "Either way, this is our last night in Evergreen."

Hours later—after Noah had calmed down enough to turn off the light and go to sleep, after Nox had opened his second Red Bull of the night, after it had gone limp in his hand and he'd dozed off sitting up . . .

Something woke him.

A sound—the puff of air, like padding footsteps on a soft surface—and a sudden brightness that washed the inside of his eyelids with color.

Sleep fought him viciously. It pinned his limbs to the bed, sealed his eyes shut, clouded his mind. He didn't think to call out. He didn't think anything, other than:

Get up!

He peeled his eyes open. Phantom white light filled the room. He squinted against it, groping around for his baseball bat. The Red Bull fell to the ground with a clatter, spilling what was left of its contents. He jumped at the sound and looked up instinctively—

The beast was there, on Noah's bed. It crouched above him, its paw hovering over his chest. The razor tips of its claws just grazed Noah's shirt.

"St— *Stop*," Nox said, voice hoarse and thick with sleep.

There was nothing ghostly about it. Nothing ghostly about the ripple of muscle in its great silvery hide, or the flick of its huge brush tail, or the indents its paws made in the mattress, or the way its head swiveled around to pierce him with all those eyes.

Nox's fingers closed around the handle of the bat. He yanked it up, holding it poised to swing, and said: "*Get away from him!*"

Without looking away from Nox, it lowered its paw—*into* Noah's chest. Its claws disappeared through his shirt, and deeper, until they were buried in Noah's rib cage. But there was no blood, and Noah didn't wake up.

Nox slid down from the bed, swinging the bat wildly—but the beast opened its jaws and caught the bat between its teeth. He tried to pull back, but its teeth closed, ripping the handle from his grasp and crumpling the metal. When it let go, the misshapen bat fell to the ground, clanging. Nox lunged, going for its tail, intending to drag it off of Noah—

But it was too late.

It withdrew its paw from Noah's chest, clutching something golden and bright between its claws—sprang over Nox's head—soared to the window in one leap—

And dissolved through the blinds.

He ran to the window, shoved it open, and stuck his head outside. The wolf loped down the side of the house, traversing a vertical wall as easily as flat ground. It was heading for the cliff—it hit the edge without slowing, and it jumped.

The last Nox saw of it was its tail, vanishing into the northern woods.

Nox stood there, paralyzed, until he remembered Noah. He turned on the light—as harsh and grounding as the phantom creature had been dreamlike and surreal—before he rushed back to the bed and shook him frantically. But he didn't stir.

"Noah?" he said. And then, louder: "Noah!"

Nothing. His eyelids didn't even flutter. Nox bent close, heart hammering, until he heard Noah's breathing. Hope made him feel suddenly weak; he had to use the bed to prop himself up. If Noah was breathing, and he had no visible injuries, then . . . he was okay. Had to be okay.

Only he still wasn't responding.

"Noah. Come on. Get up—get—"

Nox didn't know how many times he'd said Noah's name by then. That brief surge of hope soured and became an all-consuming dread. His throat closed, throttling the rest of his words before they could make it into the air. After a long moment—part of him still convinced that if he waited just a little bit more, Noah would spring up and laugh at him for worrying over nothing—he swallowed hard and dragged his hands off Noah's shoulders.

Noah wasn't okay.

That wolf had taken something from him. Out of him. And now he wasn't waking up. Nox could call an ambulance—he almost did—but as he picked up his phone and stared down at it, he couldn't bring himself to dial the number. What remedy would a doctor prescribe for a supernatural wolf attack? What had *any* doctor, any adult in their life, done when Noah had been sick all this time? None of them had known how to help him before. Noah even suspected the treatments had been faked. They couldn't trust anyone in Evergreen, and that wasn't going to change now.

In his memory, a voice whispered the words *tithe of souls*.

A strange calm fell over Nox—a sense of purpose that steadied him. There was only one thing to do: he had to find the wolf, and he had to get back whatever it had stolen from Noah.

"I'll be back soon," he promised Noah, though there was no way he could've heard. And then he didn't hesitate any longer. He ran. He couldn't waste another second—it could be miles away by now.

The stairs below the attic creaked admonishingly as he raced down them. The floorboards in the hall groaned underfoot. He was down the last flight of stairs, through the entryway, reaching for the front door, when—

"Nox? What are you doing?"

Standing at the top of the staircase, arms folded, was Thea.

8

"WHAT—WHAT ARE *YOU* DOING?" HE COUNTERED.
She had her hiking boots on and her backpack slung over one
shoulder. "Going somewhere?"

"I . . ." She took a few halting steps down. "My parents are up
to something, and they're lying to me about it. After we talked
earlier, I realized I was tired of waiting around for answers. I
need to go find them myself."

"So you're going to follow them?"

"Yeah." She gripped the strap of her bag. "Kind of. I think
they're somewhere in the woods right now. So I'm going to bike
the main road and look for their car. If I'm right, they would
have had to park it close to wherever they are and keep going on
foot. Once I have evidence, they'll have to—"

"What? Tell you the truth?" Nox said. "They're not going to
do that. You'll just get in trouble for sneaking out."

"Yeah, well, where are *you* going, smart guy?"

His chest hurt, like it was being slowly and mercilessly
crushed. "I don't have time for this. Good luck with your parents."

He threw the door open and went out into the night. Barely
detectable breezes and small nocturnal things moved through

the grasses, which stirred with a soft sigh. It was bright outside, moonlight diluting the darkness like milk clouding coffee. It made him think of Mom. Should he call her?

No time.

"Wait, Nox—" Thea had come after him. "You can't just . . . What's wrong?"

"It's Noah."

"Is he okay? Should I call 911?"

"You can if you want."

She looked from him to the house, visibly torn between following Nox and checking on Noah. He didn't wait for her. There was only one right choice here, and a smart, rational person like Thea was sure to know it.

He walked away, changing course at the last minute and going for the shed, where they kept the bikes. He thought he'd shaken her off, but she caught up a moment later, her hurried footsteps muffled in the grass.

"If I go with you, will you tell me what's going on?" she asked.

"Don't come with me."

"Not asking for permission."

He made a frustrated noise through gritted teeth and shot her a glare that had made schoolyard bullies and assistant principals alike flinch. But Thea only gave him an unimpressed look back.

"Fine," he said. "But don't blame me when you change your mind."

He borrowed Aster's bike while Thea grabbed her own.

There was no safe way down the bluff into the north woods. They'd have to go around, biking downhill along the road into Evergreen and then veering off at one of the hiking trails. The chains on the gate were too heavy for Nox to undo on his own, but between him and Thea, they managed.

The gate swung loose as they biked away, the lazy screech of its hinges following them like a forlorn send-off.

Thea took the lead when they got to the trails. She knew them by heart. He told her where they needed to go, and she picked the trail—out of dozens or more—that would get them to the right part of the woods. Or close to it, she said.

"This one's going north*east*," he called out after a few minutes.

"There aren't any paths that cut north past my house," she said. "But we can't—"

"We have to leave the path."

He braked. A few feet ahead, she did, too, wheeling the bike around to face him.

"Are you serious?" Her face was pale with exhaustion, her freckles standing out and the bags under her eyes pronounced. A few strands of her dark red hair rebelled against her braid, lunging for freedom in every direction. "You're just going to wander around in the woods—do you know how many *miles* of wilderness you're talking about? Can you at least tell me why we're doing this yet?"

"The cliff is over there," he said, pointing at its craggy silhouette against the navy sky. The house was a thorny crown at its apex. Its roof was just barely visible past the tops of the trees. Nox could even see the yellow light from the attic window, which he hadn't bothered to turn off before leaving. "So that's where I'm going."

Without waiting for her, he left the path. The sound of another set of wheels and Thea's muttered complaints followed. But the woods quickly grew too dense to ride their bikes through. He dismounted and left his leaning against a tree. A beat of silence as Thea must have hesitated, and then her rapid footsteps caught up with him.

"Listen to me for *once*," Thea said. "We're going to get lost."

"You can go back if you want."

"You said you'd tell me what was going on!" she said, even though he was almost positive he'd agreed to nothing of the sort. "So tell me. What are we doing out here?"

He hesitated, but all the reasons he'd had for keeping his secrets, which had seemed so important just a few hours ago, meant nothing now. What difference would it make if she didn't believe him? If she left him here, then he was no worse off. So he told her everything. He kept hiking, not looking at her face, not wanting to see the scorn there.

North of the bluff, the trees grew close together. The two of them made a racket fighting through the brush, their shoes smashing through dry, crackling things and their arms fending off branches that clung and scratched. They clambered over fallen logs and under low-hanging boughs and caught themselves with whispered curses when they stumbled. With the moon hidden behind the tangled canopy, Thea pulled out a flashlight. Nox just used his phone to light his way. He hadn't brought anything else; he was lucky he'd already had his phone in his pocket, or he'd have left that behind, too.

"What are you going to do if you find it?" she asked, surprising him.

Nox shrugged. He'd have to figure that out when he got there.

"And what if you don't?" she said. "What if it's gone?"

"I'm not going back empty-handed," he told her. "I can't go back when Noah—"

When Noah wasn't waking up.

There was a lump in Nox's throat, and for a horrible, humiliating second, he thought he wouldn't be able to speak ever again—or, worse, he'd speak and his voice would fail, right in front of bossy, know-it-all Thea. And somehow she'd know, without him telling her, how the first time the wolf had come, he'd frozen in fear, and the second time, he hadn't been fast enough to stop it even when he'd tried his hardest. If she'd seen him then, she wouldn't have followed him out here, that was for sure. Because she'd understand how helpless and weak he'd been when it really counted, and she'd think he didn't have the slightest chance of saving Noah.

And he couldn't let her think that, because if someone else thought it, that might make it real.

Farther north, the ground was flat, with a thick layer of fallen leaves breaking down into soft, spongy earth. It muffled his footsteps like foam. But his exhaustion was catching up with him. He was out of breath; his vision blurred.

"Nox, stop."

"What *now*?"

"We're lost."

He bit back a groan. "No, we're not."

"I lost track of where the trail was, like, ten minutes ago. I can't even see the house anymore."

She was right. The trees were so tall they blocked his line of sight to the house and the bluff. But they still weren't lost. Nox wasn't, anyway.

"Turn off your flashlight," he said, doing the same with his own.

"What?"

"Just do it."

With the lights off and the trees more spaced out here, he could see the stars again. He studied the sky for about five seconds, and then, pointing, he said: "That way's north. That way's south. You can go home if you want."

He walked on. Thea wasn't wrong—there was a lot of ground to cover. And just because the wolf had gone into the northern woods didn't mean it had *kept* going north. It could have looped around and headed for Evergreen, for all he knew. But then, Evergreen would've probably built a monument to the thing a long time ago if it had ever been sighted around there. He was guessing it usually stayed clear of town.

Thea was still following him.

"What?" he said. "Scared to go back alone?"

"I can't just leave you here."

"You could tell your parents to call a search party to come get me."

He kind of hoped she'd do that. No one was sending a search party to get a golden *something* back from a monster made of moonlight, but they'd send one after a twelve-year-old boy who'd gotten lost in the woods. And maybe then they'd find the wolf.

"I can't," she said again. "My parents spent years telling me to stay on the path and to never go into the woods at night without one of them, and I brought you here anyway. I'm not just going to abandon you after that."

"Call them, then."

"There's no reception here."

He shrugged. "Just quit fooling yourself."

"What?"

"You're not doing this out of the goodness of your heart. Say what you want, but you being here has nothing to do with wanting to look out for me."

She was quiet for so long he almost thought she wasn't going to reply. Finally, she said, "It did at first."

"But not anymore. So what gives?"

"This could be my only chance to find the truth about what's wrong with Evergreen."

"Why do you care?" he asked. "Didn't you say you were gonna move away as soon as you could?"

"I need to know, or it'll haunt me forever," she said. "All these mysteries will be stuck in my head, and it'll be like I never left, no matter where I go."

They fell silent. Nox felt more and more hopeless with every passing second.

Then something changed. He couldn't place it at first—couldn't tell which of his senses had gone on alert. At last, he heard it: a steady, repetitive *thwack, thwack, thwack.*

Thea tugged at his sleeve, but he shook her off. As they neared the source of the sound, he made out a glow in the distance. The trees grew twisted and bent, unlike the tall pines they'd passed before. The light threw shadows into their craggy, grooved trunks, so they looked like ghastly faces, with pits in the bark like mouths open in agony and black gashes like eyes.

An acid-blue butterfly perched on one of the trunks. Its wings were made up of subtle translucent panes like stained glass, the blue so bright it almost glowed. But each wing was about the size of his fist. Its body was covered in white fur, its spindly little legs twitching.

"It's a moth," Thea said, staring at it with a rapturous expression. "I've never seen anything like it."

"I thought moths were brown."

"Not all of them. Look at the antennae—they're kind of, uh, feathery? And its wings are open. Butterflies usually rest with theirs closed." She leaned closer, not blinking, and muttered under her breath, "Maybe I can catch it. . . ."

She pulled her backpack around to the front of her body as if to take out one of the jars she kept in there.

"We're here to help Noah, *not* add to your spooky bug collection," he said. "Come on."

As the light grew brighter, and that rhythmic sound grew louder, Nox counted more and more of those blue moths. Dozens. Maybe hundreds. They dotted the tree trunks with their wings splayed open, fluttered overhead, bloomed from the canopy like diseased flowers. Some were smaller than the first one they'd seen, and some, horribly, larger.

At last, through a gap in the trees, a cabin loomed out of the darkness. Firelight spilled from its window, the source of the flickery glow that had led them here. Moths crawled over its walls and flew lazily around the porch.

Out front, the biggest man Nox had ever seen was chopping firewood, his black hair tied back and immense shoulders heaving. The sound they'd heard was his axe. He raised it high over his head and then swung it down, a clean *whoosh* through the air, followed by that satisfying *thwack*.

Thea got in front of Nox and shook her head frantically.

Nox knew you didn't walk up to strange adults in the middle of the night, in the woods, far away from anyone who could hear you shout for help. Not if you had any common sense. But if this guy lived out here, then he probably knew about the wolf. Maybe he'd even seen it. He might be the only other person in the world who had. Nox stepped around Thea and into the firelight.

9

THE AXE FROZE ON THE UPSWING, AND THE woods were dead silent.

Firelight painted one side of the man's face and threw the other into shadow, turning him all orange and black, like a jack-o'-lantern. Still, Nox could make out a bearded jawline as hard as granite, and eyes so dark they could've been inkblots. He lowered the axe and set it down carefully. Only when he straightened did Nox realize how broad he really was.

Something in Nox went off like a siren. If he'd been a dog, his hackles would've risen.

A rustle from behind told him that Thea stood at his shoulder. That was the only thing that kept Nox from retreating. Charging in had been his idea, so he couldn't back out now.

The man sighed. "What, in the name of all things holy, are you kids doing out here at this time of night?"

He had a low, rough voice to match his rough hands. Chipped fingernails, a cut over one of the knuckles. Calluses, probably, though Nox couldn't see them from here.

"I'm sorry, sir," Thea said. "We—we went into the woods on a dare, and—and now we're lost. We'll leave."

"That's not true," Nox said.

"Nox!" she hissed.

The woodsman raised a bushy eyebrow. A moth alighted on his shoulder and crawled over the back of his neck, disappearing. He didn't seem to notice. Nox suppressed a shiver of revulsion.

"I'm looking for something," Nox said. "An animal."

The man crossed his arms. His biceps threatened to burst the seams of his shirtsleeves.

"The only things out here are raccoons and coyotes," he said firmly. "And I'm too busy to be babysitting you. Get out of here."

Nox bristled. *Babysitting?*

"Too busy . . . chopping wood at three in the morning?" he said.

The woodsman chuckled. "Go away, kid. Go home."

He picked up his axe. A second later, the *thwack, thwack, thwack* resumed.

They trudged back into the forest, past the trees with the howling faces, past the infestation of moths, until they reached the place where the shadows ate up the firelight. There, Nox stopped. The woods blocked their view of the stranger, and, more important, his view of them.

"He knows something," he whispered to Thea.

She shook her head rapidly. "This is weird. I want to go home."

"Go, then," he told her. He was tired of her saying she wanted to leave and then not leaving. "I'm going to find out what this guy's hiding."

He made a circuit around the cabin, tiptoeing over fallen leaves that crunched under his shoes. Thea trailed along after him like a freckly shadow. Once he was sure they wouldn't be seen, he crept toward the edge of the clearing again. Moths covered the back of the cabin, their bright wings soaking up the moonlight, providing a faint and spectral illumination. When one drifted off the wall and into the trees, he could've mistaken it for a ghost, a spirit of the woods.

He had been hoping to find a window so he could just take a peek inside. But there was only a door.

Nox crept away from the trees, waving Thea off when she tried to follow him. It was best for only one of them to be out in the open. The sound of the woodsman's axe beat steadily in the not-so-distant background. As long as he was occupied, Nox didn't have anything to worry about.

He crossed the backyard, over the wildflowers and scrubby patches that looked like a vegetable garden. Slowly, he reached for the doorknob, holding his breath, part of him expecting an alarm to go off the second his fingertips made contact—

"Nox!"

Thea's voice was a strangled, fearful whisper. He spun around, heart racing, fully expecting to see the woodsman looming over him.

But there was no woodsman. It was only a hare, crouched halfway between the cabin and the trees, regarding him with its beady eyes. It was the same dazzling white as the wolf. In front of its long ears, a pair of antlers jutted from its head.

His mind came up with a dozen rationalizations in the span

of a second—it was fake, it was a trick, it was a pet in a silly outfit. But it had the lean, rangy body of a wild thing, and its fur parted around the base of the antlers in a way that made it clear they weren't stuck on top but growing out of its skull. It was real. It was as real as the wolf had been. He looked at Thea, his shock mirrored in her face—and saw the woodsman coming up behind her.

Nox didn't have a chance to cry out a warning before the woodsman had snatched her by the arm, almost lifting her off the ground.

Thea shrieked, scaring away the moths on the wall. The antlered *thing* took flight, slingshotting into the woods.

"Sorry," the woodsman said, gruffly, and released her. She backed away and swiped a long stick off the ground, holding it up threateningly. He lifted his hands in a gesture of peace. "I didn't mean to scare you. Just don't want you bolting and getting even more lost."

"That didn't look like a raccoon to me," Nox said.

The woodsman made an exasperated noise.

"Any chance you'd believe me if I told you it was a rabbit with a birth defect?" he tried.

Nox and Thea shook their heads.

"Great. Then I guess you'd better come in."

Having the woodsman's permission to enter the cabin made the idea lose its appeal. Thea must have been on the same page, because she said, "No. We can talk out here. You're a stranger, and—we're not going anywhere with you. Right, Nox?"

"I liked you better when you were calling me *sir*," he told her, rolling his eyes. "Anyway, I'm not a stranger. *I* live here. *You're* the strangers."

He did have a point there.

"So. I'm going inside. You're free to follow, or not."

He strode past Nox and opened the door. Firelight streamed out and painted a golden ribbon through the woods. Before Nox could get a look inside, he'd closed the door behind him.

"Let's get out of here," Thea said, still brandishing her makeshift club. "He's a creep."

"So you . . . *don't* want to know more about the thing we just saw? Or the moths?" Nox said. Thea looked stricken. Of course she wanted to know. She was supposed to be an expert on all the local creatures. How could she resist the temptation of two brand-new, completely unfamiliar species? "If he wanted to hurt us, he would've done it already."

"It doesn't make sense that anyone lives out here," Thea said. "There's not supposed to be anyone in this part of the woods."

He shrugged. "I'm going inside. I guess you can stay here."

"Nox, wait!"

But he was already following the woodsman through the door.

10

THE CABIN WAS ONE ROOM WITH A SMALL kitchen in the corner and a bed near the door. There were no photographs, but shelves built into the walls held books on herbal remedies, foraging, animal physiology, forest nursery, and some fiction here and there. Moths fluttered around the hearth, the firelight sheathing their wings like gold plating.

"If you're going to stand there, at least shut the door," the woodsman said. He stood at the counter with his back to them as he poured steaming water from a kettle into three mugs.

They did. Then, feeling awkward, Nox went to one of the chairs at the tiny table and sat down. Thea took the other chair, and the woodsman put the mugs in front of them.

"What are your names?" he asked.

Thea frowned and didn't say anything.

"I'm Nox," he said. "This is Thea. Who are you?"

"My name is Adam Motte." He dragged over a stepladder from the kitchen to sit on; it put him at about eye level with Nox and Thea. "I'm no one."

"What was that thing outside?" Thea asked reluctantly.

"Jackalope," Adam said. "Harmless."

"Those aren't real."

"Okay."

When he offered no further explanation, Thea huffed. "And these moths—what are they called?"

He set his mug down on the table and held out his hand. One of the moths fluttered into his palm. Nox's stomach squirmed, but he couldn't look away. Its wings, outstretched, were nearly ten inches across, its size even more striking against Adam's large hand. It crawled up his fingers, antennae quivering.

"These?" he said. "They're eris moths. They lay their eggs in the bark of the moros trees outside." He gave his hand a twitch, and the moth flew away. "But you didn't come all this way to talk about them."

"You're right," Nox said, and again recounted the story he'd told Thea earlier.

Adam's expression grew shadowed and grim. He propped his elbow on the table and leaned heavily against it.

"I thought maybe you'd seen something from the Night-wood," he said in a low, troubled voice. "I just didn't think you'd seen *that*."

"Nightwood?" Thea said. "What's that?"

"So you know what it is," Nox said eagerly. "The wolf, I mean."

"The lunar wolf belongs to Zahna, Keeper of Night and Warden of the Wilds. She lives in the Nightwood." He nodded at Thea. "And to answer your question, the Nightwood is wilderness unlike any you've encountered in your short lives. It's darkness where there should be light, and death where there should be life. And it's no place for children."

Adam put his mug down with a soft thud. He leaned back, massive arms folded over his barrel chest. "You're not the first people to come upon the Nightwood by accident. I've rounded up plenty of strays before. Sent them back to safety. It's why I can't bring myself to leave this place behind. I'd like to help you now, like I've helped those before you. But if Zahna sent her familiar to take something from your brother, it's gone."

"How do I find her?" Nox asked.

"You don't want to find her."

"But if I did."

Adam studied him gravely, the firelight turning his eyes into shadowy gulfs. "You're not going home no matter what I say, are you?"

"No," Nox said.

Adam rubbed a hand over his beard, looking conflicted. At last, he stood, pulled a pen and notebook off a shelf, and tore out a sheet. "I'm only telling you this because if you get lost, you're dead. Lord knows I don't need that on my conscience."

He did a quick, rough sketch that quickly filled the page. At first it didn't look like anything to Nox, just a scribble, crooked and tangled lines with tiny, barely decipherable symbols here and there. But then he understood. It was a map.

"You're really helping us?" he said. For the first time all night, he felt something approaching hope.

"I . . . shouldn't," Adam grunted. His pen stilled, and his dark eyes met Nox's for an instant. The worried crease in his forehead smoothed out as his expression softened. "But I

understand why you need to do this. I had a brother, too, once."
He gave a short laugh. "No, he was a friend, but he *felt* like a
brother. Sometimes I forget he wasn't."

"What happened to him?" Nox asked.

"He's gone," Adam said curtly, bending over the map again.
"Nightwood took him. That's what it does."

"Is that why you . . . *round up the strays*, like you said?" It was
none of his business, but he couldn't hold the question back.
Maybe this was what had happened to everyone who disappeared from Evergreen—they'd just gotten lost someplace they
couldn't come back from. "To stop more people from getting
hurt."

"I live here anyway. Easy enough to keep an eye out. Now
shush, boy, I'm concentrating."

A pang of sympathy made Nox's chest ache. He understood
Adam. It was disturbingly easy to picture himself growing up
to be a grumpy old recluse without Noah. Even Thea relaxed a
little, biting the corner of her lip as if deep in thought while she
watched Adam work. Finally, he straightened.

"We're *here*." Adam jabbed the bottom left corner with the
end of his pen. "Zahna's watchtower is *there*. If you go too far,
you'll reach the Web"—he prodded the top right corner of the
map—"so make sure you *don't*. It's walled off, but you still don't
want to get too close. Avoid it at all costs. And stay on the path.
It has its dangers, but it's nothing compared to the rest of the
woods."

"And you're saying that things like the jackalope and the
lunar wolf live there," Thea said. "But . . . why? How come they

exist there but not anywhere else?"

"Most places aren't like here," Adam said.

"But *why?*" Thea insisted.

Adam looked like he was rethinking his decision to invite them inside. "Look, it's complicated."

"Try me," Thea said.

"Okay," he said, drawing out the word. "Well. There are places in this world where other dimensions— I guess that's where we start. So, most people think of our reality as being defined by four dimensions. There are three spatial dimensions—length, width, and height—plus the temporal dimension, or time. But there are *other* dimensions beyond that."

"Like string theory?" Nox said. It was a physics thing; there was a lot of physics in astronomy.

Adam, who had just started to warm up to the subject matter from the sounds of it, visibly faltered. "No— I— Sorry, do they teach string theory to middle schoolers these days?"

"Isn't that, like, multiverse stuff?" Thea said.

Adam groaned. "Stop. I am not teaching quantum mechanics to strange, ill-mannered children at this hour, or preferably ever. No, I'm not talking about the multiverse, or any version of string theory that you'd find in a modern-day physics journal."

"Then what?" Nox prompted.

"The next dimension is *chance*—the spectrum of the probable to the improbable, the highly likely to the all but impossible," Adam said. He counted the rest on his fingers. "Beyond that is the dimension of *chaos*, as well as the dimension of *fate*, that which creates fixed points in history, events that cannot be changed or averted. And yet another is the dimension of night. There are others, but that is the one that most concerns us right now."

Thea didn't look remotely impressed. "What kind of research has been done to prove anything you just—"

Adam raised a hand for silence. "I have no proof except what you can see with your eyes. You don't have to believe me. In fact, I encourage you not to."

Nox was a skeptic at heart, but he also enjoyed watching Thea fume as some unkempt stranger breezily informed her that her entire understanding of reality was false, so he said, "Okay, right, so there are other dimensions. What about them?"

"So," Adam said, "every one of these dimensions plays a role in our reality. It's like—like different colors of paint blending together, all of the dimensions interacting and forming something new, forming what we know as our world."

"Paint?" Nox repeated, with great scorn.

Adam shot him a look of disbelief. "You were fine with string theory, but you don't understand *paint*? Never mind," he said. "The point is, these forces define the limits of reality in the same way that space and time do. But there are places and times and circumstances that allow some of these dimensions to exert a greater influence over the world than they usually do. The Nightwood is one of those places. It's a part of the world ruled by the dimension of night. When you go in there—just don't expect things to look the way they do out here."

"What about Evergreen?" Thea said.

Adam frowned. "What about it?"

"Weird things happen there. People go missing, or they see things in the woods, or—"

She broke off. Nox had a strange feeling that she had stopped herself from saying something else.

"When you build houses next door to the supernatural, you'd best not be surprised when it comes knocking to say hello," Adam said gruffly. "Yes—the Nightwood's boundaries are fixed, but that doesn't mean things can't slip out every now and then. Those who venture into the woods around here have a decent chance of seeing or feeling something out of the ordinary."

Nox had so many questions he didn't even know where to begin. But there wasn't time. Noah was in trouble. The key to saving him was in the Nightwood. So that was where Nox had to go.

"You're right," Thea said, crossing her arms stubbornly. "I shouldn't believe you. I'll look for my proof with my own eyes."

Nox picked up the map, studying it. "So there's a path we have to take? How do we get there?"

"Come with me," Adam said, heaving himself to his feet. He seemed all too ready to be rid of them. They left behind the warmth of the cabin as he led them outside, through the backyard, and into the woods. There, Adam pointed out a faint, mostly scuffed-out trail that Nox had completely missed.

"We're on the outer edge of the Nightwood. This path will take you over the border," Adam said. "After a few minutes, you'll reach a fork in the road. The left path is a shortcut that will bring you to Zahna right away. The right path is the long way around, at least one or two nights' hike through the woods. But that's the one you'll have to take."

"Why would we take the long way?" Nox protested. "I don't have two nights to waste."

"Because the other one is guarded by the Wayfinder," he said, "and he'll only let you pass if you answer his riddle."

That sounded sinister and all, but Nox was stuck on the "shortcut" part. A shortcut was *exactly* what they needed.

"We can handle a riddle," Thea said, sounding miffed.

Adam threw up his hands in exasperation. "You can try. But listen well: do *not* answer the riddle unless you're absolutely sure you know the correct solution. Not if you want to get back home to your brother."

Nox folded up the map and tucked it into his pocket.

"You're just gonna send two kids into the woods by themselves?" he said innocently. "What kind of adult are you?"

Adam raised a bushy eyebrow. "You're not *my* kids."

"You could come with us. Be our guide."

That elicited a hearty laugh. "If you want to do this fool thing, then go on. No one's taking responsibility for you except you."

Well, it'd been worth a shot.

"And one more thing," Adam said as he turned to go. "Some of the beings you'll encounter in the woods are harmless, like the jackalope. Some are dangerous, but they can be bested as long as you keep your wits about you. But the one thing you don't want to cross is the Devil."

Thea frowned. "You're not talking about the Evergreen Devil, are you?"

"Not exactly. The Devil of the Nightwood is far more than what the local legends say. The Web is his territory, but he ventures out as he pleases. If you hear the beating of his wings, you run the other way. Got it?"

Wingbeats? Nox thought.

But before Nox could say another word, Adam Motte left them without so much as a goodbye. There was a short-lived burst of light as he opened the door to his cabin, and then the sound of it clicking shut.

Thea switched on her flashlight again, but Nox kept his phone light off to conserve the battery. The shadows lay thick and soft as wool.

"You really went out of your way to piss that guy off, huh?" he said, after a minute of walking. He knew they'd left Adam's property when he could look into the woods and see only the pines and maples he expected. No moros trees. No warped wooden faces making him jump when he glimpsed them from the corner of his eye. But the occasional moth still fluttered past.

"*Me?*" she said. "You tried to break into his house."

"You almost whacked him in the face with a stick."

"That was self-defense."

"He was nice. He gave us a map." It was a crudely drawn map, but at least he'd *tried* to help them. And he hadn't told Nox he was making things up.

But Thea scoffed. "*Nice* isn't always the same thing as *good*."

Nox had no idea what she meant by that. He would've asked, but then the beam of the flashlight fell across a split in the path up ahead. It was just like Adam had said: two forks, one veering off to the left and one to the right. Nox and Thea stopped in the middle.

On the left, the branches had been trimmed neatly away from a wide, spacious path. The ground was smooth as pavement and clean of leaf litter, as if it had been swept. A breeze stroked gently over his cheek, carrying with it the muted fragrance of a distant meadow. It didn't look wild. It looked welcoming and cared for, more akin to a palace promenade than a remote trail in the woods.

The right fork—what Adam had called *the long way around*—was its polar opposite: narrow and cramped, with raised tree roots and dips in the earth and wet-dark patches of mud waiting to glue their shoes to the ground. The air smelled of stale, algae-choked waters and the spicy, bitter, green scent of an old forest. A few more years, and Nox wouldn't be surprised if this path disappeared, consumed by the woods once and for all.

"I don't see anything," Thea said, peering down the left fork. "Maybe the Wayfinder's asleep?"

"Maybe," Nox said.

He didn't have high hopes they'd be able to avoid the Wayfinder and his riddle, but they had to try. Turning left, they took their first few halting steps down the path.

A deep, reverberating sound made the ground shake beneath their feet.

There were sounds that had weight to them, sounds that took up space like a physical presence, and this was one of them. It came again and again, one after the other.

Footsteps, coming closer.

11

THEA MADE A PETRIFIED NOISE, LIKE A SQUEAK.

"He's just going to tell us a riddle," Nox reminded himself as much as her.

"How do we know Adam was right?" she said, in a high, airless voice.

Another footstep made the ground judder beneath them. Nox pointed the flashlight ahead, but the beam bounced in his trembling hands, sending whips of shadow flying in every direction.

A cloud drifted away from the moon, dispelling the darkness.

The Wayfinder was as tall as the trees. Taller, even. His skin was bark, mossy and crusted with sap. A long, leafy beard swung down his chest. From his wooden face jutted a twig nose under black stone eyes and two fern-tuft eyebrows.

When he was barely ten feet away, close enough that another couple of steps would've brought him within crushing distance of Nox and Thea, and Nox was willing his legs to *move, run, get me out of here*—

The Wayfinder sank into a crouch, peering down his long nose at them.

"Are you here," he said, in a coarse, solemn voice that somehow echoed, as if it had come from the depths of a cavern, "for the doors?"

"What *are* you?" Thea had gone straight from fear to breathless awe. "Like an elf or something?"

Right, that's how you get someone to help us, Nox thought. *Call him an elf.*

"I am Myte, the Wayfinder," said the thing that couldn't have looked less like an elf if he'd tried. His breath was hot as desert wind and smelled of kindling.

"We're trying to get to Zahna's watchtower," Nox said hastily, in case Thea was planning to accuse the scary giant of being a merman next. "Adam Motte said this way was a shortcut."

"You *are* here for the doors," Myte rumbled. The air went tight and staticky with pent-up energy, the way it did before a lightning storm. Something in Nox's peripheral vision shifted. He dragged his eyes away from Myte. Then he blinked rapidly, sure he had to be seeing things.

But he wasn't. The doors were real.

Six doors in total, three on either side of them, not connected to anything—just standing free in the woods like misplaced pieces of a dollhouse. They didn't—couldn't—lead anywhere.

But Myte said: "The place you seek awaits you beyond one of these doors. The toll for safe passage is the answer to my riddle."

"But which door gets us to Zahna?" Thea asked doubtfully. "And where do the others go?"

Myte tilted his head thoughtfully, his beard rustling. Its

leaves were ablaze with autumn colors, all red and orange and yellow. Nox wondered if he'd shed them soon and grow new ones in spring.

"That way," Myte said, sweeping his hand at the door nearest and to the left of Nox, which was oval-shaped and made of mother-of-pearl, "a priceless treasure and a cold, swift death await you."

He indicated the neighboring door, a granite arch with a crystal handle. "The second will take you to night's end, at a junction of earth and sky where great fortune may be found. But your death there will be cold and slow."

The third door was pale and oddly ridged. After a moment of study, it dawned on Nox that it was made of bone fragments—many small broken animal bones pieced together. Of this door, Myte said, "Therein lies the forest's heart and its most watchful eyes. Nothing there passes unnoticed."

"What, no death?" Nox said weakly.

Myte smiled, lips pulling back under his beard to reveal a row of checkered wooden teeth. "Depends on how fast you run."

He informed them that the fourth door, which was made of polished ebony, would take them *to the heavens themselves and a hell like no other.*

"But this passage is sealed," Myte added, "and even I cannot open it."

The fifth was the plainest door of all, the one made of pine with an ordinary brass knob. Myte said: "It leads to refuge, but it is guarded by strangers without faces or names."

The sixth and final door was liquid shadow, with hints of what might have been light or glitter or flakes of metal shifting so subtly within it that Nox thought his eyes were playing tricks. It had no handle and no frame.

And Myte said only, "I am too afraid to find out where that door leads. But you may look and tell me what you see."

Nox didn't want to look. He just wanted to be pointed in the right direction and left alone.

Thea, however, was bubbling with excitement. "Did you *make* the doors? Why are there six of them? Why do they all go to different places? Do they all lead to other parts of the Nightwood, or do some of them go elsewhere? Why is that one sealed? How long—"

"Can we just hear the riddle?" Nox said, cutting her off.

Myte wrapped his huge arms around his knees, dislodging an owl that had settled on his shoulder; it flew away with a disgruntled hoot. He fell silent, as if collecting his thoughts.

At last, he said:

My roots are strong but do not grow.
In my crown, I wear a yellow jewel.
No sap flows through my veins. I am not alive,
but there is life within me. What am I?"

Nox gaped at him. "Huh?"

Thea was muttering to herself. "Roots and a crown. A tree? A tree with yellow flowers? No, it can't be a tree if there's no sap. Maybe it's another yellow plant. Forsythia. Yarrow. Daffodils? Those are sort of crown-shaped. But this is a riddle, so it can't be something obvious."

"You can take your riddle and shove it up—"

Thea grabbed Nox's sleeve and turned them around so their backs were to the Wayfinder. "Don't lose your temper. It's a riddle. *Think*."

"Think about what? Things that have *roots*? We're in the *woods*. We'll be standing around naming plants all night."

"Maybe it's a metaphor," Thea mumbled, frowning into the middle distance. "Or a trick question. I don't understand the 'not alive' part. A seed? An . . . egg?"

Nox looked over his shoulder to find Myte watching them intently.

"What happens if we get it wrong?" he asked.

Myte smiled again. Some of his teeth were so black they looked like gaps. "Then you're mine."

Nox decided he'd rather not know what he meant by that.

"Fine," he said. "Come on, Thea. Let's go."

"I can get this!" Thea insisted. "I know I can."

"Even if you come up with something, do you think you'll be confident enough to stake your life on it?"

Thea hesitated, which was answer enough for Nox.

"We have to make it back to Noah," he said. "No matter what."

"Leaving?" Myte said.

Nox wondered if they were going to have to run.

"Yes," he said cautiously. "We don't have a solution. We're taking the other path."

Myte sighed, his hot breath gusting over them.

"No one ever even tries," he said dejectedly.

He stood and ambled away, his hand brushing at the trees as

112

he went, dislodging a cascade of leaves. Nox and Thea waited until he was out of sight. Then they hurried back to the crossroads.

They stood there in shocked silence as they caught their breath, at the base of the only other path available to them. The long way around.

"Nox, let's go back," Thea said desperately. "This is bad."

"I can't."

"If Noah isn't waking up, we need to tell Mom and Dad so they can help him. He would want you there."

"*I'm* going to help him. Your parents haven't done anything for him so far, so why would now be any different?" Nox half shouted; he'd forgotten, for a moment, where they were. His cheeks felt hot and his eyes prickly; his shaking hands had clenched into fists.

"I know you're scared, but maybe the best thing you can do is be with him!"

"You wanted to know what was going on, too."

"I've seen enough." She gestured at the endless woods around them. "What are *we* supposed to do in a place like *this*? If the Wayfinder was bad, what do you think someone called the *Keeper of Night* is going to be like? I'm still not convinced any of this is real—maybe we're hallucinating, maybe *we* need medical attention as much as Noah does—"

He opened his mouth to argue, and then stopped. Arguing didn't work on Thea. He had to *reason* with her. He'd told her to go home, but the truth was . . . he had never done anything alone. Not really. Not anything that mattered. He'd always had Noah. The louder one, the more popular one, the braver one. How was Nox supposed to do this—the scariest, strangest, single most important thing he'd ever done in his life—by himself? Thea was a poor substitute for Noah, but at least if she was there, Nox wouldn't be alone.

"You're a scientist, right?" he said abruptly.

Thea looked taken aback, like she was shocked he'd remembered something like that.

I listen sometimes! he thought. *It's not that weird!*

"A conservationist," she said after a beat.

"Okay, and isn't science all about—testing new ideas? Finding out that maybe things we thought were true really aren't?"

Thea nodded reluctantly.

"Mom says success in the sciences is finding out you were wrong," she said. "There are no facts, only theories based on experimental observations. No proof, only evidence for or against a hypothesis, and you can always find new evidence."

"Look at the evidence that's right in front of us," Nox said. "Look at what we *just* saw. How can you say it's not real?"

She was silent.

"And if this is real," he pressed, "then don't you think the wolf I saw might be real, too? I know everyone thinks I'm a liar, or I'm out of my mind with, like, *grief* or something—"

"I don't think that."

That shouldn't have made him falter, but it did.

"Yeah, well. Good," he said, gathering himself. "If I'm right, then no one else can help him. The only thing that can save Noah is here in the woods."

From her silence, Nox knew he'd won.

It didn't feel like much of a victory, though.

"All right." She adjusted her backpack strap and faced the path. "Let's get this over with."

12

THE PATH STARTED OUT TIGHT AND HALF-overgrown, so they had to fight their way through, but then it widened like the opening of a funnel, and they spilled out into the middle of the Nightwood. The shock of meeting the Wayfinder faded from memory like a bad dream, overwritten by their new, grim reality.

They heard a lone whippoorwill whistling its own name. The rustling in the dark could've been a breeze or could've been small rodents scampering through the brush. Insects, too, went mostly unseen, but they made themselves known with the occasional low whir of their wings as they darted close to him and Thea. Their world was small, ending where their light did, but the Nightwood was vast, and the calls of its inhabitants traveled far.

When a high-pitched yowl in the distance made him jump, Thea said, "Just a fox," as if he'd asked. The yowl went on for a while. And then it cut off.

But there was no such thing as silence in the woods. Soon, the howling began. One at first, and then a chorus, all overlapping. And these weren't the low, haunting, respectable howls of a wolf, but an unholy shrieking that made Nox's skin crawl.

This time, Thea said nothing. Nox caved first.

"Are those coyotes?" he asked nervously.

"Yeah."

"Should we, uh . . . be worried?"

He was already worried. But Thea shook her head.

"No. They're not close enough."

By then, there had to be miles of wilderness between them and home. Even with the map, Nox felt adrift. No one would be able to come to their aid if they needed it. No one would know they were in trouble. Not even Adam. They were truly alone. It would be all too easy for someone to wander into this place and disappear forever; he was increasingly sure that was what had happened to at least some of the people the Evergreen Devil had allegedly taken. Adam couldn't save every lost soul.

Nox jumped, again, at a sharp call that he'd have *sworn* was coming from somewhere close by, maybe a city block away. Deep and growly, like the baying of some kind of demonic dog. Then it slid into a plaintive keening. Like the cry of a human baby.

Nox shivered. "What was that?"

"Bobcat," Thea said. Her expression was tense. "Let's go faster."

The path widened again, and the tree canopy opened up overhead. The stars were oddly bright—brighter than he'd ever seen them—so they no longer needed the flashlight. Fireflies appeared, first a handful and then dozens, drifting lazily between the crooked maple pillars tottering away in every direction. The woods were fragrant with night-blooming flowers. He nearly lost Thea because she kept stopping to examine them.

"We'll never get anywhere if you keep doing that," he snapped, the third time it happened.

A noise like dry leaves crackling underfoot made his breath catch.

What was that?

Neither of them were moving. Over Thea's head, in the direction they'd come from, the path disappeared into pitch blackness. Empty.

There was no such thing as silence in the woods. But it was silent now.

"You don't get it," Thea was saying, bent over a stalk of pink-and-white trumpet-shaped blooms. "This is tropical. It shouldn't be able to survive here."

It was nothing, he told himself. *An animal. You're in the woods, scaredy-cat. What did you expect?*

"Just come on," he said tersely. She opened her mouth as if to argue and stopped. He willed her not to comment on the tension in his face, the death grip he had on the flashlight, and she didn't.

Their footsteps crunched over a thick layer of leaves. He strained his ears for more animal noises.

"Wait," he said, throwing out an arm to stop her.

Another barely detectable noise stopped, too, half a beat later.

Something was tracking them.

"You hear that?" he asked.

Thea nodded, eyes wide. "Is it getting any closer?"

But the only way to find that out was to keep going. The noise sped up when they did; it slowed down when they did, too.

"What do we do?" she asked under her breath.

Nox shook his head. "Do you think it knows . . . ?"

Did it know they were on to it, he wanted to ask.

"We need to lose it," Thea said, so quietly Nox barely heard her. "Maybe we should run."

"It'll follow us."

If he looked behind them at the path again, would it still be empty? Or would he see something there in the dark this time?

He didn't look.

"Then what?"

"We have to leave the path," he said.

"We—we can't do that. It's . . ."

"What? Dangerous?" he said. "It knows where we are. We need to get away."

Thea bit her lip. "Fine."

"When I run—"

"I'll be right behind you."

"Sure you can keep up?"

"Screw you."

He grinned to himself. The adrenaline was kicking in.

"Okay," he whispered. "One. Two . . ."

On three, they bolted, crashing heedlessly through the woods and making an obscene amount of noise. He couldn't hear whatever was following them anymore, but it could probably hear them. He hadn't thought about that, the obvious flaw in their plan. But then came another sound, one that sent relief coursing through him: running water. Something that could cover their footsteps and maybe stop them from being followed.

He veered in that direction, Thea following. The ground sloped downhill and became softer, giving under their weight. The dull roar of the river drowned out their ragged breathing. Nothing had caught them yet. Maybe they'd done it—they'd lost whatever was tailing them—

He lost control as he slid the final few feet down the slope, broke through the tree line, and finally stumbled as his shoes stuck in the muddy bank of the river. A pained hiss escaped him as his knees and forearms took the brunt of the fall. The momentum rolled him onto his side; only a rocky outcropping at the edge of the water stopped him from falling in.

"Nox! Are you all right?" Thea skidded to a stop beside him.

He turned onto his back, aching and muddy all over, and pressed a finger to his lips for quiet. She clapped her hands over her mouth. They held their breath and listened.

But there was nothing. No footsteps. No one coming for them. Only the buzz of insects and the croaking of the toads some ways up the bank.

Nox climbed to his feet.

"I guess it's gone," he said, hushed.

"Or it's just being quieter now." She rubbed a hand over her arm, as if she had goose bumps, and peered around anxiously.

Not wanting to double back right away, they followed the curve of the river, still heading mostly in the direction they'd been going before. A couple of eris moths glided overhead and then swooped down over the water, dampness beading on their fuzzy bodies. These were smaller than the ones at Adam's place. One of the toads eyed them. Its tongue snapped out, snatched a moth by the wing, and dragged it into its mouth.

Instantly, the toad shriveled up like the life was being sucked out of it. A disgusting, slimy liquid drained from its body and into the river. In seconds, all that was left was a desiccated husk, which flopped into the water like a used candy wrapper and floated away.

Thea covered her mouth with her hand. "The moth poisoned it. That's not . . ."

She didn't need to finish her sentence. They both knew that wasn't normal.

The other toads watched the surviving moth hungrily. Thea scooped up a rock and tossed it into the water. Startled, the moth fluttered back into the safety of the trees. The toads fled, too, ducking into the water and paddling away.

After a while, the river veered off in another direction. If they followed it any longer, it was going to take them off course. They had to get back to the path.

"Wait," Thea said. "We need to rest."

Nox started to protest, but she cut him off.

"If we don't take breaks, we'll be too weak and exhausted to deal with this . . . Zahna person," she pointed out. "And if whatever was following us comes back, we won't have enough energy to run away."

His stomach grumbled, as if agreeing with Thea.

"Fine," he said. "Just for a few minutes, though."

They found a dry spot to sit by the riverbank. Thea produced two handfuls of berries from her pockets, washing them and then passing half to him.

"Wha— Where did you get these?" he asked. She might as well have conjured them from thin air like a magician.

"I've been collecting them on the way. They're safe, I promise." She pulled a few strips of bark from another pocket and split those with him, too.

"That was smart," he said. "Thanks."

Her smile in response was bewildered and pleased at the same time, like a compliment was the last thing she'd expected. He felt kind of bad. She *was* smart. Brave, too. She didn't have to come with him, but here she was anyway. Maybe he could stand to be less of a hostile jerk to her.

But he was a hostile jerk to everyone, so really he was just being fair.

Thea had also gathered dandelion leaves, mint, and violets. They ate in silence. He was wiping his hands off on his pants, trying not to think about what Noah would say if he'd caught Nox coexisting peacefully with Thea—in fact, trying not to think about Noah at all—when something nudged his shoe.

And then he was underwater.

There wasn't any time for him to hold his breath; one moment he was on land and the next he was in the river. It was *frigid*. His bones turned to ice and he sank like a lead weight, or he would've, except whatever had a vise grip on his ankle snapped like a whip, and the world thrashed around him. He no longer knew which way was up. Reflexively, his mouth opened in a gasp, and icy water flooded his lungs.

White-hot pain seared his chest as his body searched for oxygen and found none. The thing holding his ankle flung him around again. It was trying to break his neck, some distant, calm part of him thought. There were spots in his vision now, tricking him with the illusion of light.

One of his hands went to his throat, as if he could somehow squeeze the water back out. With the other hand, he scrabbled weakly at whatever was holding on to his ankle. His fingers slipped on something glossy-smooth—scales? He felt a bump where the scales gave way to bony claw, and only then did he realize that the claws were digging into his flesh, and that he was bleeding. He only felt a sting, insignificant compared to the agony in his lungs.

He forgot what he was doing, forgot that he was trying to make the thing release him. All he wanted was to breathe. All he knew was the need for something that was completely out of his reach.

I'm gonna die, he thought. A helpless rage wrung itself from the battered remnants of his consciousness. He was never going to see Noah again.

At the place where his fingers met bone, it was as if something was being pulled from him, pulled *through* him. Was that part of drowning? Could he feel his life slipping away? Deep in the water, a pair of eyes glowed. He couldn't tell if they were close or just huge.

The grip on his ankle disappeared. But Nox was dizzy, weak,

the spots of color in his vision blooming like fireworks going off in his head. The water frothed around him again, and he was tossed this way and that; whatever was in the river with him made an awful noise, a groan like an engine—

A cold, tight grip closed around his wrist. It must have grabbed him again. Nox couldn't fight anymore.

Everything went black.

The next thing he knew, he was on solid ground, expelling what felt like the entire river from his lungs.

"*OhmygodNoxareyouokay?*" Thea said, her voice very fast and oddly muffled. He worked his jaw until his ears popped.

"What happened?" he coughed.

"Look," Thea said. Something crumpled and translucent floated in the water. It kind of looked like a deflated balloon, except it was the size of a circus tent. It shimmered faintly in the moonlight, glinting with the ghostly purple-blue imprint of scales.

"What am I looking at?"

"The thing that grabbed you shed its skin," Thea said, with something that sounded a lot like reverence. Nox took back all the nice things he'd thought about Thea earlier.

"I was in the water with that?" he said.

"But I don't know why it would go hunting when it was about to molt."

She said *hunting* so calmly, like Nox hadn't been the prey.

"Is that why it left?" he asked.

"It must be. Some animals are vulnerable after they molt. Like crabs. And tarantulas." Her face lit up, like talking about hairy, poisonous spiders was the highlight of her whole night. "They're soft for a bit afterward because their new exoskeleton is still hardening. And some insects stop breathing for around an hour until the old one has finished coming off." Knowing Thea, she was just getting started. But one look at Nox's face and her teeth snapped shut with a click. With a great amount of restraint, she added, "I just don't understand why it happened now."

Nox's fingers dug into the mud of the riverbank. He remembered touching a clawed appendage, remembered that strange tugging sensation within him, but . . . maybe it was normal to feel that way when you were drowning.

"Let's just get away from the water," he said.

The climb left Nox winded and shaky. They stopped on the edge of the path to regroup. Thea must have fished him out herself, because she was almost as soaked as he was.

She only gave herself a minute to rest before she was up again. "We need to build a fire."

"Something was following us," he protested half-heartedly. "A fire will give us away."

"We don't have any clothes to change into, and we're all wet. We can't risk hypothermia."

This was an argument he was glad she'd won; he wanted to be warm again almost as much as he wanted real food. They gathered stones for a firepit and filled it with twigs, bark, and leaves. By the end, he was shivering, his fingertips turning blue. Luckily, Thea had a book of matches in her backpack—it was the one she took on her hiking and camping trips with Aster, not the one for school, which was why it was so well stocked with supplies. The flame caught with a crackle and a snap.

"You know what you're doing," he said with reluctant appreciation. It had been his idea to come out here, but Thea was the only one of them with any survival skills.

"Yeah, you'd have frozen to death without me," Thea said. "That's the second time I saved your life tonight."

"Bragging isn't very heroic of you."

"Not bragging." She fed the fire until it roared. "I'm just saying . . . you owe me one."

"Feel free to let me die next time."

She rolled her eyes. "I just want you to trust me. We're in this together now. Right?"

The warmth of the fire was already seeping into his skin. He'd stopped shivering. It kind of killed him to admit it, but Thea was right, even if she had to be right in the most annoying way possible.

"Fine," he said.

A temporary truce. Just to get them through this nightmare.

They sat in silence after that. It wasn't long before he noticed that Thea was nodding off next to him. He wasn't inclined to get up yet himself.

A few more minutes, he told himself. *Then I'm waking her up.*

But it felt as if only seconds had passed before his eyelids grew heavy. He was out cold before he could finish his next thought.

13

WHEN HE STIRRED, THE FIRE WAS LOW, GNAW-
ing away the last pieces of kindling in a bed of embers. A big
black bird sat in the tree across the path from where he and
Thea had settled down to rest.

He thought it was a bird, anyway. Its dark wings were so
long they almost brushed the ground; they dangled limply as
if the bird was asleep, or maybe dead. He couldn't see its face
among the leaves and shadow. And he was still so tired.

His mind conjured up the cardinals flitting up and down
the road from the Day house to Evergreen. He dozed off to that
sunny memory.

The next time he woke up, it was in a panic as he remembered where they were and what they were doing. He couldn't
believe he'd fallen asleep at a time like this. He sat bolt upright.

"Thea—" he started, intending to wake her up, too, but then
his eyes locked on something on the other side of the path. A
pair of black wings dangling from the tree branches.

His heart hammered wildly against his ribs. Cold fear swept
through him. He dragged his gaze up the length of those
wings—and they weren't bird wings at all. They were leathery

and smooth and tipped with sharp points like spurs. In the darkness of the forest canopy, a pair of eyes glinted back at him.

Nox let out a strangled scream before he could stop himself.

The wings twitched, and then the rest of it moved, too. Nox couldn't see it properly—not in the dark, when his eyes were still bleary from sleep—but it was *big*, bigger than any bird. It retreated, dragging its wings with it. There was a *thump* and a rustle as if it had dropped to the forest floor, and then strange half footsteps, like something with a limp was hurrying away.

"Nox?" Thea mumbled, sitting up. Nox swiveled to look at her, his heart still pounding. She hadn't seen it. "W'happened?"

"Something was watching us. It's gone now."

She winced, her hand rising to press against the back of her neck, which was probably killing her after she'd slept upright against a tree with her chin practically touching her collar. Nox wasn't in much better shape.

"Watching us?" she said. "The thing from before?"

"I think so. It . . . it had wings."

Thea glanced at him sharply. He was certain that she, too, was remembering Adam's warning about the Devil. *If you hear the beating of his wings, you run the other way.*

"My phone's dead," he said, waving it. It had been in his pocket when he'd gotten dragged into the river and was probably beyond saving. "Check yours. What time is it?"

She checked. "There's something wrong with it."

The phone was on, but the digits that should have showed the time were set to all zeroes.

"Okay, wait here," he said, standing.

"Shouldn't we go? If we're being followed . . . being *watched . . .*"

Nox hesitated, but now that the initial terror had faded, he could think clearly. "We were asleep for who knows how long, and it didn't do anything. It ran away as soon as I saw it. So . . . maybe it'll leave us alone if we ignore it."

Thea didn't look convinced. Nox wasn't, either, but they needed to get their bearings. He found a tree with a few decent footholds and scrambled up. Once he'd climbed as high as he dared, he stopped, surveying the sky. It took him longer than it should've, because what he was seeing was impossible. He sat there clinging to the tree for a few long minutes, the bark scraping his clammy palms, his skin prickling with a slow-building alarm as his mind cast around for a logical explanation for what he was seeing and did not find one. Finally, he clambered back down and turned to Thea.

"The constellations are, uh . . . not in the right place," he reported.

She gave him a blank look. "Meaning, what? They moved around?"

"No, like, you can see Virgo right now."

"And that's . . . bad," she guessed.

"Apocalyptic. Like the sun went out. That, or we just slept for months."

She gave a thoughtful hum. "I don't think we would have slept through the destruction of the sun. And if we were unconscious for that long, we would've starved or frozen to death by now. There's got to be a rational explanation for what's going on."

Her lack of a reaction to what was *literally* earth-shattering news was so irritating that it grounded him immediately.

"Okay, so . . . the position of the stars changes during the year because of how the earth revolves around the sun. Right? The stars aren't actually moving, but we are. We're looking at them from a different position relative to the sun."

"Right," she said, nodding along.

"The constellations in the zodiac are the ones that the sun appears to pass through during the year. So, like, in January, the sun is in Capricorn."

"I didn't know you were into astrology."

"This isn't astrology, it's astronomy. The point is, from late September through October, the sun is in Virgo. That means you *can't* see Virgo this time of year, because the sun is blocking it out. So why is Virgo, like—" He gestured wildly in the direction of the sky. "*Right there?*"

"Is there any chance you misidentified it?" Thea said.

"Thea, if I can't identify Virgo, assume I've been body-snatched," he seethed. He had also found Leo, another constellation that shouldn't currently be visible. Orion, meanwhile, had been high in the sky when they'd fallen asleep in the middle of the night, but now hovered near the horizon—which was where it would have been located in the late morning.

"Okay, okay!" she said. "Let's assume it's daytime. The sun's not gone, but we can't see it from here. I think that's more likely than a full-blown Armageddon. There's some kind of meteorological phenomenon limited to this part of the world that makes it look like it's always nighttime here."

She bent to tie her shoelaces like that was the end of it.

"That's it? That's your theory?" he said.

"I wouldn't call it a theory. A theory is supported by evidence, which we don't have. This is more like . . . a guess." She raised her eyebrows at him, as if challenging him to come up with a better one. "You were on board with all those things Adam was saying about the . . . dimension of night. I told him I wanted proof, and maybe this is it. It's a start, anyway."

She climbed to her feet, brushing off her clothes. Sleep had had opposite effects on the two of them: Thea seemed energized, ready to move forward, and Nox felt like he was slowly falling apart. Suddenly he wondered if going back wasn't the better option after all. More than anything, he wished he could talk to Noah.

But that wasn't going to happen even if he did go back now.

He took a deep breath and forced down the fear that had him in a choke hold all of a sudden. In its place, he summoned the rage that had been simmering deep inside him from almost as soon as he'd arrived in Evergreen. Rage at whatever was making Noah sick, at Mom for separating them, at Weston for not believing him, and most of all at the lunar wolf for what it had done. He pulled the anger around him like a favorite jacket, familiar and protective.

"Okay," he told Thea. "Let's keep going."

They huddled together over Adam's map. Thea prodded the lower center of the page.

"There's the river," she said. "That's where it curves away from the path." She traced her finger up the smudged line that represented the trail. Zahna's watchtower was marked with a triangle, deep in the woods. Adam had drawn a dotted line at the safest place for them to go off the trail. It was perilously close to what he'd called the Web, and practically on top of a symbol Nox hadn't noticed before: a clock.

He pointed it out. "What do you think that means?"

"I don't know," she said. "But it doesn't look like we can avoid it, so I guess we'll find out."

Nox decided not to worry about it. Adam hadn't steered them wrong yet. If whatever awaited them at the clock was dangerous, Adam would've warned them, like he'd warned them about Zahna and the Devil.

As they walked, Nox learned to be grateful for small victories. Thea finding a patch of nontoxic mushrooms for "breakfast"; the constant, steadying presence of the North Star, which at least assured him they were still going in the right direction; the path under their feet, which—although it was hard to see at times—felt like a safety tether, keeping them connected to the world they'd left behind and ensuring that they could find their way back.

He still sometimes heard that faint sound underneath their footsteps, a sound he could now identify as the *step-drag, step-drag* of the thing that had watched them sleep. Thea heard it, too, and their silence was uneasy. But it never seemed to come any closer, and it didn't show itself again.

The night wore on, the sky deepening to indigo and then

lightening to navy. The autumn foliage was a cold fire eating up the stars. The trees grew tall and ancient: pines broad enough to carve a house out of their trunks, oaks with leaves that more resembled sleds. The path had them climbing over and under roots that were thick as small hills. He flinched away from centipedes the size of his forearm and struggled to hear anything over the chirping of the crickets. The canopy blocked out the stars, so they had to use Thea's flashlight again. He had no idea what they'd do when the batteries died.

The eris moths were their only companions, and they, like the trees, grew to impossible sizes. Some of them had bodies three feet long, monstrously huge, their luminous wings dyeing the woods a watery blue. The larger moths stayed clear of them, perching on branches far over their heads or meandering through the air. Maybe that meant there was a giant moros tree somewhere in the Nightwood, too. Nox could picture it, how it would loom over them in the moonlight with a face like a fallen god's. But they hadn't come across it so far. They hadn't seen any moros trees other than the ones around Adam's cabin, for that matter.

When something shifted in the woods up ahead, Nox's first thought was that whatever had been following them had finally decided to make its move.

He stopped short; his eyes strained to pick the outline of black wings from the shadows. When had it circled around them? Was it really the Evergreen Devil, or just something that looked like it?

But the figure that emerged from the trees was pale and wingless.

A moose clopped onto their path. It was pure white, from its hooves to its antlers, and stood around ten feet tall. Nox was pretty sure moose didn't get that big. He was also pretty sure they were only supposed to have one head. This one had three. The leftmost face crunched a pinecone between its stone jaws. The one in front had its gaze trained on Nox and Thea, eyes black and watchful in a way that reminded Nox forcefully of Adam.

"Stay calm," Thea whispered. "Maybe it'll go away on its own."

"Doubt it. We don't have that kind of luck."

He was going to suggest they make a break for it when the middle face said, "Greetings, trespassers."

Yeah, that checks out, Nox thought. *Would've been weirder if it* didn't *talk*.

He glanced at Thea, but she didn't look afraid. She wore an expression of deep concentration, like she was taking an exam.

"How do you know we're trespassers?" Nox said.

"The smell," said the rightmost face. "Unmistakable."

Their voices were identical, slow and deep. It wasn't a human voice; the words slid heavily from its jaws, like at any moment they might dissolve into low animal moans or swell into bellows of rage.

"Right, sorry. We'll just go back home, then," Nox said, but as he made a move to step off the path, the moose reared its heads and stomped its hooves, agitated. He froze.

"We are the deity of ephemeral things," said the right face. "*I* am the lord of the first cloud that crosses the waning moon each month."

"I am the lord of the hundredth leaf to fall in autumn," said the left.

"I am the lord of shadows at midnight," said the middle face. "And I have a proposition for you."

"Uh, sure. We're listening." Under his breath, Nox added, "Think we can outrun it?"

Thea shook her head minutely.

"I wish to borrow time off your life," said the middle face. "I will take five minutes from you, and midnight will last five minutes longer here in the woods, just for tonight."

"What does that mean for me?" Nox asked.

"You'll hardly even notice," said the lord of midnight shadows. "You'll simply die five minutes sooner than you were meant to, be that in a day or fifty years from now. Five minutes, and we will bestow upon you a blessing."

The leftmost face bent to graze on a cluster of ferns, stretching its neck and taking the other two faces with it. It managed to get one mouthful before the middle face jerked them upright again.

"I don't know," Nox said, stalling.

"Gods don't hand out blessings to just anyone, you know," the lord of midnight shadows said, starting to sound a little peeved. "You could show a little gratitude."

"Uh . . . yeah, thanks," Nox tried.

"Not interested? Humph." The lord of midnight shadows stamped his front hooves, each of which was bigger than Nox's head. "Maybe I'll take your whole life, then. Right here and now. How does that sound?"

Stall better! he thought.

"How—how exactly are you going to split those minutes?" Nox said. "Does Shadow get everything? Seems a little unfair to me."

"I got the last trespasser," said the right face, which was in charge of clouds or something.

"No, no," said the left face, which owned one specific leaf and probably knew he'd gotten the short end of the stick. "The boy is right. Shadow thinks he's the leader."

Nox nudged Thea's shoulder, and they began shuffling backward.

"I'm in front. That makes me the leader."

"Not this again!"

The three faces dissolved into a full-fledged argument, its neck whipping back and forth as each one tried to take over.

Nox and Thea ducked off the path, got as far away as they dared, and hid behind a tree. After a while, they heard the fighting break off into abrupt silence, followed by an inhuman sound of fury as Shadow and his brothers realized their victims had escaped. They paced back and forth, their hoofbeats restless and agitated, before padding away.

"We should wait here for a bit," Thea whispered. "In case it doubles back to look for us."

Nox nodded. In the darkness and silence, the seconds dripped past slowly, reluctantly, like water caught on the rim of a gutter, each drop clinging until its own weight dragged it over the edge.

"How did you do that?" Thea said after a while.

"I'm good at pissing people off."

"You've got that right."

"You weren't even scared of that thing," he said. "You looked at it like—"

The shadows hid her expression, but he felt her tense up. Her breathing changed.

"Like what?" she prompted.

"Like you were thinking about something else. Kind of a weird time to zone out."

"I didn't zone out."

"Is there something you're not telling me?"

"No," she said quickly, and then: "I mean, nothing important."

Right. That was comforting.

"Does it have something to do with why you're here?" he pressed.

"I mean . . ."

"I knew it," he said. "I knew that excuse you gave me about being *haunted* by the *mystery* was a load of—"

"No! That was true," she insisted. "I just left something out."

"Uh-huh."

"It's not like it's some big secret. It doesn't really matter if you know or not."

"Okay, so tell me."

"Fine." After a silence, she spoke again. "Mom and I used to live in Portland and come up to Evergreen for camping trips. One time, something . . . happened."

"What did?" he said quietly.

"I was eight, so I don't remember it that clearly." Her voice dissolved in the air, like rain so gentle it turned to mist before it hit the ground. "We'd put out the campfire, and we were in our tent, about to go to sleep. And then we heard something move outside. Something big. Mom thought it was a bear. That's what she told me it was, later.

"She whispered that I should be very quiet, but don't be afraid, it'll go away by itself," Thea said, the words barely audible. "But it didn't. It stopped outside our tent, just breathing. Loud and hard, like the way a dog pants when it's too hot. I don't know when Mom started to get scared. I just remember her holding me really tight with her hand over my mouth. And I don't know how long we stayed like that. After a while, it went away."

"It did?" Nox could see it all like he'd been there himself: Aster hiding a much smaller Thea in her arms; the darkness scrubbing the red from their hair and turning them into anonymous shadows; a shape outlined on the wall of their tent, blocking out the moon.

"We—we thought it did," Thea said. "And then everything happened really fast. Mom crawled out of the tent and picked me up and started running. She didn't take any of our gear, and she didn't tell me what was happening. She just carried me and ran away. And whatever was in the woods . . . it wasn't gone. It must have been hiding nearby, and it saw us leave.

"It chased us. I could see it over Mom's shoulder." Thea's whisper had gone patchy, as if her voice was failing her. "Everything was dark and all I could hear was Mom's breathing in my ear, fast and scared. But I remember it was really big and white. Kind of like Shadow just now. But whatever followed us back then, it almost glowed. Just like the wolf you saw, and the jack-alope. So now I'm *sure* it came from the Nightwood."

Nox was more confused than ever. That story didn't explain why Thea had come here with him—it did just the opposite. If *he'd* gone through something like that, he'd never want to go outside again.

"How did you get away?" he asked.

"Mom found the road. She ran right in front of a set of head-lights. Almost got hit by a car," Thea said. "Guess who was driving it."

"You're kidding."

"Nope. Dad was coming home from a late shift. He unlocked the doors and told my mom to get in. The next thing I remember is getting to the hospital. That's how he and my mom met."

"Super romantic."

"Mom must have thought so, because they got married a year later," Thea said. "I was so mad Mom wanted to move up here after what happened to us. I mean, it makes sense, 'cause Dad has the house here and everything. And I don't think Mom liked living in the city. Eventually, I stopped being scared and just wanted to know what really happened. The truth."

Nox chipped at the bark of the tree with his thumbnail.

"So . . . Weston wasn't surprised when he found you, huh?" he said. "Just let two strangers get in his car without asking any questions?"

"I know what you're implying, and you're wrong," she said instantly. "My parents don't have anything to do with what happened to Noah. They wouldn't hurt anyone."

"Maybe it's just your dad."

"It's not."

They didn't talk again until they decided it was safe to return to the trail. Once they got there, he switched the flashlight back on.

And the light fell on something with black wings, which stood no more than three feet away from them.

It was a patchwork thing like a rag doll made of wood and mud and stone. One of its wooden legs had broken off, and it balanced precariously on the other. It had a twisted spine and a clay rib cage stuffed with leaves, and its face was a featureless slab of bark with onyx chips for eyes. Its long, leathery wings brushed the ground, limp—but they were the only part of it that looked like it had ever belonged to something alive.

It hopped, once, and the sound of its wings dragging through the leaves woke Nox from his shocked stupor. With a strangled shout, he swung the flashlight at its face like a club.

Thea shouted his name in alarm; the rag-doll thing jerked backward, its wings shifting over the ground with a dry rasp. Nox drew his arm back again, aiming for its hollow rib cage, but Thea grabbed his wrist.

"Nox, *run*!" she said.

"Why should we?" he snapped. "What's it gonna do, give me a splinter? I wanna know what this thing wants from—"

Its wings flexed and then spread wide, sending clouds of dirt into the air as they started to flap, and Nox broke off, shielding his eyes. Silhouetted against the night, those wings were massive, and its eerie carved face terrifying as it rose to hover over them. It tilted forward and dove at them.

He let Thea pull him away; they fled, its wingbeats following. The sound was horribly familiar; they were the same wingbeats Nox had heard almost every night for weeks. It had been watching the Day house all that time.

"What—do we—do—now?" Thea panted.

"Keep running!"

"We'll miss the turn," she said. "We'll run straight into the Web."

And if the Web was the Devil's territory, and if the thing chasing them was the Devil, then that was the last place they wanted to be.

"We won't miss it," he said, needing to believe it.

Nox's lungs and sides were burning, but he didn't dare slow down. The path grew so tight they couldn't go on side by side. He risked a look back for the Devil, but it was too dark—he couldn't see it. He could only hear its wingbeats, following them tirelessly. And then—

And then they faded away, and the only sound was his and Thea's loud breathing.

"Thea!" he called. "I think it's gone."

She slowed to a stop, panting. "Why would it just leave?"

"Maybe it—"

Something over Thea's shoulder caught his eye: a glimmer of light, deep in the woods.

"Maybe it what?"

"*Shh*," he said. "Look."

Between the black silhouettes of the trees, something moved, radiant silver and quick as a ghost. He took a few halting steps forward.

"Nox, we—we don't know what that is," Thea said, hushed.

"It's the lunar wolf," he said. "It has to be."

He stepped off the path, eyes fixed on the depths of the forest. He turned off the flashlight, afraid it would startle the wolf away, and held his breath as he crept forward. His heart hammered. He didn't know what he'd do when he came face-to-face with the lunar wolf again, but he couldn't let it get away this time.

A bough overhead creaked as if about to collapse. Nox looked up: a dark shape moved over their heads, blending with the shadows of the canopy. The Devil, he thought—it had come back for them.

"Look out!" Thea shouted, but it was too late.

Something heavy collided with him, sending him face-first into the dirt. The air slammed out of his chest. Whatever was on top of him moved, a pair of knees digging into his back, a hand shoving his head down when he tried to lift it. Something sharp pressed against his neck.

"Stop *moving*, outsider," said a girl's voice, and that was when he figured out the heavy something on top of him wasn't a Devil, but a person.

14

HIS CHEEK GROUND INTO THE DIRT. A THUD accompanied by a high-pitched yelp told him Thea had been shoved down, too. Nox's arms were wrenched painfully behind his back, his wrists lashed together, and then he was yanked to his feet. His gaze darted in every direction, searching wildly for that celestial glow he'd seen—but it was gone. The woods pressed close around them, the darkness undisturbed beyond the flashlight one of his captors carried.

There were three—no, four of them. Bandanas were tied over their faces and hoods pulled down over their heads, so that only their eyes were visible.

"Let me *go*!" he said, struggling so hard he nearly wrenched his shoulders from their sockets. The rope dug into his skin. He was livid. He'd been *so close*. The lunar wolf had been right *there*.

But the girl's grip on his wrists was unyielding. With her free hand, she pressed something cool and hard against his throat—a long piece of sharpened stone. He went still, pulse pounding against the edge of the makeshift blade.

"How did you get here?" she demanded.

"We *walked*," he bit out, conscious of his throat moving against the stone dagger.

"Sounded like you were in a hurry to us." That was the one who'd tied Thea up, and who held her in place now with a gloved hand on her shoulder. He was the tallest of the bunch. "Did you want everything within a five-mile radius to know where you were? If so, job well done."

Nox stared at him. He didn't . . . *sound* very old. And he was the only one big enough that he could have maybe been an adult. The smallest of them, watching the proceedings from the sidelines, couldn't have been more than four feet tall.

This realization came as no relief to Nox, not with his hopes of catching up with the lunar wolf dwindling to nothing. He should've been able to defend himself from someone his own age. They shouldn't have gotten the better of him so easily.

"V-Violet? Look at this." The voice was almost too soft and timid to hear. It was the fourth and last of the group, bending to pick something off the ground and then holding it up for the girl to examine.

Their map. It must have slipped out of the pocket of his jacket when the girl—Violet—had tackled him.

"It's the Nightwood," said the shy kid. He had chin-length dark hair framing his face beneath the hood, half-pinned messily under the floral scarf that covered his nose and mouth.

"We didn't mean to come here," Thea said quickly. "We were running from—"

She cut herself off, biting her lip.

"F-from what?" the boy asked apprehensively.

"I . . . I don't really know."

"Could've been anything," the tall one said. "Thanks for leading it here. Much appreciated."

"Relax for once. Whatever it was, there's no sign of it now."

That had been a new voice. A fifth person slouched up the path with his hands in his pockets, inexplicably wearing ski goggles and an oversized coat.

"We have to take them back to the settlement," Violet said. Then Nox and Thea were being forcibly walked off the path. He fought and dug his heels in, trying to slow their progress. The back of his skull connected with something hard—Violet swore—and he tore away from her. But he didn't get far; the big guy caught the hood of his jacket, reeled him in, and threw him over his shoulder like a sack of dirty laundry.

"Let go!" Nox yelled.

"Don't think I won't gag you."

"Why are you taking us with you?" Thea asked.

"We don't let outsiders wander around," the guy carrying Nox said. "You could get hurt, or cause trouble in the woods, which means problems for us."

"And we need to know how you got this map," said Violet. She had dark brown eyes and light brown skin; that was all he could see around her mask. Her hand touched gingerly at her jaw, where Nox suspected a bruise was forming.

"We—" Thea began.

"Don't tell her," Nox snarled. "We don't need to answer their questions."

"Maybe they can help us," Thea said. "We got it from someone called Adam."

Violet's eyebrows shot up under her hood. "Adam sent you here?"

"Kind of," Thea said. "We told him we were going into the woods no matter what he said, and he gave us the map because he figured it was better than letting us get lost. We're looking for someone called *Zahna, Keeper of Night and Warden of the Wilds.*"

"*Looking* for Zahna?" Violet said. "Why would you do that?"

"Maybe they like the idea of having their heads mounted on her wall," the big guy suggested. Nox contemplated kicking him in the stomach. On the one hand, he'd probably get dropped and crack his skull open. On the other hand, he'd die happy.

After a few more minutes, Nox's captor said: "If I put you down, are you going to try to run again?"

"No," Nox lied.

"He's obviously lying," said Violet.

But he put Nox down anyway, and before Nox could even think of running, he was distracted by the sight ahead of them. Light, radiating into the sky from behind a wall made of felled trees, which had been cut down to equal sizes, lashed together, and staked deep into the ground. Soon he picked up voices, and beneath that, the gurgle of running water. They came up to a gate, and Violet whistled. A sentry appeared at the top.

"Violet!" he said. "Hurry and get in. We're locking up."

"What happened?" Violet asked.

"Trouble."

Someone out of sight heaved the gate open; light flooded the woods, so bright Nox had to squint until his eyes adjusted. Beside him, Thea gasped. The wall encircled a riverside campsite, except calling it a campsite felt like an understatement. It was more like a small town. The colorless moonlight bled into the pulsing gold of countless lanterns and firepits. Dozens of simple huts and tents dotted both sides of the river, though a light mist hung over the water and half obscured their view of the other side. Overhead, suspension bridges and zip lines connected a network of tree houses. Rope ladders dangled down the trunks, swaying lightly.

Nox and Thea were herded through the gate as the sentry climbed down from his post to meet them.

"Newcomers, huh?" the man said, sparing them a cursory glance before returning his attention to Violet and the others. "They're lucky you spotted them. Deadlock, head over to the woodworkers, yeah? They could use an extra pair of hands restocking arrows for the archers. Patch, take Betty to the safe house—the other children are there already. Nine—" He broke off to glare at the boy with the goggles. "Just stay out of trouble."

"It's like you have no faith in me," Nine said, unconcerned.

The big guy—Deadlock—nodded and left without a word. Nox wasn't sorry to see him go. The shy kid, Patch, went after him, and the short one who hadn't said a word the entire time followed; Nox guessed that was Betty. That left them with Violet and Nine. Behind them, the gate was already being dragged shut by a second guard working a pulley system.

"Violet—" the sentry continued.

"Where's Mom?" she said, interrupting.

"The usual place. You might catch her if you hurry, but—"

"Thanks!" Violet said, already jogging away. The sentry shook his head and returned to his post.

"HEY! We're still tied up!" Nox called after her. Nine snickered, and Nox rounded on him. "Untie us!"

"Why should I?" he said, and then laughed at Nox's outraged sputtering. "Just kidding. Gate's locked anyway, not like you're going anywhere."

He pushed up his goggles; under the reflective lenses, his eyes were an alarming traffic-cone orange. Nox wondered suddenly if he'd been wrong to assume that their captors were human. He had never seen a person with eyes that looked like that. But Nine was already picking apart Thea's bindings and then turning to get Nox's. He held out his wrists silently, deciding not to ask.

"What exactly is going on?" Thea said.

"We'll have to follow Violet to find that out," he said. "Unless you want to wait here. I'd give you the tour, but I don't think now's the best time."

"Violet still has our map," Nox said, rubbing at his wrists where the rope had started to chafe.

"This way, then." Nine strolled away. Reluctantly, Nox and Thea followed. He led them down the pathways between the tents, lantern-lit and adorned with zigzagging strings of flowers and colorful bandanas. Mosquitoes, fireflies, and moths darted from campfire to campfire, unperturbed by the people gathered around them. No one was panicking, but a tension hung thick in the air—the way it felt before a thunderstorm in the city, when the sidewalks were full of pedestrians scuttling home, and the shops were packing away their outdoor tables and signs. Like something was coming.

No one else in the settlement had their faces covered, Nox realized. Just Violet, Nine, and the others who'd caught them in the woods.

Someone called out, "Okay there, Nine?"

"Yup!" he said.

"They going to see E and R?"

"If we can find them."

"E and R?" Thea asked.

"Echo and Radar," Nine said. "Echo's the closest thing we have to a leader. Radar's her second-in-command."

They tracked Violet to a large canvas tent in the middle of the sprawling campsite, beside a taller figure with a shock of black hair cropped short, heavy-rimmed glasses, and a mark on the side of her nose as if she'd rubbed it with ink-stained fingers.

"Why can't I help?" Violet was asking her.

"You're not ready yet," the woman said.

"I thought you said it was under control."

"It *will* be, but— Oh! Are those new folks? Welcome!" the woman said, her expression brightening as Nine approached with the two of them. "See? You already have a job, Violet. Stay with them until you hear the all clear. Echo and I will talk to them later, when everything's settled, yeah?"

"But—" Violet said.

The woman pressed a distracted kiss to the top of her head and hurried away, leaving Violet to fume, fists clenched, as she watched her go.

"Did you find out anything?" Nine asked.

"Bog witch headed toward the wall. Mom wouldn't tell me what direction it's coming from, though."

Violet threw open the flap of the big tent and disappeared before Nox could get a word out about their map. Nine slipped inside after her.

"We should go with them," Thea said under her breath.

Nox was going to grind his teeth into nubs at this rate. "Do we have a choice?"

Inside, every inch of the tent was covered in maps, tacked up on the walls and across the small table in the back, which also held a lantern, ink pots, empty water bottles serving as makeshift pencil holders, compasses, rulers, and sheafs of clean grid paper.

"Radar made these," Nine said. "She's been mapping out the Nightwood for years. The parts of it that can be mapped, anyway."

"Was that her outside?" Thea asked, with a glance at Violet, who had bent over the table to examine a map that was spread open over its surface.

"Yeah. She's probably gone to meet up with Echo."

"Great," Nox said pointedly. "You definitely don't need *my* map, then."

Violet straightened suddenly. "Northwest by west. Are you coming?"

"I don't know," Nine drawled. "Let me see if I can fit you into my busy schedule—"

She grabbed Nine by the wrist and dragged him to the entrance, only to stop short and turn back to glare at Nox. "You too! I can't let you walk around alone."

"Give me back the map first," he demanded.

Violet opened her mouth to fire back at him, but Nine interjected.

"Stick with us, and we'll answer any questions you have," he said. His strange orange eyes were as bright as signal flares in the dimly lit tent. "After this is over."

They climbed a ladder, crossed three suspension bridges that wobbled nauseatingly, went around the back of a tree house, and clambered onto one of the branches that supported it.

"Go on," Nine said, behind them, when they hesitated. "It's sturdy. Just use the same handholds she does."

Violet's route took them into the highest branches, until they could step off onto the roof of the tree house. From there, they had a clear line of sight over the top of the wall that encircled the campsite, and an unobstructed view of the stars. He thought about climbing onto the roof of the Day house with Noah and felt a pang, so he quickly tore his eyes away from the sky, looking out into the dark woods instead.

Violet stood on tiptoe, eyes scanning the night. Then she stretched out an arm, pointing. "There."

Beyond the golden light that emanated from the campsite, the forest was dense and dark. Then something shifted out there in the shadows, a flicker, like a fish tail breaking the water's surface for an instant before disappearing, hidden behind the trees.

Nox inhaled sharply, leaning forward to try and catch another glimpse. That was . . . He thought that had been . . .

Another flash of movement in the dark, and then it was visible in a break between the trees: a tall, thin, luminous white figure, brilliant with moonshine just the way the lunar wolf had been. Nox's heart tripped at the sight of that familiar haunting glow. It moved so smoothly it might've been gliding; he couldn't say if it was or wasn't, because it wore a kind of cloak, a shroud that fell all the way to the forest floor. An animal skull covered its face—something with a long snout and large, sharp teeth. The bleached bone and dark cavities of the eye sockets made Nox shiver, a half-remembered dream whispering in the back of his mind. As the figure glided through the forest, it brushed up against the trees; wherever its shroud made contact, white rot spread over healthy bark, mushrooms sprang up, and the autumn leaves withered and dropped like stones. It left black patches of decay under its feet, as if a dark carpet unfurled behind it as it walked.

"Is it a ghost?" Thea asked, her voice hushed.

"No. The bog witch is part of the Nightwood," Nine said. "Its touch kills instantly."

Far below, someone whistled a single shrill note. Arrows shot out of the woods from every direction; ropes were tied to the ends, crisscrossing in front of the bog witch as the arrows buried themselves in the trunks of the trees. When the last arrow had been fired, the ropes made a pattern like a giant game of cat's cradle, pulled taut. The bog witch kept gliding forward as if it didn't see the rope trap there. Nox watched with bated breath—would it pass through the ropes like a phantom, the way the lunar wolf had gone through the window glass?

But when it made contact, the bog witch's weight sent little tremors through the trap, and bent and strained the cords that swiftly tangled around it. It struggled for a moment, thrashing, and Nox was sure it had been caught—but then it executed a strange, sinuous motion and slipped between the ropes, the hem of its shroud fluttering as it twisted and glided through the gaps. The way it moved reminded Nox, revoltingly, of a giant centipede.

"It didn't work," Thea said nervously.

"Wasn't supposed to catch it. They're just slowing it down," Violet said. "Keep watching."

A dozen small fires burst into existence: torches, burning in the hands of the people who rushed in to surround the rope trap. The bog witch made a hissing, rattling noise and whirled away from the light, as if it hurt. Three more sharp whistles cut through the night. The torch bearers shifted, leaving a gap in their ranks, and the bog witch fled toward the darkness.

Only then did Nox notice that a lone figure stood in front of the rope trap. She had a hood on, but her muscled arms were bare. She knelt, a rifle in her hands, her eye lined up with the scope as she aimed.

The bog witch slithered out of the rope trap, alighting on the ground at its full height, towering over the markswoman for a single heart-stopping instant as it regarded her with its terrible empty eyes.

Then, in a streak of motion like a python's strike, it lunged. From the flowing folds of its shroud, a spindly hand appeared, the fingers tapering to unnaturally long points, curled into a claw.

Seconds before they made contact, the markswoman fired. The rifle went off with a bang. Her shot knocked the bog witch off course, its whole body jolting from the force of the impact, and then it toppled sideways in a flutter of silvery white to land on the ground, which turned slowly black underneath, as if with a spreading bloodstain.

There was a brief silence underscored by the gasp of the torch fires. And then a commotion broke out below as people swarmed around the bog witch and the markswoman, who was getting to her feet and tugging her hood down to reveal a tall woman with a buzz cut and a jagged scar across her nose. She was giving orders to the others, but Nox couldn't make out the words from up here.

"That's Echo," Violet said worshipfully. "There's nothing in the woods that scares her."

"Is it . . . dead?" Thea asked, with mingled awe and horror.

"Nope," Violet said as she dropped back down to sit beside them. "Just a tranquilizer dart. We're allowed to hunt enough to survive, and we can defend ourselves when something threatens the settlement, but we're not allowed to kill anything that glows white like that. One of Zahna's rules."

"So what are they going to do with it, then?" Thea asked.

"They'll transport it back to the bog," Nine said. "If they can find it. The boglands move around sometimes."

"Get it now?" Violet told them. "If we hadn't caught you, you could've walked right into that."

He opened his mouth to argue, but then he remembered what he'd been doing seconds before Violet and the others had stopped them: chasing that elusive flash of silver-white, letting it lure him off the trail, like a peabrained fish following a hypnotic light straight into a predator's teeth. It seemed likely now that what he'd seen hadn't been the lunar wolf at all.

Monsters were real and they lived in the dark. Everyone started out knowing that, on some level—an intrinsic knowledge that small children had, which you forgot or unlearned as you grew up. He'd walked into the dark looking for his monster, but the Nightwood wasn't a closet or the space under the bed. Here, there was no telling how long the dark went on, and room enough for many more monsters than just the one.

15

"SO YOU ALL LIVE HERE? *WILLINGLY?*" NOX ASKED.

"No, all this is an elaborate ruse just to mess with you," Deadlock said. They had met up with Violet's friends after the bog witch had been dealt with and things around camp seemed to be settling back down. Nox was no more fond of them now than he had been when they'd been tying him up and dragging him through the woods.

"We like it here," Violet said. "Obviously."

"Obviously," Nox echoed. "'Cause who needs sunlight anyway?"

"But how did you all *get* here?" Thea asked. "There's so many people—at least a couple hundred."

"Kidnapping, mainly," Nine said.

"He's joking. No one got kidnapped," Violet said. "Everyone who's here *wants* to be here. Most of us got lost in the woods and found their way here by accident. Some of us came from nearby towns, like Deadlock, and others were hikers who wandered off a trail and stumbled into the Nightwood. Like me and my mom. Anyone who stays gets a job. They hunt, or trap, or cook, or build. Or they're lookouts, like us—it's our job to warn the settlement if anything dangerous comes our way. Or to rescue lost strangers. Who, by the way, are usually grateful for our help." She gave Nox and Thea a pointed look. "Some *do* leave, but a lot of people decide that what's in here is better than what's out there."

"What's that mean?" Nox asked. *"Better than what's out there. Out there is only the entire rest of the world."*

"Uh, yeah, and everything in it sucks, in case you haven't noticed," Violet said. "Go on. Tell me what's happening in the world. Tell me if there's a reason we should go back."

"There's—" Thea began, and stopped. "Okay, so the climate's not in the best shape. And neither is the government. And then there's the growing class divide, and education policy is a mess, and—"

"Wow," Nine said. "When you put it like that, how could we resist?"

"Because!" Thea said. "Because if we don't fix it, then who will?"

To this, the lookouts responded with a round of hearty laughter. Thea's face went a little pink.

"So you all ran away from the real world because you couldn't handle it," Nox said, irritated, though he wasn't sure why. Any other time, if Thea had told him earnestly that she wanted to save the world, he would've laughed, too. Didn't mean he liked it when *they* did it, though.

"Y-yes," Patch said. His hands twisted anxiously at the end of his floral scarf.

"Don't agree with him when he's mocking you," Nine said,

exasperated. Beside him, Betty—who hadn't yet spoken and was the only one whose face was still covered—raised a hand to her mouth as if to muffle a laugh.

"Wh-why not?" Patch mumbled. "It's true."

"You said people come from towns nearby, right?" Thea asked hopefully. "What about Evergreen?"

"I don't think we have anyone from Evergreen," Violet said. "Which *is* a little weird, since it's so close. We send a team there when we need to top up on supplies every few months."

Violet had pulled down her scarf but left her hood up, revealing a round face with a button nose that made her look younger than she probably was. Without the mask, her resemblance to Radar was obvious. To Nox's grudging relief, her first order of business had been to make sure he and Thea were fed. He couldn't care less about what life was like in this city of cowards and runaways—which they all referred to, pretentiously, as *the settlement*, since it had no real name—but Thea spent the entire meal interrogating Violet and the others about it.

Camp Chickenshit held communal dinners at long wooden tables, where they served the deer and rabbit meat their hunters procured, trout their fishermen hauled in, edible plants their foragers retrieved, and root vegetables cultivated using a grow-light setup their farmers had rigged in a few of the tree houses. They had builders to keep those tree houses in good shape, as well as the huts and bridges; seamsters who worked with animal pelts supplied by their trappers; and lookouts to monitor the surrounding areas and warn the community of impending dangers.

After they'd eaten, Violet took them to one of the tree houses near the edge of camp—a makeshift headquarters for the look-outs, with a crow's nest at the top that stuck out like a middle finger. It was going to be a *lot* harder to sneak out from up there.

"I'm scared of heights," he told her flatly.

"Want me to give you a piggyback ride?" Deadlock offered, straight-faced.

They glared at each other other until Thea sighed and went up the ladder first. Deciding he just barely preferred Thea's company to Deadlock's, he followed. The inside was strewn with blankets and sleeping bags, and hand-drawn maps were tacked on the walls, showing different parts of the Nightwood in detail. Violet must have gotten those from Radar. Moonlight poured in through a square opening cut into one of the walls for a window and the hole in the ceiling where another ladder led up into the crow's nest. Violet lit a lantern in the corner. She tugged her hood down absently, revealing purple hair.

"Is that why they call you Violet?" Thea asked.

"Pretty much," Violet said. "It's a trail name. We all have them."

"What's that?"

"A nickname that other hikers usually give you," she said, sitting against the wall with her legs stretched out in front of her. It seemed she'd resigned herself to Thea's endless ques-tions. "Even those of us who didn't start out as hikers get a trail name if they decide to stay."

"So then what's your real name?" Nox asked.

"Whatever name she chooses is her real name," Thea said.

Discomfort flashed across Violet's face almost too quickly for Nox to process it. But then she shrugged. "I don't remember."

He rolled his eyes. "Okay, I get it. You don't have to tell us."

"I mean it," Violet said, fidgeting. "I've been here a long time, and . . ." She trailed off into an awkward silence.

"How long?" Thea prompted.

"Um . . ." Violet sighed. "I lost count. I think it's been ten or eleven years."

"You mean you were born here?" Nox said, mystified.

Violet tugged at her sleeves, watching the entrance to the tree house as the others climbed in. "No," she said finally. "I was twelve when I got here. But no one ages in the settlement."

"So you've been the same age for ten years?" Nox said with rising horror. He tried to imagine being stuck in middle school forever and decided instantly that he'd sooner lie down on the nearest set of train tracks.

"Cool, right?" Nine said, hoisting himself up last and perching on the edge of the opening. "Fountain of youth's got nothing on this place."

As Nine and the others shed their hoods and scarves and coverings, Nox's jaw dropped. Nine's coat turned out to be hiding a pair of stubby wings. He wore a band T-shirt that had seen better days, with slashes cut into the back to let the wings stick out. Patch probably would've been a high school freshman. He was skinny and tall and slouchy the way a lot of them were, so he looked stretched out like an old rubber band—except he also had a pair of black-tipped cat ears and a short tail, the fur tawny with dark streaks. At Nox's open gawking, his ears flat-tened self-consciously, and he twitched the tail out of the way so it was hidden behind his back. The smallest one, Betty, couldn't have been more than eight or nine years old; she had curly black hair and a red backpack, and Violet said her trail name came from some old cartoon character. When she pulled down the bandana around the lower half of her face, it was mottled with spots a little bit darker than the rest of her skin tone—kind of like a hyena, maybe. They were on her hands, too, under the gloves she wore.

Violet threw her scarf at Nox, hitting him in the face. "Stop staring."

"Where else am I supposed to look?" he sputtered, balling it up and lobbing it back at her.

"What . . . happened to all of you?" Thea asked.

Nine shrugged. "Once you've been in the Nightwood for a few years, you start to change. Only the kids, though. And . . . mostly just us, since we've been here the longest. We're not sure why—Radar thinks the magic is changing our DNA, and that adults aren't affected because their bodies are fully developed. But that's just a guess."

"Jukebox thinks she's growing a horn," Patch shared timidly.

Nine scoffed. "I told her that's just a zit."

"But she's been here almost as long as me. She's p-probably next."

Nox frowned at Violet and Deadlock. "What about you two?"

Without the hood, Deadlock reminded him unpleasantly of Zack Millard, big and lumbering with dirty-blond hair. His thick blond eyebrows had a slight upward slant toward the middle, so it looked like they were drawn in a permanent furrow of concern.

He tapped his chest with his knuckles, producing a dull knocking sound. "Exoskeleton. It's kind of patchy, though."

"Like a roach?"

"Pretty much," he deadpanned. Unlike Zack, who had a nasally smear of a voice, Deadlock talked in a monotonous drone.

"That's disgusting," Nox said.

"Wow!" Thea was plainly over the moon about getting to hang out with real-life mutants. "Violet, do you . . . ?"

Then she looked embarrassed for asking. Violet shot her a grumpy look but pulled up her sleeve, revealing shiny green scales, like a snake's. Thea opened her mouth—Nox would've bet a brand-new Xbox that she was going to ask how far up the scales went—but then she reconsidered and closed it again.

"Does it hurt?" Nox asked before he could stop himself. He had been reminded, unwillingly, of Noah's condition and the spreading gray patches on his skin.

"No. It's just a side effect of staying here," Violet said. "We're part of the Nightwood now."

Her eyes were drawn to something above Nox's head. It was one of the eris moths, floating in through the window to alight on the wall.

"I'll get it," Deadlock muttered, and stood as if to scare it off.

"No, wait!" Thea said. She pulled a jar from her backpack, the kind with air holes poked into the top, which she used to gather specimens on her hikes. She snuck up on the moth and trapped it in the jar, nudging it inside with the lid before sealing it in. Then she held the glass up to her nose, gazing at it rapturously. "I've been dying to get a closer look at these."

"I answered your questions," Violet said. "It's your turn. What do you want with Zahna?"

"I never agreed to take turns," Nox said.

"She doesn't take appointments," Deadlock said. "And we're not helping you find her. She's one of the Keepers of Night. We just follow her rules and stay out of her way."

"*One* of the Keepers," Thea echoed. "How many are there?"

"Three. Zahna is the Warden of the Wilds—she protects the wilderness, the quality that keeps the Nightwood pure and untamed. They all sort of have their own territory." Violet unfolded the map—*Nox's* map—and pointed at the upper righthand corner, the place Adam had called *the Web* and told them to avoid. "That belongs to the Warden of the Dark."

"The Devil," Thea said quietly. She shared an uneasy look with Nox. The memory of the winged creature that had chased them through the woods was fresh in his mind. "But why are they in charge? What's so special about them?"

"How much do you know about the Nightwood?" Nine asked. "If you've come this far, you must have noticed the whole . . ." He waved a hand in an abstract gesture. "Eternal-night thing?"

"Yeah," Thea said eagerly. "Adam told us there are other dimensions beyond time and space, and that this is a place where the dimension of night has more control over the world."

"Right. So every dimension has Keepers to watch over it.

Their powers are inherited, either through a bloodline or the choosing of an heir," he said. "The different dimensions are the forces that shape our world, and the Keepers stop their magic from overflowing and breaking the boundaries of reality as we know it. Here, where the dimension of night is dominant, the Keepers of Night rule. They can leave, but when the sun is out, they lose most of their powers."

Thea looked dissatisfied with this explanation. "So is there a dimension of morning? A dimension of midday?"

"No," Nine said slowly. "That's not really the point. It's not the time of day that matters."

"Don't overthink it," Deadlock advised.

"There's no such thing as overthinking," Thea said.

"Okay, okay," Nine said. "What's night?"

"Um, when the sun sets and it's dark outside?" Thea said, uncertain, as if she thought it was a trick question. "As the earth rotates, one side of it faces away from the sun, which causes—"

"No," Nine said. "I mean, yeah. But also no. When we talk about the *dimension* of night—night as a force that shapes the world—there's more to it than that. Night is—things that are hidden, and secrets and lies, and not being able to trust your own senses. It's fear and nightmares, and the thoughts that keep you awake when you're trying to sleep. And it's also, you know, the way you feel when you look at the stars, and the anticipation in the seconds before sunrise."

"But how do you *know* that?" Thea asked.

"The owls told me," Nine said, with a bright smile and a cheerful flutter of his wings for emphasis. It was impossible to tell if he was joking or not, and honestly, Nox didn't care.

"Give me that." Nox snatched at the map, but Violet shoved it into her pocket.

"Tell me what you want from Zahna," she said again, looking between him and Thea.

Thea put up her hands as if to say, *Leave me out of this.* "It's Nox's call."

He wanted to refuse. But . . . the lookouts knew the woods a lot better than he and Thea did. The painstakingly detailed maps on the walls were proof of that. If he was being honest with himself, he'd felt his guard go down the moment he'd seen their mutations. Their damage made it easier to trust them. Like Noah, they couldn't stop their bodies from betraying them, changing against their will. And the way they covered themselves up when they left the safety of their hideout—it was like they knew they were outsiders, even in this colony of outsiders.

"Zahna took something from my brother, and now he's . . . in trouble," Nox admitted.

"What are you going to do?" Deadlock said. "Ask her nicely to please hand it over?"

"I'm not asking. I'm gonna steal it back."

"You're out of your mind," Violet told him. "And if she thinks you're from here, we'll *all* be punished."

"She won't think that," Nox said with more confidence than he had any right to feel. "The lunar wolf saw me. She's probably expecting me to show up."

"That's even *worse!*"

Patch hugged his knees to his chest and hid his face against them. His ears flattened until they disappeared in his hair. "You're *dead*," he whimpered.

"I told you what you wanted to know," Nox said. "Give me back the map."

"No way. Then it's on *me* if you die," Violet said. "And one of Zahna's rules is that we're responsible for any humans who find the Nightwood. We guide them home or we take them in. If you want to leave, Mom will get someone to escort you out of the Nightwood once Echo's team comes back from the boglands. Until then, you're staying put."

She assigned everyone shifts to keep watch over her prisoners as they all prepared to go to sleep. In the settlement, they told time using the stars and had sun lamps to keep their internal clocks regulated. Violet said that time passed in the Nightwood the same way it did in the outside world. They didn't skip over the daylight hours; it was just that the sunlight didn't reach them in the woods.

Nox meant to stay up and wait for an opening to escape— but before he knew it, his exhaustion had overcome him, and he was out.

He didn't know how much time had passed when he woke up; it was a commotion outside that roused him, raised voices and countless rapid footsteps. The lookouts had woken up around him, but he only knew because he felt them moving and heard their confused whispers. He couldn't see anything. It was pitch-black.

"Nox?" Thea said.

"Over here," he replied. A shuffling noise as she scooted toward him, and then her hand landed clumsily on his shoulder.

"What's going on?" Her voice was rough from sleep.

"Something got into the settlement," Violet said. "I need to go see. Can someone—"

"I'll stay with them," Nine said. "Go."

"Why aren't any of the lights working?" Thea said. A clicking noise indicated she was switching her flashlight on and off, to no avail. "Even my phone. It's just black."

"Something turned off all the lights in the settlement—lanterns, campfires, everything—and it won't let us have them back," Nine said. "Radar will probably try to negotiate with whatever it is, since Echo's still gone. That's why Violet's so freaked."

Whatever had stolen all the light from Camp Chickenshit hadn't managed to suppress the moon or stars, and soon, Nox's eyes had adjusted to the faint illumination filtering in through the tree house window. The dark silhouettes of the other lookouts were climbing down the ladder, Deadlock identifiable by his broad shoulders, Patch tugging his hood over his triangular ears, Violet descending last. In the corner, Betty slept blissfully on.

"So we're supposed to just sit here?" Nox said. He got up to kneel by the window, twisting his neck to see the middle of the settlement, but the tree house was too out of the way.

"What if there's trouble and we have to run?" Thea said worriedly.

"We've never had to evacuate," Nine said. He dropped his voice low. "Anyway . . . I told Violet I'd stay with you. I never said we'd stay *here*."

His fluorescent orange eyes were piercing in the dark. Nox could just make out his sly grin.

They gave Violet and the others a five-minute head start before they followed, Nox and Thea climbing down, Nine jumping off the ladder ten feet from the ground, his half-formed wings flapping madly to slow his fall. Nine put a finger to his lips for quiet, and they crept around the outer edges of the settlement, behind the tents and the clearings with the cook fires and covered tables, until they came up on the center of camp. He heard a snatch of Radar's voice, but not clearly enough to make out what she was saying.

They hid behind the canvas tent that housed Radar's workshop as clouds rolled in overhead, obscuring the moon. It began to rain, a slow, dreary drizzle. Nox listened with bated breath, biting his lip to hold back a shiver as cold water dripped into his hair, down his neck, and under the collar of his shirt.

"I ask you one more time," a deep, familiar voice said. "Where are they?"

"I can't answer that, Lord Shadow," Radar said calmly. "I'm sorry."

"Fine!" Shadow said, with a snort that indicated he was tossing his heads and stamping his hooves in agitation. "I wouldn't bless them anymore even if they *begged*!"

Nox's stomach was in knots. The god of ephemeral things had come looking for them.

The trees all around the settlement shivered, as if the storm had intensified—and then, in a rush, all the leaves dropped as if they'd been shocked from their branches. They fell in a cascade, startling the birds from their nests. Somewhere, an owl gave a shrill hoot as it flapped away. The rain picked up in tempo.

"And as for *you*," Shadow was saying, "I suppose if you're willing to hide them, then you're willing to take responsibility for them, too. Those who refuse blessings court curses."

"I understand, Lord Shadow," Radar said.

"I won't be giving you your lights back. I'm keeping them."

"If that is your will," Radar agreed.

"The storm clouds will keep coming."

"Do I have to?" one of the other heads complained.

"*Yes*," Shadow snapped.

"Of course, Lord Shadow," Radar said. "I'm sorry the children failed to show you proper respect. We can't undo their mistake, but we will leave offerings of food and gifts beside your altar."

"As if bribery will be enough to win my forgiveness!" he huffed. "The curse will end when I feel like ending it. You might pray to the gods of mercy for that time to come quickly!"

Shadow and his brothers clopped away, the sound of their hoofbeats quickly disappearing under the rain. Nox was soaked through. He glanced over at Thea and saw, through the gloom, that her hands were clamped over her mouth.

"This is *our* fault," she whispered to Nox.

"What are we supposed to do about it?" he hissed.

"I don't know, but shouldn't we do *something*?"

"Shadow threatened to kill us, in case you forgot."

"I'm with Nox on this one," Nine said. "We need to get the two of you out of here."

They retreated. As they left, they heard Radar calling out instructions.

"We need a team to visit Lord Wick," she was saying. "See if he'll let us borrow an ever-burning flame."

"That's another minor deity," Nine told them in a whisper. "A lord of ember and charcoal. Pretty chill, for a fire god."

"When you say *god*," Thea said, "you don't mean a literal divinity, right? Because I'm an atheist, and—"

"*Shh*," Nox said.

Nine took them to a side gate that was unlocked. They struck out into the woods, and Thea's flashlight flickered back on at last. She breathed a sigh of relief. Nox's eyes stung at the sudden brightness.

"The path isn't far from here," Nine told them in an undertone.

"Why are you helping us?" Thea asked.

"Eh. You guys are bad news," he said breezily. "How did you get on Zahna's *and* Shadow's bad side? I'm just sending you off before any more of your mortal enemies come looking for you and causing trouble."

And Nine didn't even know about their run-in with the Evergreen Devil. He had a point—they were like magnets for miserable luck. Or maybe just Nox was.

"You snuck us out of the tree house before you knew about Shadow," Thea said, undeterred. "And you volunteered to stay with us before Violet even asked. You were thinking about it while everyone else was asleep."

Nine laughed. "Okay, you got me."

"So? Why are you doing this?"

"Why not?" he said. "Violet worships Echo. And Radar's never steered us wrong. But I don't think we should get to say who comes and goes."

Soon, the voices had faded behind them, and the low calls and rustlings of nocturnal creatures took their place.

"Almost there," Nine muttered. "I'll stay with you till we get to the path. If you don't know what you're looking for, you'll miss the turnoff to Zahna's watchtower and walk right into the Web."

"Having fun, Nine?" someone said.

It was Violet; she'd followed them. She came out from under cover to stand in front of them, her expression livid and betrayed.

"Aw, come on, Violet. Even if we send them home, they'll just—"

Nox jumped as a pair of huge hands clamped down on his shoulders. But this time, Nox was ready. He spun out of Deadlock's grip and aimed a punch at his stomach.

It was like hitting a solid wall. Nox swore and recoiled, hugging his hand to his chest. It hurt so bad he gave it a shake just to make sure it wasn't broken.

"Exoskeleton," Deadlock reminded him. "Comes in handy."

He grabbed at Nox's collar, but his hand closed around empty air as Nox twisted out of reach, darted back in, and delivered a sharp kick to his kneecap. Deadlock yelped and crumpled to the ground. He clutched his knee with both hands and shot Nox an affronted look, as if he'd expected a clean fight and Nox had broken some unspoken pact.

As far as Nox was concerned, there was no such thing as fighting dirty. There was only winning, or not winning. And Nox liked to win.

Nearby, Violet and Nine were having a vicious, much-too-loud argument. But where was Thea? Had she gotten away? Deadlock was hauling himself back up, and Nox was getting ready to run, when he spotted her. She snuck up behind Violet and snatched the map from her pocket.

Outraged, Violet lunged for her. Thea wheeled backward, balled up the map, and threw it over Violet's head. Nox caught it by the tips of his fingers. He laughed, triumphant, but broke off into a gasp when he almost collided with Deadlock—who was on his feet and looking annoyed beyond belief. Not even mad, just inconvenienced by Nox's existence, the way other people got annoyed at tangled headphone cords or slow-changing traffic lights. Nox swerved around him, faster and more agile than he was, and took off running after Thea.

Behind them came the sounds of a scuffle. But they faded as he and Thea raced through the woods. Nox's relief at finding the path was short-lived. They were completely turned around, and the Devil could be anywhere, waiting for them.

"Think we're close?" Nox asked, smoothing out the map and studying it.

"No idea," Thea said.

"Nox! Thea!"

Nine had caught up with them. His hair was streaked with dirt and his cheek red with the beginnings of a bruise.

"I shook them off, but I don't think Violet's gonna give up that easy," he said. "Hurry."

"You fought Violet for us?" Nox said as they scurried after him down the path. Nox had gotten into scraps on other people's behalf, but no one had ever done the same for him. He'd never needed them to.

Nine waved the question away. "We fight all the time. It's not a big deal."

"But—"

"Right here." He stopped. There was a dip in the ground— the start of a faded trail that branched off the main path, winding away into the woods. Nox never would've seen it if Nine hadn't pointed it out. "You get to the end of this trail, you'll find Zahna."

"Thanks. You really saved us," Thea said. "Look, if Lord Wick can't help you guys, I'll come back. I'll apologize to Shadow, or—I don't know, but I'll help clean up this mess."

Nox resisted the urge to roll his eyes. There wouldn't even *be* a mess at the settlement if they hadn't forced Nox and Thea to stay when they'd wanted to leave, but trust bleeding-heart Thea to make it her problem anyway.

"The settlement will be fine, don't worry. And I didn't help you so that you'd pay me back." Nine looked away uncomfortably. "I had a younger sibling. Out there, I mean. She would be older than me now."

"Then . . . why'd you leave?" Nox asked. He had assumed that anyone who stayed at the settlement had nothing to go back to.

"I had to. Anyway, she's better off without me."

"Oh."

Nine shrugged. "Everyone here's got a sob story. Deadlock ran away from home. Patch came here with his parents, but something in the woods got them, a couple of years back. Betty doesn't talk about her past. Like, ever. So I get it. And they do, too." He gave Nox a friendly push on the shoulder. "So on behalf of all of us, I'm telling you to go save your brother."

"I will," Nox promised.

Nine returned to the settlement; Nox and Thea went the other way, onto the hidden trail.

16

ZAHNA'S WATCHTOWER CROUCHED OVER THE forest like a giant daddy longlegs. Its base was made up of crisscrossing wooden struts, and the cabin at the top soared above the trees.

"Can you see anyone?" he asked Thea as they hid in the woods.

"I don't know. It's too high up," she whispered back.

A set of stairs zigzagged up to a catwalk that ran the perimeter of the cabin. Stairs were risky, though. If they ran into Zahna on the way, then they were done for.

"Think we can climb up the side?"

She hesitated. "It's a long way."

"Yeah."

"If we get caught," she said, "I'd rather be on the stairs."

"Maybe we should split up. You could wait here."

"No splitting up," Thea said sharply.

"Okay, okay. Let's go."

They crept up to the base of the tower. He put his hand on the rail and took the first step. His fingers traced the grain of the wood. It was cold as metal, like the outside of a car on a winter night.

"Nox?" Thea said. She was right behind him. "You okay?"

"Yeah," he said, and climbed.

They raced up the stairs, winding around and around the tower. There was no point in going slow. The sooner they got out of the open, the better. But even so, the climb went on for what felt like forever. He was pretty sure the tower wasn't *that* tall, but it was as though the stairs multiplied each time his foot landed on one of them. The ground dropped farther and farther away. Every now and then he glanced over his shoulder to make sure Thea was still with him, using her dark red hair as a focal point when the endless climb started to make him lightheaded. Her head was bowed, like she was counting the steps. Nox couldn't bring himself to do the same. He didn't *want* to know how many they'd climbed.

We're almost there, he told himself, willing it to be true. *We're almost there.*

But the stairs kept going and going and going, and he started to wonder whether they'd walked into a trap. Nothing in the Nightwood could be *easy*. Nothing could be straightforward, could just be exactly what it looked like.

He hated this place.

Helpless fury burned through him, and he used it as fuel to move faster, uncaring of the noise they made pounding up the stairs. He had to get out of here. He *had* to get back to Noah.

It was like he was drowning all over again: his body moved almost of its own accord, fighting for survival. Every sensation was sharper and at once very far away—the gashes on his arm and ankle burning, the sweat trickling down the back of his shirt, his muscles beginning to burn.

They turned the corner up another flight, and the catwalk was suddenly—miraculously—ahead of them. He threw himself onto the platform. Now that he didn't have to climb, it felt like he couldn't have gone another step even if he'd wanted to; he slumped against the rail, pressing his forehead into the icy wood while he caught his breath.

"Did that . . . ?" Thea said, leaning against the rail next to him. She stopped to gasp for breath. "Did that take longer than it should've?"

"I think so."

"Why do I feel like we almost got . . . stuck?"

Because we almost did, he thought. Or had they? Could he have imagined that?

He shook his head, dispelling the odd stirrings in his mind.

"Well, we didn't, so forget about it," he said. "Let's just get what we came here for."

He glanced down at the Nightwood. From here, it looked no different from an ordinary forest, clouds of dark green shadow rolling all the way up to the horizon, where they met the mountains. Gaps in the canopy gave him glimpses of the streams strewn over the ground like shattered wind chimes. He looked for Thea's house in the distance but couldn't find it.

Large windows lined the walls of the cabin, all the way around, so that anyone inside could see out in every direction. They were lucky no one was in there, because they would've been spotted the second they made it to the platform. The door was by the stairs. He reached for the handle—

A sound made him jump.

Thea's face was ashen under her freckles. They retreated to the other side of the cabin, ducked under the window, and waited.

The footsteps ascending the stairs could've belonged to a cat, they were so quiet. But when Nox peeked over the window frame, he had to stifle a gasp.

That definitely wasn't a cat.

It was Zahna.

There was no mistaking her. She was a seven-foot titan with a linebacker's build. One of her muscular arms carried a dead doe over her shoulder, and the other held a bow about as long as Nox was tall. The tan of her skin spoke of long days spent in the sun, even though such a thing wasn't possible in the Nightwood. Her armor looked like leather, bleached bone white. A tight plait kept her long white hair out of her face. It swung behind her like a chain as she kicked the cabin door open.

"In," she said, and then—

Nox dropped under the window again, heart beating wildly. Because something had followed her up the stairs. Something that shone like the moon.

The lunar wolf.

He and Thea cowered with their backs to the wall, shoulder to shoulder. If Zahna figured out they were here, they had nowhere to run.

But this was his only chance. He hadn't come here just to

hide when he was *this close* to finding what he needed to save Noah.

He covered his mouth with his hand, worried Zahna or her wolf would hear his rapid, frightened breathing. Then he gritted his teeth and got shakily to his knees. Thea put a hand on his shoulder, urging him back down, her eyes huge with fear.

He shook his head, and her hand slipped off his shoulder as he braced himself against the wall and peeked inside. Zahna had her back to him. She'd laid the carcass out on the wooden floor. The lunar wolf sniffed at it, its long snout poking into the wound in the doe's side and coming off red-tipped.

As Zahna turned away and hung up her bow, the wolf's head shot up. Nox tensed. It bounded to the door and nudged it open, sticking its enormous head around the frame. As if it'd caught a scent it didn't like.

Zahna straightened, watching it.

"What is it, Umbra?" she said.

Nox ducked as the lunar wolf withdrew its head from the door. A few moments later, he heard the door open and shut again; then those light footsteps once more. And then quiet. His nails dug into his palms. Beside him, Thea held her breath.

If Zahna was coming for them . . . If she knew they were there . . .

Each second lasted an eternity. *She's gone*, Nox thought. *She went back downstairs, she's gone.*

Unless it was a trick. Maybe she was just waiting them out.

Nox swallowed his fear. If it came down to waiting, then Zahna would definitely win. Because she had all the time in the world, and Nox didn't. Noah didn't.

Heart banging like a drumbeat in his ears, he bent low and peered around the corner.

Nothing there.

He nodded at Thea, and she did the same, checking the other side. Her shoulders slumped in relief. Just to be safe, he checked through the window again, but the cabin was empty. Zahna really had gone and taken the lunar wolf—Umbra—with her. They were in the clear. For now.

"We have to go inside," he said.

"If she comes back, we're dead."

"I know."

Thea didn't miss a beat. "Just make it fast."

They tiptoed to the front of the cabin and slipped through the door.

The inside of it was like a cross between a hunting lodge and an armory. Animal pelts strewn over the sparse furniture. Bows and arrows in every shape and size. A table pushed against the corner, carrying knives made of bone, a pair of binoculars, rope, and an assortment of other tools.

The dead doe lay on the ground, its eyes open; the limp sprawl of its limbs was almost more grotesque than the wound that had killed it. Nox shuddered, but there was no avoiding it. The cabin wasn't very large, just the one room, and he was going to have to search every inch.

"Guard the door in case she comes back," he said. Thea stationed herself outside with the door open a crack, leaving him alone.

It has to be here, he thought. The key to saving Noah was

between these four walls, just waiting for him to find it. If he could do this, he could finally go home.

He started with the table and the cabinets. But even as he opened drawers, flung their contents across the ground, felt around for hidden compartments, swept his arm across every surface—he knew that would be too easy. It wouldn't be somewhere out in the open. Next, he dug through the animal pelts, ripped the bows off their stands, upended quivers of arrows and shoved his hand inside.

He tore the place apart. Speed was more important than secrecy. And—and it felt good to destroy something of Zahna's after what she'd done. The fear of getting caught was gone. He was *furious*, and he wanted to make Zahna pay.

Not knowing exactly what he was looking for—he'd only caught a glimpse of it when the wolf had torn it out of Noah's chest—a small part of him worried he'd miss it. Or that he'd take something else by mistake. But he found nothing that even remotely resembled it. Nothing gold. Nothing that glowed.

Under the floor, maybe?

He picked a crowbar out of the pile of tools he'd knocked to the ground and began pulling up floorboards at random, growing more frantic with every passing second. Still nothing.

What if it wasn't here? What if Zahna had it on her?

Then he'd come all this way for nothing.

With a scream of frustration, he swung the crowbar around and slammed it into one of the windows. Cracks radiated out from the point of impact.

"Nox?" Thea said, rushing back inside. "What are you— Oh my god, what *happened* in here—"

He swung again, and this time, the window shattered. Thea grabbed him by the back of the collar and pulled him down, shielding him as glass shards rained on them both.

When the crashing ceased, it was eerily quiet. Except for his own hard breathing. He'd fallen into a crouch, Thea's arm over his bowed head and the crowbar still clutched tight in his hand. Cold air poured into the cabin from the broken window.

Thea straightened, brushing glass out of her hair and shaking it off her jacket.

"What the *hell*, Nox," she said. There was a razor-thin cut on her cheek.

The crowbar slipped from his grasp and fell with a sad *clunk*. He looked at Thea, blinking as if he'd just woken up.

"I couldn't find it," he said numbly. "It's not here."

She crossed her arms. "So you threw a tantrum? Ugh! Where did you look?"

He told her. As he talked, she turned a slow circle, scanning the room. She picked her way through the chaos, skirting around the holes in the ground, and disentangled a knife from a length of rope.

"There's one place you forgot to check," she said. Then she turned to the doe carcass in the middle of the room, which Nox had left alone.

"What?"

"It's not bleeding, and it looks like it's been cleaned up. So why would she bring it up here? It's not like there's space to skin it or cook it." She pushed it over, lifting one of its front legs. "Look."

The soft white fur of the doe's chest was marred by a long, straight cut that had been sewn up with black thread.

Thea held the knife over the doe and took a deep, steadying breath.

"Maybe I should—"

"*Shut up*," she said.

She lowered the knife and sliced carefully along the incision, cutting through the thread and reopening the wound. As the doe's flesh parted, golden light spilled from its chest. It was the exact same shade of gold Nox had seen a couple of days ago in the attic—the light that the wolf had taken from Noah. The knife fell from Thea's hand with a clatter.

"Holy crap."

"Yeah." Nox nudged her aside gently. This part, he could do. He pushed his hand into the doe's chest. It was cold and tacky, and the feeling made him shudder, but he stretched out his fingers until they brushed something warm.

When he pulled his hand out, he was clutching a golden pinecone.

"We found it," he breathed, hardly able to believe it. The pinecone was warm in his hands, like it had been baking in the sun all day, and its rough edges scraped his palms.

"You're sure that's it?" Thea asked.

"Yeah. It has to be."

Thea began to say something else, but a sound interrupted her: the dull scratch of claws against wood. Nox spun around just as the door swung open. Ghostly silver light washed over the room, and the lunar wolf came prowling inside.

17

ITS SIX BLACK EYES REGARDED NOX WITH
unnerving intelligence. Somehow it was even larger than he
remembered—or maybe it only appeared that way because the
cabin was so small and cramped, and because the moonlight
from outside blended into its fur, softening its outline. When it
moved, all the light in the world moved, too.

Nox clutched the golden pinecone tightly and took a half
step backward.

"You can't have it!" he said furiously.

Its puffy tail bristled. Its lips drew back in a snarl, revealing
sharp teeth in black gums. He wished he still had the crowbar.
But as he fell back another step, something crunched under his
shoe: glass from the window.

"Nox, get back!"

He barely had time to register Thea's warning. The wolf
sprang across the room, clearing the doe carcass in one powerful leap and landing with perfect grace on the spot Nox was
occupying—

But he threw himself to the side at the last second, sprawling
on the heap of animal pelts he'd torn through earlier. He swiped

a shard of glass off the ground. It was about the size of his fist and came to a point, not unlike Violet's stone dagger. His shoes slipped on the furs as he tried to get to his feet without using his hands and failed. Still prone, he brandished the glass shard threateningly with one hand and cupped the pinecone to his chest with the other. Its golden light shone through the cracks between his fingers.

The wolf advanced, less like an animal and more like a car speeding toward him on a dark road, unstoppable and dazzlingly bright. Blood dripped from his palm down his wrist; he'd squeezed the glass too hard.

He braced himself—its stance shifted as it prepared to pounce—

"HEY!" Thea shouted. "OVER HERE!"

Past the arc of the wolf's tail, Nox caught sight of Thea. She'd pulled out the jar containing the eris moth. The lid was unscrewed. The moth crawled onto the lip of the jar, fluttered its brilliant sapphire wings, and took flight.

The wolf followed the moth with its eyes, transfixed, not unlike the frogs they'd seen by the river. It turned away from Nox as the moth drifted up to the ceiling. Its nose—still red-tipped from where it had brushed the doe carcass before—pointed up, tracking it. And then:

It sprang into the air, jaws wide open, and clamped its teeth around the moth. There was a horrible *crunch*. The wolf landed, licking its chops with a long black tongue.

Then it made a noise in its throat, between a growl and a whine, and it fell over on its side, writhing in pain.

"Come on!" Thea said.

He rolled to his feet, dropping the bloodied glass shard, and ran around the wolf's twitching form to join her. Before they could get anywhere near the door, it flew open again. Zahna was there, her bow slung over her back. And she was *livid*.

Her eyes landed on the wolf, who let out another agonized whine. Then Zahna's deadly gaze turned on Nox and Thea.

"*What have you done?*" she thundered, shaking with rage.

No—she wasn't shaking. She was transforming.

Her muscles bulged like clay being molded by invisible hands. Her tan skin went gray and leathery. Spines burst through her armor in a row down her back, and her face changed, growing fangs and a long snout, like a hairless wolf. Her hands curved into three-inch-long claws.

And an inhuman roar ripped from her throat.

Thea grabbed his hand in a bone-crushing grip, and they ran for their lives, barreling around Zahna and practically flying out the door. Still at the tail end of her transformation and unbalanced on her new, clawed feet, Zahna swiped at him—and missed. Mostly. One of her claws tore through his sleeve, opening a shallow cut on his arm, but he barely felt it.

Cold wind battered them as they ran down the stairs. Tears welled up in his stinging eyes. He concentrated on getting down—*right now, faster, let us out now*—and then they were at the bottom, stumbling off onto the grass.

"Look for the door," he told Thea, following a sudden impulse. They couldn't afford to take the long way around this time.

It was so well hidden, he almost missed it. A mossy patch on the side of a tree, its edges limned very faintly with light. A lumpy stone handle half-concealed under a coat of green. He pulled; it stuck just hard enough to make his heart skip a beat, but finally it gave way, opening on a wide path bordered with wildflowers and rows of carefully tended trees. Even the breeze felt warm.

Myte's shortcut.

They squeezed through. The other side of the door was made up of animal skeletons pieced together—definitely one of Myte's. But the rest of the doors were nowhere to be found, and neither was the path to Adam's cabin.

"Maybe they change locations when Myte's not using them," Thea whispered. "We're still deep in the Nightwood."

"Let's keep moving," Nox said, and shut the door.

A cramp stabbed at Nox's rib cage as they took off running again. Within the woods on the side of the path, he thought the darkness moved. He thought he heard, under the harsh sound of his own panting, great creaking footsteps that made the earth tremble. He thought he glimpsed a pair of obsidian eyes high above him, level with the crowns of the trees. But he didn't dare pause long enough to make sure.

From far behind them came a high, vengeful scream. A hunting call.

Nox and Thea somehow found it in themselves to run faster, the woods blurring around them as they hurtled down the path. His legs burned. Despite the cold, sweat beaded up on his face and the back of his neck. The new cut on his arm from Zahna's claw and the one on his palm seared. But he still held the golden pinecone safely in his right hand, and if he could just run a little bit faster—if he could just make it a little bit farther—

Like everything else in the Nightwood, the Wayfinder's shortcut defied reason. They reached the crossroads faster than should have been possible and dashed down the narrow, overgrown trail to Adam Motte's cabin. Here, the eris moths lit their way. The mournful faces of the moros trees seemed to mouth warnings as they flashed by. They bolted through Adam's garden and threw themselves at his back door, both of them pounding on it.

They nearly fell on Adam when he pulled the door open and ushered them inside. "Didn't expect the two of you back so soon."

"Guess it's your lucky day," Nox said, doubled over and gasping for breath. Thea collapsed against the wall, wiping her sweaty face on her sleeve. Blood from the cut on her face smeared over her cheek.

Adam watched them in silence for a minute. But it was a reassuring silence—he'd gone from a stranger to a familiar face. In the warmth and light of his cabin, and in his gruff but authoritative presence, the Nightwood felt like nothing but a spooky campfire story. And in a way, it was like Adam had been with them the entire time. His map had been through as much of an ordeal as Nox and Thea had, crumpled and stolen and dirtied until it had become nearly illegible—and it had pretty much saved them.

Finally, Adam said: "Did you get what you wanted?"

With his last shred of strength, Nox held up the pinecone. Adam barely glanced at it. His eyes scanned Nox, evaluating, lingering on his injuries—and there was something in that look Nox couldn't read. Something kind of preoccupied and kind of frustrated, like he was angry at someone who wasn't in the room.

"Zahna—she's coming after us—" Nox croaked.

"You need to get out of here," Adam said. He led them to his front door, a hand on Nox's shoulder, half guiding him and half supporting him as he stumbled. "This way. Get home as fast as you can. I'll take care of Zahna."

"You will?" Nox said. "But . . ."

"It's fine. Just *go*. You don't want to be around when she gets here."

"He's right, Nox," Thea said. She hovered with a hand on the knob, waiting for Nox to catch up.

"What about you?" Nox said, and a torrent of questions he hadn't even known he had came spilling out of him. It had been building in him ever since he'd talked to the lookouts. Maybe before that. "How do you know so much about the Nightwood? What are you even planning to do when she gets here? Are you . . . ?" Here, he faltered, because the realization was still forming in his head even as he spoke the words. "Are you the other Keeper of Night?"

Thea's lips pressed together into a thin line—a decidedly unsurprised look. It all made sense now: how Adam knew the Nightwood's trails by heart, why he lived on its border, why the lookouts had recognized his name. Only now did it occur to

Nox that Violet had never said who the third Keeper was; she must have thought she didn't need to, that Nox and Thea had already known. Because they'd met Adam for themselves.

Adam groaned, exasperated. "Questions are for the classroom, boy. I don't have time to give you my life story, and you don't have time to listen to it."

"But will you be okay?" Nox said, digging his heels in. He owed Adam a lot, and how had he repaid his debts? By bringing Zahna to his doorstep and tracking mud into his house.

Adam's booming laugh made both Nox and Thea jump. "I know how to handle Zahna."

Nox gave in. He let himself be reassured. He didn't have the willpower to do anything else, not when they were so close to going home.

Adam steered them out the front door, gently but firmly, and then they were back in the forest: a moth-infested, pitch-dark, *normal* forest on a normal night where he could be sure the sun would soon rise. They fled, leaving the cabin and the Nightwood behind.

By the time they biked through the gate to Thea's house, dawn was breaking.

Almost two days spent in near total darkness left Nox blinking in shock at the sight of a candy-pink sky. It was like part of him had never expected to see daylight again. The early morning sun dabbed at the autumn foliage, waking it; the maple procession lining the driveway perked up as if to welcome them home.

The Days' car was parked out front. Nox faltered. Had they

found Noah? Had they taken him to the hospital? And had they realized Nox and Thea were missing? They had to have. But then, where were the police cars? Why was everything so . . . calm?

He had to check the attic first, on the off chance Noah was still there. He dropped his bike in front of the house, already halfway to the door by the time it hit the ground.

"Nox," Thea said quietly. "Something's wrong." Her eyes were fixed over his shoulder, on the house.

The only thing wrong was that he wasn't already upstairs. He didn't want to leave Thea with that look on her face—both anxious and resigned, her knuckles white on her bike's handlebars, her shoulders slumped like one more bad thing happening would knock her over. Thea, after all, had never left him. Not once. Not even when she probably should've.

"Noah might be—" He couldn't even finish the sentence. "Just—just wait here. It'll be okay. I have to wake Noah up, and then we can figure everything else out together."

He crashed through the front door, which was unlocked. That was a little weird. And so was the smell: sickly sweet like decay, and spicy-sharp like firewood. A familiar smell. Up the stairs, down the hall, up again—how he still had the energy to run, he had no idea. At last, he was pushing open the door to the attic, chest tight with fear.

But Noah was right where he'd left him. Overgrown black hair flopped over his eyes and curled against the pillow. His chest rose and fell slowly. Nothing had disturbed him since Nox had left.

Tears of relief burned his eyes, but he forced them back. He couldn't relax until Noah was awake. Pulling the golden pinecone from his pocket, he hurried to Noah's side.

"Noah?" he said. He tried shaking him awake, just in case, but got no response. The pinecone was reassuringly warm in his hand. He lifted it over Noah's chest and then hesitated. Would his body just . . . absorb it? But it felt so solid.

Nox had been so single-mindedly determined to take back what the lunar wolf had stolen that he'd never really stopped to think about what it actually *was*. And once he'd retrieved it, it'd been a nonstop race to escape Zahna and get back home to Noah. He hadn't had time to pause and ask himself: *What was a golden pinecone doing in Noah's chest anyway?*

He examined Noah again, more closely. All he'd paid attention to before was the fact that he was still breathing. Now he saw that the skin on his forearm—where his sleeve had bunched up—was smooth and unmarked. Nox pulled up the other sleeve. It was the same: that gray rash was gone. He turned Noah's head so he could inspect the back of his neck. The odd white sores were gone, too. Noah was healing.

An awful suspicion surfaced in his mind. He backed away with such haste he tripped over nothing, trying to get away from Noah—

It made no difference. The pinecone flew from his grasp as if pulled by an invisible force. His hand shot after it, fingers outstretched, but it was too late. It sank into Noah's chest.

Noah woke up screaming.

His eyes flew open and then shut again in pain. His body

thrashed, fingers tearing at the sheets, as the mottled gray spots sprang up on his arms again, worse than ever. They spread up under his sleeves and down over the backs of his hands. The sores popped up on his neck, traveling across his throat and up his jaw and over his cheek. As he screamed, that dark reddish-brown substance he'd coughed up before beaded at the corners of his mouth.

"Noah. Noah!" he shouted, but Noah didn't seem to hear him. He climbed onto the bed and held Noah down by his shoulders, afraid he'd knock his head against the wall. Noah's hands scrabbled at Nox's arms, his nails digging in, tears streaming from his eyes—it was impossible to say if Noah was clinging to him, or trying to push him off, or if he even knew who Nox was.

Nox couldn't stand to watch, but he couldn't bring himself to look away, either. His own eyes blurred with tears as Noah finally went limp. He was wide awake now, expression dazed and chest hitching as he caught his breath in ragged gasps.

"What . . . what's happening to me?" Noah said. He turned his head to the side and coughed wetly. And kept coughing. He pushed at Nox to let him up, and then he turned on his side, hacking until his lungs ejected another cluster of catkins, coated in that sticky reddish substance. Nox had never heard him cough that badly before. His whole body seized with it, and he struggled to draw breath in between.

When he'd finished coughing, he slumped, pressing his forehead against the pillow where Nox couldn't see his face.

"What just happened?" he mumbled. "Why . . . ?"

Nox couldn't speak. He pulled Noah's wrist up to inspect the renewed rashes. They were rough and flaky under his hands, and tougher than they'd been before. And now that he knew what to look for, he realized they weren't rashes at all.

It was bark.

At the edges of the "rash," his skin was bright red and irritated. Blood showed in one spot where the bark had broken and started to pull away from the skin. It wasn't growing *on* him. It was part of him. His skin was *changing* into bark. He checked the sores on Noah's neck next. And they weren't sores at all, but mushroom caps pushing out of his skin. Some of them were still mostly buried, only the round, spongy tops showing. Others had sprouted fully, their caps exposed while their stalks remained rooted in Noah's neck. What Noah was coughing out, then, wasn't blood, but sap.

Noah wasn't sick. He'd never been sick. He'd been poisoned. Whatever this was, it had come from the Nightwood.

That meant the lunar wolf hadn't stolen anything from Noah. It had *saved* him.

And Nox had made him sick again.

18

ONCE NOAH HAD GOTTEN OVER THE INITIAL
shock, he insisted on following Nox downstairs.

"I'm fine," he said for about the hundredth time, as if holding out hope that with enough repetition, Nox would believe him. He'd slid off the bed and was rooting around in the wardrobe for a change of clothes.

"Noah," Nox began. "I . . ."

But the words died in his throat.

Noah pretended not to have noticed his failed attempt at speech. "At least we know what's wrong with me now."

"I . . ." Nox tried again.

"I mean, I was hoping for a diagnosis that didn't involve otherworldly horrors from a land of endless night, but I still feel like this is an improvement," Noah said. "Like, overall."

When he grinned, his skin stretched around the toadstools on his right cheek in a way that looked painful.

Nox swallowed hard and forced the words out, steadier this time: "I'm so . . . so sorry—"

"Shut up," Noah said cheerfully, hopping around on one leg as he tried to pull on his jeans and a sweater at the same time. "You were trying to help."

"What if you . . . What if we can't . . ."

The guilt was so bitter he could've choked on it. He couldn't believe *Noah* was reassuring *him* when it should've been the other way around. The only thing Nox ever did was make things harder on people. Mom, the Days, Camp Chickenshit, and now Noah, too.

"We *can*," Noah said. "You know, you're being a real downer for someone who just found out that *magic* is *real*."

His eyes were huge and bright with amazement, like the fact that the magic in question was eating him alive was a nonissue.

"Magic is a nightmare," Nox told him.

Noah checked his hair in the mirror, giving it a quick finger comb.

"Are we going or what?" he said. "I wanna see this place myself."

Because this meant, of course, they had to return to the Nightwood.

"We have to get Thea," Nox said.

How was he supposed to face her after this?

His cheeks went hot with shame. He'd dragged her into danger and almost got both of them killed for *nothing*. Because he'd jumped to conclusions. Because he'd refused to listen to her when she tried to reason with him. Because he'd been so sure that he was right, that he knew what was best, especially when it came to Noah.

"I told you she was cool," Noah said. "Okay. I'm ready."

As they ventured downstairs, Nox noticed things he'd missed during his mad dash to the attic room. The moss creeping over the walls. The clover pushing up through the cracks between the floorboards. The spiders busily spinning new webs in the corners and between the balusters in the stairway.

The Nightwood was *here*, and it was claiming the Day house as its own.

Noah knelt to touch the edge of a spiderweb. When his fingertips made contact, he gasped and looked up at Nox. "You weren't kidding. It's *real*."

Downstairs, the infection was even worse. They stepped over ropy tree roots that had broken through the floor. The hall reeked of sawdust and mildew. Layers of dirt and grime clouded the windows, as if they hadn't been cleaned in a century, blocking out the morning light. Something in the walls moved—he hoped it was only rats.

The bathroom door was ajar. When Nox peeked inside, he found the sink and tub full, the water green and alive with tiny fish and frogs. He slowly shut the door, shaking his head silently at Noah's questioning look. Above them, every inch of the ceiling was crowded with bats, their furry bodies and leathery wings curled tight together. Their heads swiveled around, ears rotating as if tracking their footsteps. A million beady black eyes shined down at them.

They found Thea in the kitchen, her back to the doorway. Before her, two enormous cocoons dangled from the ceiling, each one at least seven or eight feet tall, the ends just brushing the tiles. He shuddered. Whatever was going to crawl out of *those*, he wanted to be very far away when it happened.

"Thea?" Nox said. "We, uh . . ."

He didn't know how to explain what had happened, how badly he'd messed everything up. But before he could try, Thea said, in a voice choked with tears: "We have to go back."

"What?"

She turned, wiping her eyes on her jacket sleeve. "Look at what they did to my parents!"

"Your . . ." Nox gave the cocoons a second look. Through the translucent grayish-blue membrane, he made out two familiar human faces. It was Weston and Aster. And they were *changing*. A pair of furled wings grew on Aster's back, and the beginnings of antennae had sprouted on Weston's forehead. It was a little like an accelerated version of the lookouts' mutations.

Nox's stomach clenched with nausea. "Maybe we can cut them out."

"Tried that already," Thea said, gesturing at the table, where a steak knife lay abandoned. Her eyes landed on Noah. "You're even worse than before. So I guess we got it all wrong."

"*I* got it wrong," Nox said. He could add Thea to the growing tally of people whose lives he'd screwed up.

Thea opened her mouth to reply, but a faint scratching noise interrupted them.

It was Aster. She was awake, clawing weakly at the inside of the cocoon. Through the cloudy membrane, they heard a muffled but unmistakable "*Thea.*"

"Mom!" she said, pressing her hands flat against the cocoon. "I'm so sorry. This is our fault."

With what looked like a great effort, Aster shook her head. "*No. We tried to stop him. To cure Noah. But . . .*"

"Him?" Thea said.

"Adam."

Thea swung around to meet Nox's eyes. They traded looks of horror.

"Stop him how?" Noah said, not noticing or understanding their dismay; the name *Adam* meant nothing to him.

She blinked at him in bleary confusion. *"We made a deal with another Keeper of Night . . . in exchange for her help undoing Adam's spell. But we couldn't do what she wanted. That must be why . . ."*

"No, Mom," Thea said. "We're the ones who messed up. How do you even *know* about Zahna? About the . . . Night-wood?"

"Weston knew. They found it when they were kids."

They? Nox thought. She couldn't mean . . .

"Neither of them had been there in years. But when they figured out what was wrong with Noah, Weston knew he had to go back. It was the only way to save him. So I went, too. Celia couldn't. It's too dangerous for her."

Her voice grew weaker and weaker, and nothing she said made any sense. Mom knew about the Nightwood, too? It was . . . dangerous for her? What did that mean?

"So that's why Mom sent me to you and Weston," Noah said. "She knew I wasn't really sick. But she couldn't fix it herself."

Aster's eyes slid shut.

"Mom? Mom!" Thea shouted. Her nails scratched against the cocoon until they bled. Noah tugged her hands away, gently, with his stiff bark-crusted ones. Aster didn't wake again.

Nox found Weston's phone on the table and called Mom, but she didn't pick up. It didn't really matter, anyway. Nothing she said would have changed what they had to do next.

Adam's cabin stood in the place where morning turned into night, half in the shadows and half out of it. Overhead, the pale blue sky darkened like a bruise. The eris moths fled the sunshine and congregated around the back of the cabin, where it was twilight.

The three of them had decided to sneak past Adam's cabin without confronting him and go straight to Zahna. If they could somehow convince her to help them again . . .

But that was a really big *if.*

Nox caught glimpses of the cabin as they circled it, creeping among the moros trees. Its windows were dark.

"Keep going without me," Nox told the others. "I'll meet you on the path."

"Where are you going?" Thea whispered harshly. Noah didn't try to stop him. Either he knew what Nox was thinking, or he was trying to conserve his energy. It was taking him more effort to move than usual, Nox could tell, and he kept having to muffle his violent coughing in the sleeve of his sweater.

"His fire's out," Nox said. "I just want to see if . . ."

He shook his head. He didn't want to speak his hope aloud: that Zahna had beaten Adam. That he was already dead. The fanged monster that had chased him and Thea out of the Night-wood seemed like more than a match for Adam Motte.

Unless Adam was a shape-shifter, too.

"Just go," he said, and crept away toward the cabin before Thea could object.

Without the flicker of firelight and the sound of Adam's axe, Nox had the eerie sense he was approaching someplace abandoned. A haunted house. But there were no ghosts here, not unless he counted the wraithlike faces in the moros trees. They looked even more grim and lonely in this false dusk. Moths crawled up the grooves in their trunks, the play of their pale blue light making it appear as though the humanoid features carved in the bark were moving.

Nox stopped. He turned a slow circle, examining the trees more closely and with rising horror.

Noah's affliction had to have an endgame. The bark overtaking his skin and the sap clogging his lungs weren't there for no reason. He was changing. So maybe this was Noah's fate: a full transformation into a moros tree.

Shakily, Nox laid a hand on one of them. It was cold and dry to the touch. It didn't move. It didn't breathe, and it had no heartbeat, not one he could detect anyway. If it really *had* been a person once, there was no trace of that person left now.

One of the first things he'd learned about Evergreen was that it was a place where people vanished. Evergreen blamed the Devil; Nox, meanwhile, had tried to convince himself they'd just gotten lost in the woods. But maybe all those missing people whose photos were on the sign outside the discovery center hadn't gone very far after all. Maybe they were all right here.

But why would Adam want to do that to them?

They're eris moths, Nox remembered him saying. *They lay*

their eggs in the bark of the moros trees outside. The moths were important to Adam somehow, and they needed the moros trees to survive.

Nox ripped his hand away. This was sicker than anything he could've imagined. No matter what, he couldn't let this happen to Noah. He wouldn't.

And he still had time to make things right.

Adam's cabin was empty and undisturbed. The garden, though, told a frightening story. It was torn up. Deep gouges marred the ground, and a trail of bloody footsteps ran from the yard and into the trees. Toward the Nightwood.

The others waited for him up the path, Thea kneeling to examine the bloodstains.

"Did you see anything useful?" she asked, straightening, when he caught up to them.

He glanced at Noah guiltily. "No."

"Let's go, then," Thea said. "We've got a long trip."

"How long?" Noah asked, following them up the path.

"Two nights," Nox said.

"Wait, what? We can't leave Aster and Weston that long. They looked pretty bad."

Noah scratched at the bark on his wrist, realized what he was doing, and yanked his sleeve down. He clearly didn't need to be reminded that *he* wasn't in the best shape, either.

"There's a shortcut, but we can't take it," Thea said.

"Why not?"

They told him about the Wayfinder, his doors, and his riddle.

"But what was the riddle?" Noah asked.

"Uh," Nox said. He honestly couldn't remember.

"It was about something with roots, and a yellow jewel, and it's not alive but it also is?" Thea said hesitantly.

Noah fell into a thoughtful silence, and when they got to the fork in the path, he stopped them. "We could really use a shortcut right now."

Nox recalled the silent, ominous presence that had watched him and Thea flee from Zahna. But Noah wasn't wrong—they needed that shortcut. "You sure?"

"I can't just sit around and let you save me."

Why not? he thought, stung. But he knew why not: because he'd already tried that, and Nox had let him down.

For the second time, they took the left path. They didn't have to wait long before the Wayfinder's telltale footsteps, each one like the boom of a cannon, came to meet them.

19

"YOU WERE JUST HERE," MYTE RUMBLED. NOX tensed, wondering if Myte was going to be angry with them for using his door without permission, but then he added sullenly, "And you didn't answer my question. Not even a guess."

"We . . . needed more time to think," Nox said. "Is that allowed?"

Myte scratched his chin, dislodging a few brown leaves. "I suppose."

"We look like we could be related," Noah said, holding up his hands for comparison.

The Wayfinder bent close, the moon carving patterns of light and shadow into his wooden features. His stone eyes glistened as he studied Noah.

"Even *you* must pay the toll," Myte said. That electric feeling crept over Nox's skin again; the hair on the back of his neck stood up. Without having to look, he knew the doors had appeared.

Even you. What did that mean? Why did Myte talk like he already knew who Noah was?

Noah's gaze traveled slowly over each of the doors before returning to Myte.

"Can I hear the riddle?" he asked.

Once more, Myte said:

"My roots are strong but do not grow.

In my crown, I wear a yellow jewel.

No sap flows through my veins. I am not alive,

but there is life within me. What am I?"

Noah grinned the way he did in the last stretch of a race, when he knew he'd won before he ever crossed the finish line— already anticipating the applause. "A house."

"Wait!" Thea said, wringing her hands. "Are—are you sure?"

"Not just any house," Noah added. "The house on the cliff to the south of the Nightwood. When you stand up, I bet you can see it over the trees."

Thea gaped at him. "What?"

Myte gave an earth-shaking laugh. "You may pass."

Noah held out his fist. Myte tapped it with one of his enormous knuckles.

"Not bad," Noah said. "But give me something harder next time."

"I will think on it," Myte told him, and rose to leave. All the doors disappeared except the one made of bone.

"Wait!" Nox said. "Before, when we left Zahna's watchtower, why did you let us through?"

"I only guard entrances," Myte said. "Not exits. I don't care about the other side of the door. The time you spend and the dangers you face in finding them are the price you pay."

He left, the thunder of his departure echoing through the night.

"A house? *My* house?" Thea said. "How is that the answer?"

"The roots are the foundation," Noah explained. "The yellow jewel is the light in the attic. It's not alive, but people live inside . . . get it?"

"That's *completely* ridiculous!" Thea said, affronted.

"You guys just take things too literally," Noah said. "Let me guess. You thought the answer was some kind of plant, and Nox was too pissed off to think of an answer at all." He shrugged. "Sometimes things are really simple if you try to see them from someone else's perspective."

Easy for him to say. Because while Nox was busy picking fights, Noah was figuring out how to make people like him. How to be their friend. That was why he'd solved the riddle. He'd always been better than Nox at thinking past his own feelings, especially his anger.

Adam never would've fooled him. If their places were switched, and Nox had been the one who'd gotten sick, Noah probably would've already cured him by now.

Nox's fists had clenched without him noticing. He took a breath and forced them to loosen.

"Let's just get out of here," he said.

Up close, the skeleton door looked like it was made of melting wax. But it was cold to the touch, cold as everything else in the Nightwood. He pulled it open to reveal a familiar clearing. The other side of the door hadn't moved; they climbed out of the same mossy tree they'd escaped through before. It sealed soundlessly behind them, becoming invisible again.

Splotches of drying blood marred the stairs of Zahna's watchtower. By the end of their ascent, Nox and Thea were shaken and disoriented, just like last time. But Noah was unaffected. He hadn't even broken a sweat. At the top, he paused by the rail to study the panoramic view of the Nightwood, the same way Nox had his first time up here.

"Have we . . . ?" Noah said.

"What?"

Noah dragged his eyes away from the woods and blinked dazedly at Nox, as if he'd forgotten he wasn't alone. The white toadstools sprouting over the side of his face had grown, each of them an inch tall now, and the skin around their trunks was red and irritated. He scratched at it absently.

"Have we been here before?" he said.

"What do you mean?"

"It doesn't feel . . . familiar to you?"

"Familiar? Sure. Reminds me of *The Blair Witch Project*." Nox really didn't want Noah leaning over the rail like that when he was this spacey. It made him uneasy. Less like he thought Noah was going to fall; more like he sensed Noah might jump. "Come on. She's in there."

Noah smiled crookedly. "Who? The Blair Witch?"

"Worse."

Thea pushed the door open. The destruction they found beyond it was so complete that Nox at first assumed Adam must have chased Zahna back here, and what they were looking at was the result of that battle. And then he realized, with a flood of shame, all of that damage was the aftermath of his search earlier.

He remembered tearing through the furniture. What he didn't remember was how utterly *wrecked* he'd left the place.

The broken window admitted a whistling wind. Drawers and cabinets hung open. Floorboards were splintered or missing. Polished bows with broken strings lay among a chaos of glass and furs. And in the middle of it all was Zahna, Keeper of Night and Warden of the Wilds, halfway transformed.

The top half of her face was human, her eyes glaring up at Nox and the others as they invited themselves in, but she still had a snout and fangs. Her shoulders bulged with muscle, and patchy fur showed through the tears in her leather armor. She bled heavily from a deep, canyonlike wound that sliced in a crescent from her rib cage to her lower back. It was as if someone had tried to sever her in two.

"Oh my god," Thea whispered.

The lunar wolf's head rested in Zahna's lap, eyes shut. Its moonlit glow had dimmed so much he could've mistaken it for one of the lifeless pelts he'd left crumpled on the ground.

"She's alive, if you were wondering," Zahna rasped. Her snout plainly wasn't meant for human speech, because the words came out half growl. "If you care about such things."

"I'm—I'm sorry," Thea said. "I thought she was going to hurt us. I was the one who . . ."

Zahna shook strands of sweat-damp white hair from her eyes, examining Thea as if to judge her sincerity.

"Clever of you to use the moth that way," she said reluctantly. "It *would* have killed her, if she hadn't coughed most of it out."

She nodded toward a wet lump on the ground, a crumpled blue wing and fuzzy body coated in saliva. Nox suppressed a shudder of revulsion.

"She may not recover," Zahna added. "Only time will tell."

"It wasn't Thea's fault," Nox said quickly. "It's mine. She was only here because of me. All of this—coming here, stealing the . . . the pinecone—it was me."

Zahna's eyelids fluttered, like she was on the verge of passing out.

"Adam deceived you," she said. "I can hardly blame a child for failing to see through him. I suppose I did expect more of you, though, knowing your mother. She never fell for Adam's tricks."

"Noah's sick again because of me. Can you . . . can you help him? *Please*," he forced himself to add. "He shouldn't have to suffer because I screwed up."

"Umbra might yet die," said Zahna. "Why should I care what happens to your brother?"

At the sound of its name, the lunar wolf stirred. Its head twitched in Zahna's lap, three of its six black eyes opening so that it could cast a pained, accusatory look at Nox.

We pretty much poisoned her dog, Nox thought guiltily. *I wouldn't help us, either.*

"Weston and Aster made a deal with you," he said. "Make one with me, too. If you help Noah, I'll . . . do anything you want."

"*We* will do anything," Thea said.

"There is one thing." Zahna's fingers combed lightly through Umbra's fur. "One thing that only you can do."

"Me?" Nox said, weakly. Nox couldn't think of anything *only* he could do, except maybe top the national record for number of suspensions before high school, or history tests failed, or hours of *Candy Crush* played on his phone in the dark at two a.m. when he couldn't sleep.

Her snout opened and closed, as if she was trying to yawn, but then it receded until her whole face was human again. She grimaced in pain, blood showing between her teeth.

"You and your brother," she explained. Her voice was clear and melodious. Nox would've called it pretty if he'd heard it anywhere else. "I gave the task to your elders in hopes they'd find a way around it that I couldn't. But in truth, I knew it was impossible. That what I asked wasn't fair. That was why I held up my end of the deal, even though they couldn't hold up theirs. I should have known that it would alarm you when your brother fell into a healing sleep. I didn't account for that. Nevertheless, what's done is done, and you're here now. . . ."

She trailed off, as if debating whether it was worth asking Nox at all.

Nox came closer and sank to the ground in front of her and Umbra. He could smell the sick iron tang in the air around them and see the sheen of sweat at her hairline.

"Just tell me what to do," he said, trying to channel the confidence with which Noah had answered Myte's riddle.

Despite the exhaustion and blood loss, Zahna's gray eyes were clear and alert.

"I need you to go into the Web and retrieve something for me," she said. "A weapon."

"That's the Devil's territory," he said.

"Yes. If you must insist on using that ridiculous name."

"And he's . . ." He twisted around to look at Thea, who crossed her arms as if to ward off a chill. "He's after us."

Zahna laughed, startling him. "After you? How do you expect a dead man to be *after* anyone?"

"*Dead?*" Nox asked. "But—that thing with giant bat wings has been following us since we got here. If that's not the Devil, then what is it?"

"What you saw was a puppet," Zahna said. "Adam killed the Devil, stole his wings, and used them to make a servant—a half-living abomination sustained by the Nightwood's magic. But the puppet was of no use to Adam. It did not respond to either punishment or reward, and it was too clumsy and inept to complete even the smallest of tasks. So he set it loose in the woods. I don't know if it will harm you. I don't know if it's even aware of the things it does."

"Then why was it following us?" Thea said.

The mechanical petting motion of Zahna's hand on Umbra's neck ceased. "I can't be certain. Let me tell you what I *do* know, instead. After the Devil was murdered, his territory sealed itself off. The Nightwood grew an impenetrable wall around it. Now only his descendants can enter. *That* is why I need you."

"I don't understand," Nox said, because what she was implying was— No. He had to have heard wrong.

But Noah seemed to understand perfectly well.

"Because we're his sons," he said. "Right?"

20

IT WAS THE FIRST THING NOAH HAD SAID TO
her. He stepped over the deer carcass and sat beside Nox. His
eyes drifted over Zahna's shoulder, toward the window, at the
sky mottled in shades of charcoal and indigo.

"Is that why I feel like I've been here before?" Noah asked.

"No," Nox said, not an answer to a question, just a refusal to
accept what he was hearing, and one that was mostly reflex, like
lifting your arms to shield your face when something flew at it.
"That's impossible. We're *human*."

Okay, so Nox didn't know anything useful about their dad.
Mom had no pictures. No stories she was willing to share. He
could've been anyone. But Nox had always taken it for granted
that their father at least wasn't a *monster*. That *Nox* wasn't a
monster. Despite his temper. And the way he scared people
without even trying all that hard. And how he liked fighting a
little more than he'd ever wanted to admit, how he even kind of
craved it sometimes.

He had to force himself not to turn around and look for
Thea's reaction. The thought of Thea knowing they might
be the Devil's sons was almost worse than actually *being* the

Devil's sons. Like maybe if there had been no other witnesses he could've walked out of here and pretended this conversation hadn't happened.

"You are human," Zahna agreed. "The Devil, Adam, and I came into being from the realm of night. But your mother is human, and in a union that crosses between realms, the child always takes after the mother. In short, you cannot be half Devil. But you *are* his sons. And you—" She tilted her head at Noah. "You are his heir. His firstborn child."

Nox opened his mouth to correct her mistake—and then, reconsidering, looked at Noah instead.

But Noah avoided his eyes.

"Is that why Adam did this to me?" Noah said, showing her his hands, the knuckles so scabbed over with bark that Nox doubted he could bend them.

"To help you understand, I must go back to the beginning," Zahna said. "There have always been three Keepers of Night. Myself, Warden of the Wilds. Adam, Warden of Life and Death. And your father, Warden of the Dark. The three of us got on well, for the most part. Your father and Adam were especially close. Like brothers."

That sparked a memory in Nox: Adam at the table in his cabin, drawing them a map, and the sadness in his voice when he'd said, *I had a brother, too, once. He's gone.*

Gone because Adam had murdered him.

"We reach the height of our power in the dead of night," Zahna continued. "At twilight and in the early hours of dawn, we retain only a fraction of our abilities; by day, we lose them entirely. Keepers in general tend to stay in the places where their own realms are dominant; but the realm of night is the youngest of the lot, and our power pales in comparison to the others. Adam has always resented that."

"So he wanted to do something about it?" Noah guessed.

Zahna inclined her head in a weak nod. "The Nightwood is more than just a place of magic. It is like a stopper in a leak; if its borders were broken open, night would flow from here unchecked, eradicating the daylight and plunging the world into eternal darkness. That was what Adam wanted; but it could not be done without the other two Keepers."

"And the Devil wasn't on board," Noah said. "He stopped him."

There was something complicated in his voice, hopeful and triumphant and a little sad.

"I agreed to do as Adam wished," she said. "Open the border or do not, it matters little to me. But the Devil refused point-blank. They argued about it for ages—years—but neither of them would yield. In Adam's view, the Devil alone stood between him and his grand ambitions. So when Adam acquired a weapon strong enough to kill another Keeper, he saw it as an opportunity he couldn't pass up."

Nox knew what was coming, but he dreaded it anyway. He held his breath.

"Adam waited for him to be vulnerable, and he got his chance on the night you were born." Zahna didn't try to soften the blow; maybe she knew nothing could. "Your father didn't know the attack was coming until Adam was nearly upon him, and then it was all he could do to keep Adam away from your mother. Adam slew him while your mother fled with the two of you."

Absolute silence. Umbra stirred in Zahna's lap and then subsided, dropping back into a deep sleep. Zahna watched them impassively through weary, half-lidded eyes. Nox glanced at Noah again, and this time found Noah already looking back at him, face drained of color.

"She saved us," Noah said at last, turning back to Zahna. "But why did Adam want us dead?"

"If a Keeper dies without either a direct descendant or a chosen heir, the remaining Keepers of their realm can bequeath their power to another, one we deem worthy of it. Adam meant to kidnap you and raise you as his pawns. But he didn't expect Celia to slip through his fingers. The Devil's power had passed to you, so the Nightwood's borders could not be broken without you, and Celia had taken you out of his reach. Before he could begin to follow her, it was dawn in the outside world, and he is powerless by day. By the time the sun set that evening, Celia was gone, and Adam had no way of finding her. He tried, make no mistake; he has made short excursions away from the Nightwood, attempting to track her down, but Celia proved adept at disappearing."

Nox thought about how often they'd moved, and how Mom had always had a good reason for it—the rent had gone up, or she'd found a better job three counties away—and wondered whether all that time she had been looking over her shoulder, watching out for Adam's looming shadow.

"Adam cannot stay away from the Nightwood for long,"

Zahna said. "With only two of its three Keepers present, the Nightwood's magic grew chaotic and destructive; we had to beg a Keeper of Time to lend us her power and assist in stabilizing the forest. Even with her aid, we could not spare Adam for long. If Adam had known how much trouble your mother would cause him, I believe he would have killed her first. And if he'd known he wouldn't be able to get back into the Web, he wouldn't have left his weapon there. He would have left the Devil's wings instead."

"Why did he want his wings?" Noah asked, nose wrinkled with disgust.

"He thought that if he could make the puppet live, it might serve as a stand-in for the Devil—it would take his place as Keeper but be obedient to Adam." Zahna gave a low, rasping laugh that turned into a cough. "Of course, it didn't work. So, to finish what he started, he needed to persuade you to cooperate with him. That is why he sent a moros seed to infect you. It could find you where he couldn't. Celia would recognize the moros seed's magic, and he expected that she would grow desperate and come to him for help, instructing you to do his bidding. He knew she would do anything to save her son's life."

Nox's fists were clenched in his lap, nails digging into his palms. Why *hadn't* Mom done it? Why *wasn't* she willing to do anything to save Noah?

He was ashamed at how selfish these thoughts were, but he couldn't shake it. He'd take eternal night in a heartbeat if the alternative was losing Noah. If anyone had asked him, up until about ten seconds ago, he would've said that Mom felt the same way. The fact that she didn't was a betrayal of the worst kind.

Noah, leaning forward and listening raptly to Zahna, didn't look the least bit surprised or upset by what she'd just said. Of course—he would never have wanted Mom to put him before the fate of the world. He'd have been devastated if she had.

"Adam did not account for the possibility that it was not him she would go to," Zahna was saying, "but *me*. And that she would send a friend in her place—the companion who had followed her on all her adventures in their youth."

"My dad," Thea said quietly.

"Indeed. I sent Umbra to watch over you and used my own powers to slow the effects of the moros seed's poison, but I cannot extend my reach very far for too long. It is why your mother sent you to Evergreen."

"And why I felt worse whenever I left," Noah said, realizing. "Like when I went to the hospital for a fake checkup. That's why they made me do my classes online, too. I'm not immuno-compromised. They just knew that going to school in Grayville would make the moros seed poison me faster, because I got too far away for you to help me. But wasn't Adam mad at you?"

Zahna choked on another laugh. "I concealed it from him. He assumed it was your own power that protected you. And he was partly right—an ordinary human succumbs much more quickly to the moros seed, but you have night magic in your blood. Still, he was prepared to wait it out, certain your mother would give in soon enough and unaware of the measures I was taking against him. He must have been pleasantly surprised when *you*, Nox, showed up on his doorstep instead."

Dread and self-loathing twisted inside Nox, snakelike, choking the air out of him. He had been so intent on listening to the story that he had detached himself from it, hearing it from a distance like a tragedy that had happened to someone else, and not one he had played a role in.

"For Adam, it was a windfall," Zahna said, cold in her frankness, not that he thought her sympathy would have made a difference. "My treachery had been uncovered. Noah would soon be dead, and then Nox, the only possible remaining heir, would be within reach; Adam would not need Celia at all. I do not believe he hopes for your cooperation any longer. Knowing how close you came to escaping him, and understanding that Celia will never yield to him, he will take no more risks; if he catches you again, he will almost certainly kill you both and compel me to name a new heir with him."

Nox's anger dwindled away to nothing, until he just felt hollow. He didn't have a right to be angry with Mom. She *had* been trying to save Noah, even if she hadn't come here to confront Adam herself. And it had *almost* worked. It was Nox who had ruined everything, played right into Adam's hands, and almost doomed not only Noah but the entire world.

He was the one who'd failed everyone he cared about.

But he couldn't think about that now. He had to pull himself together. He was done taking charge, making decisions it wasn't his place to make, and screwing everything up. He'd do whatever Zahna and Noah wanted. Adam had wanted a pawn, so Nox would be a pawn—just not for him.

"All I have to do is get you this weapon, and then you'll cure me?" Noah asked. "That's it?"

"Yes," Zahna said. "That's it."

"Are you going to use it to kill Adam?"

"Who cares?" Nox muttered.

"No. The Nightwood needs him," she said. "But if I have the weapon, I can use it as a deterrent. I can keep him in check."

"What kind of weapon is it?" Noah asked.

"An iron axe."

"Adam has an axe already," Nox said.

Zahna laughed darkly, her hand dropping to cover the gaping wound in her side. "Believe me, I know. But that one's just an ordinary tool. It can do a great deal of harm, but it can't kill someone like me or your father. The one you're looking for is special."

"So we'll know it when we see it?" Noah said, with a wry smile.

"You will."

Noah nodded. His fingers tapped distractedly on the floorboards. "Anything else we should know?"

"It would take many nights to tell you everything you *should* know," Zahna said. Her eyes fluttered shut. "As for what you *need* to know, I've told you all I can think of. Go now, before your time runs out."

"Wait, I still—" Noah stopped. "Did she fall asleep?"

"Passed out, more like."

"We're defenseless," Thea said, speaking up at last. "We

219

should take some weapons of our own."

Of all the reactions Thea could have had to what they'd just learned, this was both the most baffling and the most reassuring. He watched her sort through the wreckage. She picked up a crossbow and studied it with grim satisfaction. "This should work."

"You know how to use a crossbow?" Noah said, sounding impressed.

"No. But I took a few archery lessons at summer camp, and I bet it's easier to learn than a normal bow. If I can just figure out how to load it . . ."

Thea was scarily efficient as she gathered the arrows that went with it, stuffing them into her backpack, where the ends stuck up past the open zipper. She set aside one to use. It took her a few tries to figure out how to draw back the string and latch it into place—there was a click when she managed it—and how to slide the bolt into position.

In the meantime, Noah explored the rest of the cabin. Nox examined a dagger that had gotten kicked under the table. It was sheathed; he drew it to reveal a serrated blade about the length of his forearm. But when he tried to imagine putting it to use, he just pictured Adam yanking it out of his hand and shoving it between his ribs. He shivered and put it down.

"I bet Thea would give you a crash course in archery if you wanted," Noah said, wandering over to where Nox stood.

Nox shrugged. He didn't think he'd take to a long-range weapon. He glanced at Thea, who wasn't paying any attention to them, and then back at Noah's wan face. "Are you okay?"

"Ugh. My head's spinning," Noah said, with a crooked half smile. "She told us a lot, but I still have so many questions. What about you?"

Nox thought about how sorry he was, how terrified of making another mistake that Noah would have to pay for, how little he trusted his own judgment right now. But none of that was helpful, and he wouldn't burden Noah with it.

"Fine," Nox said. "I just want to get this over with and get out of here."

Noah laughed. "Yeah. That about sums it up."

Thea held the crossbow awkwardly against her shoulder, aimed at the door, and fired. The recoil made her falter back a step.

"You okay?"

"Yeah. Just wasn't ready for that."

She loaded the crossbow again, faster this time, and didn't budge even an inch when she fired. Her aim wasn't perfect, but she *did* hit the door.

She took three more practice shots before she was satisfied.

"Okay. I'm ready," she said, collecting the arrows, which left deep puncture marks in the door. "You taking anything?"

"No," Nox said. If it came to a fight, he'd rather use his fists.

Noah cast one last distant look around the room. Nox followed his gaze to Zahna, slumped on the ground with her fingers limp in Umbra's fur, and Umbra, motionless except for her six closed eyelids twitching slightly. Did lunar wolves have nightmares?

At last, Noah shook his head. "The axe is my weapon."

Thea hitched her backpack strap higher on her shoulder. She held the crossbow easily at her side, like she'd been doing it her whole life. "Then let's go and get it."

They ended up back where they'd started: on the half-vanished trail that wove through the heart of the Nightwood. The flashlight sliced through the trees. Tattered scraps of sky showed through gaps in the canopy. None of them spoke. There was nothing to say.

They had barely made any progress before the branches rustled overhead.

It was probably a bad sign that none of them were prepared for something to go wrong this soon. Noah froze; Nox swung the flashlight up wildly, looking for the source of the noise; Thea lifted her crossbow, but it wasn't loaded, so he didn't know what she thought she was going to do with it. A big, dark shape dropped from above to land in front of them.

"Hey!" Nine pushed up his goggles, his stubby wings fluttering excitably. "You're alive!"

Hastily, Thea lowered the crossbow. "Nine! Are you out here alone? Is everything okay at the settlement?"

"Holy crap," Noah said. "Are those *real*? That's so cool!"

Nine twitched one of his wings up over his shoulder, showing off his glossy feathers. "What, this? Nah. It's nothin'."

"Back already?" someone said, coming up from behind them and making Nox jump. It was Violet, of course. She pulled down the coverings on her face so she could scowl at him.

"Yeah, and we're fine, no thanks to you," Nox shot back. "How's Deadlock? Still recovering?"

"Please. You don't hit that hard." She directed her glare at Noah next. "Who's *that*? You never said there were two of you."

"I told you she took something from my brother. I—"

He stopped. His pride had taken enough of a beating today. Tonight. Whatever. The last thing he needed now was an *I told you so* from someone who'd decided to be twelve forever.

"Are the lights still out at the settlement?" Thea asked.

"Yeah. Mom and a few of the hunters left to get help, but Lord Shadow isn't exactly quick to forgive," she said. "We could be stuck for months while he cools off."

Personally, Nox thought that holding grudges should disqualify you from being a god of ephemeral things. But he supposed *god of ephemeral things except for when I'm in a bad mood* didn't sound as impressive.

Meanwhile, Noah had his sleeve pulled up to his elbow so Nine could gawk at the spreading rashes, with the air of someone showing off.

"You're practically one of us," Nine said approvingly.

"Except if *he* keeps changing, it'll kill him," Nox said. "Zahna won't help us unless we go to the Web and . . . get something for her."

"You can't go in there," Violet protested. "There's an—"

"Impenetrable wall? Yeah. For us, it's, uh. Penetrable," Noah told her. He scratched at his cheek again and winced when one of the toadstools half peeled away, bleeding where the base broke off his skin.

Violet gaped at him. Nox couldn't tell if she was more freaked out by his face or what he'd said. "What are you talking about?"

Thea put a hand on Violet's shoulder. "You know the Nightwood better than we do. What's the fastest way to get where we need to go? We don't have time to get lost."

"*What* are you doing with a crossbow?" she said. And then, voice jumping up an octave: "Did you take that from Zahna? Did you *steal* it?"

"Does it matter?" Thea said with poorly concealed guilt.

Violet looked around at the four of them, probably coming to terms with the fact that no one was on her side. Nine, the filthy traitor, at least had the decency to avert his gaze.

"Fine!" she said, pulling roughly away from Thea. "If you boneheads want to get yourselves killed, I won't stop you." She stuck out her hand. "Give me the dang map."

Nox had almost forgotten he still had Adam's map. Reluctantly—wishing he could've burned it instead—he handed it over. She laid it flat on the ground and borrowed a pencil from Thea. They huddled around her while she sketched out a route for them.

"Here," she said at last, returning it. "But whatever happens to you next is *not* my fault."

Yeah, no kidding, Nox thought. *It's mine.*

"If you survive, come visit us back at the settlement," Nine told Noah as they stood. "If you think these are cool"—he shook out his wings—"then just wait till you meet the others."

With a sheepish look, Noah reached out. "Can I . . . ?"

"Sure." Nine stretched his wing out to its full, modest length. Noah's crooked fingers brushed it. And Nine jerked away, hard, like he'd been electrocuted. "What just—"

But whatever he was going to say cut off on a strangled gasp. He staggered, as if something had shoved him and he'd lost his balance. Noah moved as if to steady him, seemed to think better of it, and snatched his hands back again, unable to do anything but look on in horror with the rest of them as Nine collapsed on his hands and knees. His goggles slipped off and hit the ground hard enough to crack one of the lenses. Feathers flew everywhere.

Nine's back twisted in pain as his wings grew. The muscles stretched and new feathers sprouted, tawny with black speckles, until he had a set of full-fledged eagle owl wings with over a ten-foot wingspan. They made frantic little flapping motions, kicking up a breeze.

Violet was the first one to get over her shock. She rushed to his side.

"Nine!" Her hands hovered over him, as if she was afraid any touch would set him off again. "Are you all right?"

He sat up shakily, wings dragging on the ground. His neon eyes were huge in his blanched face. "I'm—I'm fine. I think."

"I don't know how I did that," Noah choked out. "I'm so sorry."

Nine turned that shell-shocked look on him. "Are you kidding? You just gave me *real wings*." All of a sudden, he was beaming. "I can probably fly with these!"

He got to his feet and gave the wings an experimental flap,

but he clearly hadn't been prepared for how heavy they were. His arms windmilled for balance.

Violet stood, too, and shot Noah the sort of look that could've killed. "What was that?"

"He didn't do it on purpose!" Nox said.

If he sounded unsteady, it wasn't because of what had just happened. It was because he suspected that whatever Noah had done, Nox could do it, too. *Had* done it. The river monster that had almost drowned him—it had molted after he'd touched it. It had grown. Just like Nine's wings.

Zahna had said there was no such thing as being half Devil. But he wasn't sure she was right about that.

"But how did he—"

"I don't know, but we really have to go," Nox said abruptly, pocketing the map.

Nine's grin faded. "Maybe we should go with you. I mean . . . strength in numbers, right?"

"We're needed at home," Violet said. "Besides, if they wanted our help, they'd ask for it."

There was an awkward silence. Maybe he was imagining it, but Nox felt like everyone was waiting on *him* to fill it.

But he didn't say a word.

They followed the route Violet had drawn on the map and the hastily scribbled instructions she'd added at the bottom. After half an hour of walking, the imposing trees at the heart of the Nightwood gave way to groves of stunted oaks and skeletal pines. But even these soon tapered off as the soil grew loose and rocky. The sounds of the night receded, too. For all he'd complained about the racket the crickets made, their absence now was unnerving. And the wind didn't howl. And the whip-poorwills bit their tongues.

And at the place where the forest dropped off, a wall of thorns towered over them.

Tall as a cliff, all black and tangled. The barbs were so sharp Nox's skin prickled at the sight of them. Their tips caught the moonlight like beads of dew.

A machete couldn't have cut through that. Nox was half-convinced this monstrosity ate machetes for breakfast.

But as soon as Noah was within touching distance of the thorns, their vines shuddered to life. They snaked over and under one another, disentangling themselves, withdrawing. Making a gap in the wall.

Nox glanced at Noah, who shrugged. Thea adjusted her grip on her crossbow.

They stepped into the Web side by side.

21

A MOONLIT PATH STRETCHED BETWEEN ROWS
of tall black trees, their roots and branches tangled. Ropes of
thorny vines bound them together, and each thorn was about
the size of Nox's hand.

The message was clear: stay on the path.

It was a stark contrast to the dense, unruly forest they'd
trekked through up to this point, but there was no relief in the
open passage before them. It felt abandoned and desolate.

Every time they ventured into another part of the Nightwood, it was like discovering a new shade of darkness. If
Adam's cabin was twilight and Myte's crossroads was dusk—if
the depths of forest where the trees reached colossal proportions
were midnight and the settlement was the break of dawn—the
Devil's Web was the blackout of a new moon.

Although there was no danger in sight, a nagging sense of
unease took root in Nox's chest. He told himself it was only his
imagination.

"Greenbrier," Thea murmured, running her finger along one
of the vines. "I've never seen it grow like this, though."

A rustle in the canopy startled him, but it was only a dove

taking flight. There were more bats here, too. They huddled among the autumn leaves, roosting upside down like rows of muddy teardrops.

Noah followed his gaze. "You think maybe our dad was a vampire?"

That word—*dad*—set his teeth on edge. It felt wrong.

"No," Nox said tightly.

"What makes you so sure?"

"I'm not. I don't care what he was," Nox said. "All I know is that it's his fault this is happening to us."

"It's a little bit Mom's fault, too."

"No, it's not. Maybe he hypnotized her, or—"

"You mean . . . like a vampire?"

Nox glared at him. "Let's just go."

They went. The back of his neck prickled with the sense they were being watched, but when he looked around, there was nothing to see but the corridor of trees. Except for the occasional whisper of the bats shifting in their roosts, the woods were deathly quiet. A few eris moths had filtered into the Web after them, settling on the tree trunks and drifting lazily over their heads. The only other sign of life was the hare that scurried across their path. It paused, long brown ears folded back and large eyes peering up at them curiously. Then it crossed into the opposite row of trees and vanished. Soon, the path forked: they could continue left, right, or straight ahead.

"This isn't natural," Thea said, stopping.

The new paths turned off from the original at a precise right angle, and they were all identical. It was like someone had designed this part of the Nightwood on a game board.

"You see it, right?" Nox said. "It's a maze."

"Why, though?" Thea asked. "There has to be a reason for it."

"Maybe he was protecting something. You know, like a pregnant girlfriend?" Noah wandered into the clearing where the paths intersected, studying each of the three diverging routes in turn. "Maybe he lived in the center of the maze. With Mom."

The idea of Mom playing house with bargain-brand Batman was so ridiculous Nox short-circuited like a waterlogged phone. He decided, for his sanity, to pretend this conversation wasn't happening.

They kept going in the same direction. The route they'd chosen soon made a sharp right. The way the forest walls grew, they couldn't see down the next part of the path until they had already made the turn.

Nox was first around the corner. There, he stopped short. He didn't have time to backpedal before the others followed, almost colliding with him.

"What's wro—" Noah started to ask, and then broke off as he saw it.

The huge, furred shape that took up most of the path shifted. It was a tiny movement, a twitch, as if it were about to sneeze. Then it went still again.

It was the largest animal Nox had ever seen—some kind of wolf, but much bigger than Umbra or even Shadow. Its flank was like a shaggy hill; its immense hind paws rested on one side of the path while a snout the size of Nox's entire torso lay on the other. They'd have to climb over it if they wanted to keep going.

It was asleep, he realized. A glint of pale gold was all he

could see of its eyes, which were closed to slits, rolling slightly under their heavy lids. Its breathing was audible, great gusts of air that drew his eyes to its black nose and yellowed fangs.

They retreated slowly, inch by inch. None of them made a sound.

Before he withdrew around the corner, one of those large yellow eyes flickered open.

Nox didn't know if it saw him. He just kept going, backing out of sight and then spinning around to run at full tilt to the fork in the road, Noah and Thea at his side.

They stopped when they got there, trembling and out of breath. Nox covered the flashlight so as not to give them away if they'd been followed. The path was utterly silent and dark, but Nox's mind was filled with visions of being chased by something they couldn't possibly outrun; his eyes played tricks, convincing him that the shadows moved.

Without speaking, they picked another direction and scurried away. It was a long time before any of them dared make another sound.

He'd thought the maze was empty, but he had been wrong. They weren't alone here.

They went down corridor after corridor of thorn trees, the stars overhead providing an unobtrusive illumination. Nox kept track of the turns they made, but being able to retrace their steps was only half the challenge: they still didn't know where the axe was, and as they wandered deeper and deeper into the maze, it grew difficult to stave off the feeling of hopelessness. This place was *huge*. The axe could be anywhere. It would take *days* to search the entire thing, maybe weeks. They hit a dead end and back-tracked; they took the second of two paths, hit another dead end, and had to backtrack even farther. And then Nox started to lose track of where they'd been. The trees were uniform, like ranks of charcoal soldiers, and each new corridor looked just like the one before and just like the one that would come after.

This is useless, Nox thought. Would it have killed Zahna to warn them that the Nightwood came equipped with a beast-ridden labyrinth? Heck, Adam might have been a ruthless, power-hungry murderer, but at least he'd had the decency to scrawl out a map for them.

He was uncomfortably reminded of the story of the Mino-taur. Before Theseus slayed it, young tributes were sent into its labyrinth every nine years to be devoured. The myths never really lingered on those victims, or even bothered naming them most of the time, but now Nox could vividly imagine their last fearful moments—being hunted down and eaten, or perishing slowly after getting lost.

He glanced over at Thea, who stopped at every intersection and made notches in the trees using the tip of an arrow to mark which turns they'd taken. If she was discouraged, she didn't show it.

Noah sidled up to him as they walked, bumping his shoulder against Nox's. "So . . . did he make all this? All by himself?"

Nox shrugged. "I don't know. Someone had to have made it, I guess."

"Think *we* could do something like that?" Noah asked. "One day?"

"Zahna said we're human," Nox reminded him, hating the awe and wonder he could hear in Noah's voice. Why was Noah so interested in the magic that was even now trying to kill him? What did he see in any of this that was worth wanting?

Didn't he want what Nox wanted—for everything to go back to normal?

"I know," Noah said, "but—"

He broke off as they came up on another fork in the road.

"Is this one different?" Thea asked, sounding tentatively hopeful.

The path that branched off to the right was like all the ones they'd seen before, a wide and moonlit opening between the thorn trees, which stood tall, upright, and close together, so that there was no seeing anything over or through them. But they had been favoring left turns so far; and this time, the left fork looked—unfinished, like the Devil had begun carving it out and then had to stop midway. The thorn trees on either side bowed into each other, until their branches tangled over-head and allowed only sparse patches of light to seep through the canopy. They couldn't see very far down the path; it curved gently away into darkness.

It didn't look particularly inviting, but this was their first break from the monotony of the other paths. Maybe they were getting somewhere.

The decision was unanimous; they turned left.

The trail was winding, more like the route they'd taken through the middle of the Nightwood than the clean lines of the maze. The path grew narrower, and the branches of the thorn trees formed a tunnel that felt almost protective. Fireflies made up for the lack of moonlight and further reassured him. There had been no buzzing insects in the path where the wolf dwelled. A couple of eris moths alighted on the long greenbrier thorns as they passed by.

The arched ceiling of branches split apart overhead as the path gave way to a clearing. It was an unnatural, perfect circle. Crows perched in the tops of the thorn trees, preening and squawking at one another. And in the middle, bathed in the drifting golden glow of the fireflies, stood an old-fashioned grandfather clock. It ticked softly.

"What's that doing here?" Thea murmured.

"We should take a look," Noah said. "It might be a clue to solving the maze. Right?"

Noah looked at him, but Nox only shrugged helplessly, despite the twisting anxiety in the pit of his stomach. Every decision Nox had made so far had been the wrong one, so if Nox felt like they should turn around, then they should probably do the exact opposite.

Cautiously, they entered the clearing. When nothing sprang out of the bushes to stop them, they approached the grandfather clock, examining it. It had a swinging pendulum in a wooden case that looked brand-new, untouched by wind or rain or the scratch marks of curious animals. Its brass face shone, the minute marks delicately inscribed within it. But it was missing its hands, so it was impossible to tell the time.

"Can we open it?" Thea said. She ran her fingers along the side of the case, but there was no seam, and no visible latch.

The pendulum was behind a layer of glass. The clock face was exposed but couldn't be pried off. She went around the back to continue her inspection.

Noah's brow furrowed. "I . . . don't know what this means."

"I guess it's more complicated than Myte's riddle," Nox said offhandedly.

Noah gave him a strange, thoughtful look. "You think it's like a riddle?"

"I mean . . . I don't know," Nox said, shifting uncomfortably.

"Or a puzzle, maybe," Noah said.

Tick-tock. Tick-tock. Tick-tock.

A crow fluttered its wings and then settled down. The clock chimed, and they all jumped. Once, twice, three times. Its hollow, bell-like toll went on for what felt like ages. Ten, eleven . . . and then it was silent again.

"Does that mean it's eleven o'clock?" Noah asked.

"We don't know that it's set to the right time," Thea said. "I don't think it matters."

Noah bit the inside of his cheek, deep in thought. "This has to mean something. Should we try and figure it out? Or should we just . . . go back and take another path?"

He glanced at Nox again.

The idea of standing around wasting time made Nox's fists clench in his pockets, but he didn't want to drag Noah away if he thought this was important.

"What do you want to do?" he said.

Noah studied his expression for a while longer, and then nodded.

"I think it's a dead end," he said. "Let's turn around."

Nox kept his relief to himself as they did just that, Noah leading the way and Thea lagging a little behind, glancing over her shoulder at the mysterious clock.

"Forget it," Nox told her. "Maybe it's just there to mess with our heads."

"I guess," Thea said, clearly unsatisfied with this.

Noah stepped out onto the path, barely two feet ahead of them.

The moment he did, something slithered down from the trees. Noah shouted a warning, and Nox jumped back on reflex. Greenbrier vines were moving across the opening to the path and weaving themselves together as if spun by invisible spiders. In seconds, the web was so high Nox couldn't see over the top of it. It was a wall blocking their only way out of the clearing, a smaller version of the one that had sealed the entrance to the maze. And Nox and Noah were on opposite sides of it.

"Nox! Thea!" Noah shouted. "Are you okay?"

He and Thea traded grim looks.

"Fine," Nox called back. "Just stuck."

"Why'd it only let me out?" Noah said, frantic.

"Perks of being the heir?" Nox said. "Don't worry. We'll get out. Just . . . don't move."

"Where would I even go?"

After several more minutes of calling back and forth with Noah through the barrier, doing three full circuits of the clearing as they searched for a break in the thorns that might conceal a secret exit, and going over every square inch of the grandfather clock, Nox and Thea reconvened in the middle, defeated.

Nox was ready to set the whole maze on fire and be done with it. He was outvoted.

"It's like Nox said—this is a puzzle, so we just have to solve it," Noah called through the thorns.

"I didn't say it was a puzzle," Nox grumbled. "I don't know what it is."

The clock chimed again, and they jumped. These chimes were softer than the hour toll had been, rising and falling in a whimsical melody before stopping. Afterward, the clock ticked on peacefully.

"Have we been here an hour?" Nox asked Thea in a tense undertone.

"Definitely not," Thea said. "And it only rang four times, not twelve. Sometimes old clocks chime every quarter hour. Like the one in the upstairs hallway at home."

"There's only one weird thing about the clock, right?" Noah called. "It's missing its hands."

Personally, Nox thought the weird thing about the clock was everything. But, sure, the missing hands.

"So that's our clue," Thea said. "Maybe we have to put the hands back on the clock."

None of them thought it was going to be as straightforward as finding two little brass bits to stick onto the clock face, but Nox and Thea searched anyway. They looked for hidden compartments in the tree trunks—because if Nightwood trees could conceal doors, why not lockboxes for clockwork pieces? But what little they could see or touch of the black trees beneath their greenbrier wrappings revealed no secrets. They poked at holes in the shadows between the tree roots, tried to move the clock and check underneath it with no success, and scoured the clearing again with the flashlight.

Noah said, "You think I could climb over the—"

"No!" Nox snapped. Noah would tear himself to ribbons scrambling over what was essentially a barbed-wire fence.

"Okay, fine," Noah said. The shuffle of his footsteps told Nox he was pacing, probably as frustrated as Nox was right now.

"Can you see anything on the path that looks out of place?" Thea asked.

Nox tuned out the rest of their exchange. If the clue they were searching for was out there with Noah, then Nox couldn't do anything about it; better for him to focus on the clearing. What was he missing? Other than the clock itself, the only things there with them were a few eris moths and fireflies.

His eyes drifted up, into the forest canopy, where the serrated leaves of the black trees made razor-like shapes against the navy sky. The watchful eyes of the crows glinted back at him. They mostly hadn't moved from their perches, shuffling around sometimes but not taking flight. And, although Nox chalked it up to his imagination, he had the odd feeling that in the time since he'd last paid them any attention, they had gotten bigger.

The clock chimed again, marking the half hour with eight jaunty notes that, considering their predicament, felt more mocking than cheerful.

When the music ended, the final note seemed to hang in the air like the ghost of a firefly, illusory and bright. Noah and

Thea had fallen silent, listening, and neither of them spoke for a long moment afterward. Nox didn't think he was alone in feeling a rising sense of despair. They'd barely searched any of the maze before they'd walked right into a trap. How long would they be stuck here?

"That's another clue," Thea said out of nowhere.

"What?" Nox said.

"The chimes. And the time. We know it's half after eleven according to the clock. And maybe the music . . . the pattern of the chimes . . ." She hesitated. "I need to think."

"I've been thinking, too." He aimed the flashlight up, passing its beam over the branches where their audience of crows regarded them. He was sure of it now—they were bigger, and when the light passed over their faces, their eyes flashed red. "Count them. There's one over there. Two right there. Three . . ."

He turned a slow circle, dragging the light along the perimeter of the clearing, and Thea gasped as she understood. There were no numbers on the clock face. It was the clearing itself that was numbered, with the crows marking the hours.

"What? What's going on?" Noah asked.

Thea explained. Nox was still lost in thought. The crows at hour twelve fluttered their wings with distinct irritation when he aimed the light at them. One of them called out harshly, as if in reprimand, and the sound was piercing and musical and ominous as the chime of the clock.

He shivered. Maybe they weren't crows after all.

"If the birds represent the hour marks," Thea said, "then the clearing is like a giant clock face. Nox! That's it!"

"What's it?" he asked hopefully.

"It's us. We're supposed to be the hands on the clock." She moved to stand in front of the tree that contained seven crows. "Go stand by eleven. If I'm right, then at eleven thirty-five, it should let us out."

It was as good a plan as any, so Nox did as he was told. Then they waited. Thea counted the seconds under her breath. Nox kept his own time silently in his head.

Nothing happened.

After about three minutes had passed, Thea's shoulders slumped. "I guess not. It's definitely past time now."

"It was worth a try," Nox said, wondering whether he should float the fire plan again. Then his eyes widened. "Remember what you said before? That the chimes matter somehow? So . . ."

She brightened with renewed hope. "Maybe we can only get out when the clock chimes!"

They weren't sure how much time they had left, so they took their positions immediately, Nox remaining at eleven and Thea moving to nine, for 11:45. If it had been four chimes at the quarter hour and eight chimes at the half hour, the next should be twelve chimes.

The ticking of the clock resounded dully through the clearing. It bounced around the inside of his skull, fast becoming Nox's most hated sound in the world.

"What if this doesn't work?" he asked, too quietly for Noah to hear.

Thea's eyes were fierce with determination. "It will work."

The clock chimed—

Four notes—the greenbrier vines at the exit shivered, disentangling themselves, and Nox and Thea took off running at the first sign of movement. As the thorns parted, Noah's pale, worried face reappeared.

Eight notes—Thea made it to the exit first and threw herself across the threshold. But already the vines had started to weave themselves back together, zipping shut from the bottom up to the top.

Nine, ten—Nox was a second behind her, but a second was too much. The thorn barrier was waist-high already. He skidded to a halt before he could impale himself on one of its daggerlike barbs.

"No!" Noah shouted, hand rising as if to reach for him, but Nox shook his head, warning him off.

Eleven, twelve—Noah was forced to pull his hand away; he and Thea disappeared from view, leaving Nox alone in the clearing, ears still ringing with the echoes of the clock's chime.

"Nox! Are you all right?" Thea called. "I'm—I'm sorry, I thought—"

"It's not your fault," Nox said. "I was too slow. Or maybe it's designed to only let one person out at a time."

"How are you supposed to get out if you're by yourself?" Thea said. "You need at least two people, one to be the minute hand and one to be the hour hand—"

"Remember what time it is?" Nox said. "It's about to strike midnight. Or maybe noon. I don't know. But that means—"

"Oh! The minute and hour hands would be in the same place anyway!"

"I'm reconsidering the fire plan," Noah said tensely.

"It's fine," Nox said. "We figured it out."

"What if something goes wrong?"

Nox didn't say anything, but he had a fair idea of what might go wrong.

The hour birds had grown again—he could no longer delude himself by referring to them as crows. They'd more than doubled in height and were closer in size to falcons. Their eyes had gone a burning red that pierced through the darkness, little hovering flames surrounding him on all sides. They watched him hungrily.

22

"I'LL BE FINE," HE CALLED TO NOAH.

He turned off the flashlight and threw it over the barrier; it would only slow him down. Then he took his place at twelve, under the biggest flock of hour birds, listening to them shift overhead. They stretched their wings and croaked softly. He kept his eyes on the exit, one foot behind the other, preparing to bolt the instant he heard the first bell.

Thea counted the minutes for him, which helped, because his mind was a blank canvas. The ticking of the clock buzzed in his head like an insect, incessant and impossible to ignore, and then with time just becoming white noise. An hour bird at eight cocked its head at him, eyes flashing like the blade of a knife.

"It's been ten minutes," Thea called. "Get ready."

She stopped counting after that; they weren't sure how many minutes had passed in the initial shock of Nox being stuck in the clearing, so they couldn't keep time with complete accuracy.

He breathed in and out evenly. He wasn't a runner like Noah, but he had picked up on proper form from him. When all this was over, Noah would be back out on the track. Picturing it—Noah healthy again, winning his first race in a year—Nox realized he'd shifted unconsciously into Noah's usual starting stance.

He could feel his heartbeat in his throat, behind his eyes, a hard and rapid staccato. Directly over his head, an hour bird gave a fierce, sharp cry.

The ticking of the clock lapsed for a millisecond of absolute silence.

The clock rang for the hour—the first bell like a gong, hollow and resonant—and Nox bolted. He didn't wait to see if the thorn barrier was parting; he couldn't slow down long enough to check. He would just have to hope he wasn't about to turn himself into a human pincushion.

Distantly, he heard something like the sound of a gale battering at the forest; it was the rush of wings, he realized, as the hour birds took flight. They dove at him. Something sharp slashed at his arm, a beak or a claw. He kept running, but then pain sliced across his other shoulder—black feathers flew at his face, and he swerved, stumbled, almost fell. His arms came up to shield his head as a whirlwind of feathers engulfed him, spinning him around, flashes of pain raining down on him as the hour birds struck at him again and again, while his momentum kept carrying him forward without knowing if he was still going the right way—

A rough hand closed on his wrist. And then he was being pulled from the chaos, and running, running, running—

His foot caught on something, and he collided with Noah, sending them both crashing to the ground. Nox rolled away, arms up to either defend or fight, but—

The hour birds were gone. He was looking up at a ceiling of tree branches. The thing he'd tripped over was the thorn barrier, which had been a foot high when Noah had dragged him over it but was now resealing itself, slowly hiding the clearing and the circling, disgruntled hour birds. Their sharp cries overlapped with the toll of the clock, which rang out once more—a resounding twelfth note—and fell silent.

"Are you all right?" Thea said, helping Noah up.

Noah broke into a fit of hysterical laughter.

"I can't believe that worked," he said as he caught his breath.

"What worked?" Nox said, dazed. Something tickled his hand, and he jumped—but it was only blood, his own, dripping from one of the cuts on his arm. He wiped it away. Then he realized, much too late, what Noah had done. "Why did you go in after me?" he said, furious. "Those things could've killed us both!"

"I had a feeling they wouldn't hurt me, and I was right," Noah said.

Thea moved to sit by Nox, opening her backpack and digging inside. "Nox, roll up your sleeves. We have to clean and bandage those cuts."

"We don't have time for that," Nox said. The relief of making it out had come and gone in a flash. Noah was still riding high after his rescue, grinning wide, and Thea was in work mode. He didn't want to bring them down when they felt hopeful, but they needed to get back on track. They still had the entire rest of the maze to get through.

"Some of them are bleeding pretty bad," Thea said, refusing

to budge. "We won't finish this any faster if you get dizzy from blood loss."

"Just let her," Noah said.

Since arguing would take longer than giving in, he grudgingly let Thea clean the wounds with alcohol and wrap them with bandages. There was a nasty one on his side under his ribs, but mostly, he'd gotten off lucky.

Thea made them all eat an energy bar and drink some water from her pack before she let them move again. Then they backtracked to the last intersection, all of them subdued and tired. Noah stopped them before they could take another path.

"We need to figure out something else. This isn't getting us anywhere." Noah knelt shakily and patted at the ground. It was getting harder to ignore the fact that his transformation was hindering his ability to move. He got up, wincing, and ran his hands along the trees, carefully avoiding the thorns.

"What are you doing?" Nox said.

"Dad must have had a way of getting through the maze himself, right?"

"You don't have to call him *Dad*," he said, the words bursting out of him. "Just because Mom thought it was a good idea to date the Jersey Devil doesn't mean he's *Dad*."

"We're not in Jersey," Noah said.

"Um, Nox, maybe we shouldn't be so loud," Thea whispered.

"And now we have, like, magic powers? I mean, when I touched Nine's wing . . ." Noah's breath caught. He blinked down at his hands, as if they belonged to someone else. "And the clock trap didn't work on me. So if I can get this place to . . . I don't know . . . recognize us? Then maybe it'll show us a shortcut."

"We don't have powers!" Nox said. "*I* don't, anyway."

He shoved down his all-too-persistent memories of the river monster and the staircase.

"You sure?" Noah said, even though he couldn't possibly know what Nox *wasn't* thinking about. "I don't mind that part. If I'm gonna be sick, I might as well get powers out of it. It's my radioactive spider."

A headache was building behind his eyes. The near miss in the clock trap and the time they'd lost was weighing on him. After almost three days of hiking, his entire body hurt, and his various injuries—from the cuts he was reluctantly grateful Thea had insisted on treating, to the many scrapes and bruises he didn't even remember getting—certainly didn't help. And they still didn't understand how to get through the maze, and *everything* was counting on that, and Noah, whose life was at stake, was wandering around like he expected the trees to spring to life and start talking to him.

Nox grabbed his arm and swung Noah around to face him.

"Why are you treating this like a joke?"

"Guys," Thea said. They ignored her.

Noah's smile disappeared, expression transforming into something hard and furious. Something that looked like it belonged on Nox's face.

"I'm sick of bad things just *happening* to me," he said, pulling roughly out of Nox's grip. "At least I can finally *do* something now. I'm not stuck at home hoping I don't die!"

"Guys!"

"*What?*" Nox snapped, turning around.

Thea faced the way they'd come, her crossbow loaded and aimed into the darkness.

"Do you hear that?"

They listened. It took a moment before Nox's ears picked it up: a muffled *thump*-drag, *thump*-drag, getting closer with every passing second.

"What is that?" Noah whispered.

"The Devil," Nox told him. "What's left of him, anyway."

"Should I shoot?" said Thea under her breath.

Nox hesitated. "Maybe it knows how to get through the maze."

"I wanna see him," Noah said.

"It's not really our . . . It's not really him."

"I know, but . . ."

The shadows shifted at the far end of the path, and a tall silhouette came bouncing into view. In the split second between one hop and the next, the distance and the dark and Nox's own tired eyes played a trick on him. He saw with icy clarity the true Devil, flickering there in the puppet's place like a hologram: a broad-shouldered, black-eyed figure like Adam, with the chalky complexion and dark hair he'd passed on to Nox and Noah, his powerful wings tensed for flight and a crown of greenbrier thorns on his brow.

The puppet hopped again, and the illusion broke. Its limp wings trailed sadly along after it. Moonlight bathed its wood-and-clay frame, the leaves in its rib cage making dry *shushshush* noises, the broken stub of a leg poking uselessly at the air. It didn't even have arms.

Thea lowered the crossbow. Beside him, Noah's shoulders slumped.

Told you, Nox thought, though he had to push down a twinge of disappointment, too.

The puppet showed no sign of seeing them there. But Nox was pretty sure it *could* see. Somehow. He hadn't forgotten the way it had watched him and Thea while they'd slept.

He moved to stand in front of it as it reached the clearing.

"Can you help us?" he said, suppressing the urge to recoil. He hated the way it moved: sort of twitchy and quick, like the skittering of a giant insect. "We—"

It hopped around him and past Noah. He gave it such a forlorn look that even Nox, whose sympathy muscle had atrophied long ago, felt a little sorry. The tips of its wings drew parallel lines in the dirt as it ventured down the fork that pointed straight ahead.

"Let's follow it," Noah said. "You were right before. Maybe it's going to the center of the maze."

Nox never should've said that. He didn't really believe it. Maybe the puppet *was* being pulled along by some remaining scrap of the real Devil's personality—but more likely it was the supernatural equivalent of a squirrel, and they'd get nothing useful out of chasing it.

Also, it gave him the creeps.

But Thea said, "It's better than wandering around without a plan."

Nox wanted to argue, but then he remembered what had happened the *last* time he had been convinced that something was evil and out to get them. So they followed the puppet as it went right and left and right again.

Noah half stumbled, a quiet, bitten-off curse escaping him, but he caught himself before he fell.

"What's wrong?" Nox said.

"Nothing. Just . . ." Noah didn't meet his eyes. "It's getting harder to bend my knees."

The infection was spreading faster than before. Maybe because Zahna wasn't using her own powers to hold it back anymore. Guilt burned inside Nox like acid. But they couldn't slow down. Their only hope was to get through the maze.

"Do you hear that?" Thea said, moments later.

There was a low roar in the distance, punctuated by the occasional splash. They were near a river.

The sound of the water grew deafening, until Nox felt like the river was right under his feet. After a few more turns, the path ended at an expanse of streaming silver. The water pounded over a stony bank, foam frothing over its surface. The opposite shore was a murky, tree-lined smudge in the distance.

Nox inhaled deeply. "It smells like the beach."

"It's salt water," Thea said, surprised. She knelt beside it and dipped her fingers in.

The puppet came to the river's edge and paused as if deep in thought, hopping in place for balance. The walls of the maze ended just short of the water, so there was a sliver of riverbank to walk along. He looked up and down its length and saw where the tree line stuttered—gaps that marked where other paths in the maze met the river.

With a *whoosh* like fire catching, the Devil's wings spread open, almost whacking Nox in the head. At their full breadth, they were nearly as wide as the path. The puppet hopped once, twice, and then, with a mighty flap of its wings, it shot into the air and soared over the river.

"HEY!" Nox shouted. "You can't just leave us here!"

But it could. It flew off with all the grace of a drunken stork, its skinny body dangling lopsided between its wings, bobbing up and down in the air, at one point dipping so low its sole remaining leg almost got pulled into the rapids. It landed on the opposite bank and hopped away into the darkness.

Noah rocked back on his heels and gave a frustrated huff. "So much for that."

"I guess we'll have to find another route," Thea said, though she couldn't hide her disappointment, either.

"If the Devil made this maze for protection, then the closer we get to the center, the harder it'll be," Nox said. "What if we *have* to cross the river to get there?"

"It's too risky. Look at that," she said, jabbing a hand at the water. The center of the river churned violently, the foam gnashing like a set of teeth. "We'd get swept away before we even got close to the other side."

"You're right. I just . . ." Nox bit the inside of his cheek, gathering the words to voice something that had been bothering him. "How do we know the center of the maze is where we're supposed to go? *If* that's where Mom was, then the Devil wouldn't have fought Adam there. He'd have led him somewhere else. The axe could be *anywhere* in the maze."

"But getting to the center is probably a good start," Thea said.

"Hey, Thea?" Noah interrupted. "Do bulls live in the woods? Like . . . usually?"

"Huh? No."

"Cool. So what's that?"

Nox and Thea looked up. Something moved on the far shore: a black bull with stark white horns. It pawed at the ground.

Thea raised the crossbow. It was still loaded from earlier.

"What are you waiting for?" Nox whispered.

"I—I don't want to hurt him!"

"You've got to be kidding right now—"

The bull waded into the water until it was chest-deep. The rapids didn't seem to bother it.

"Thea," Nox said, trying not to panic.

She pulled the trigger, squeezing her eyes shut at the same time. Her aim was true; the arrow sank into the bull's shoulder. It bellowed angrily, tossing its head, and did not slow down. They might as well have poked it with a needle.

"Don't think that did anything," Noah said thoughtfully, as if it hadn't yet occurred to him to be concerned.

Thea fired again. This time, her arrow streaked across the river and sank into its eye. The bull let out a roar that resounded through the air, as if the water were reflecting it, doubling it in magnitude. Blood poured down its face and into its jaws.

She gasped. She must have aimed for the shoulder again and gotten lucky.

"Wow, that was a *literal* bull's-eye," Noah said appreciatively.

Thea fumbled for another bolt.

"No time!" Nox said, flinging out a hand to stop her. "We need to—"

The bull dipped its head, showing them the tips of its horns, and charged.

23

THEY RAN.

The riverbank was all black muck, slippery in some places and sticky as glue in others, so their shoes kept catching in it. Openings into the maze flashed past them, its tree-lined paths wide and dark and empty. Thea's braid whipped behind her like a tassel.

The bull's foghorn bellow blared louder and closer than before, so loud Nox almost lost his footing. It was gaining on them.

He chanced a look back but saw nothing except dark water. And Noah. He was struggling to keep up, his legs stiff, his teeth gritted with effort. Nox slowed down; Noah waved him away. What was he supposed to do, leave him there? Another backward glance confirmed his worst fears—a glint of reflected light, water sluicing off a rippling hide, and the bull was rising from the river. Its remaining eye met Nox's for an instant, alight with malice.

Nox took a deep breath of cold air that scalded his lungs.

"Thea!" he called. "On my signal, we get away from the river!"

He listened as the bull's heavy breathing and grunts grew louder, as the splashing in the shallows closed in on them. Another look back—it was right behind Noah. One final push onto the bank, and it would gore him.

"Now!" he shouted.

Thea dove left. Nox caught Noah's arm and dragged them both after Thea while the bull charged past. He was counting on it not being able to slow down fast enough to make a sharp turn, especially in the water.

They scurried into the cover of the trees, taking turns at random, thinking only of getting away from the river. Far away. Could a bull track them by scent? He really hoped he wasn't about to find out.

Only when they couldn't hear the water anymore did Nox begin to relax.

"I think it's gone," Noah said as they slowed to a stop. He doubled over, one hand rubbing at his knee.

Nox's shirt clung to his skin with sweat. For once, he was grateful for the chill in the night air. "We're even more lost than before."

Not that they'd been doing an expert job at navigating in the first place. But before, at least, he'd had a sense of where they'd started.

"We could double back," Thea said reluctantly. She wiped her sweaty face on her sleeve. "Keep following the river. We'd have to be careful, but . . ."

Nox hesitated, instinctively checking with Noah. But Noah wasn't paying attention to them. He stared down at his left hand, closing and opening his fist with apparent difficulty.

"Noah?" he said. "You okay?"

"Yeah. It's just my hand. It's, uh . . ."

He held it up. Bark had grown over his pinkie and ring finger, fusing them together; he couldn't even bend them anymore. Over his knuckles, the bark had broken, and blood beaded up in the cracks. Nox's stomach lurched.

"It's going to be okay," he said, determined to make it true. He turned to Thea. "We can't go back. It's too risky."

She nodded. "Forward, then."

It wasn't long before they reached another four-way intersection. To the left, the canopy wove together overhead to form a tunnel of trees, and the path went narrow and serpentine, just like the one that had led them to the clock trap before. Nox ran a short way down it to check, and their suspicions were confirmed—it opened onto another clearing with another grandfather clock. Shivering, he returned to the others. Straight ahead, the ground was dappled with pools of what *might* have been water, only there hadn't been a storm all night and there was no sign of recent rainfall anywhere else in the maze. The right path was clear, straight, and uniform, like the rest of the maze, which meant it was probably safe but also got them no closer to *solving* it.

They stood in the middle, none of them wanting to be the one to choose. He was about to admit that Thea had a point, that going back to the river was their best shot, when a sound came from the path to the right, the one Nox had mentally categorized as *safe*:

A metallic clank. A heavy thud.

At the end of the path, something in the darkness glinted.

"Let's get out of here," Thea said apprehensively. "Forward?"

Nox and Noah agreed, and they took the middle path.

At first, it was easy to avoid the wet spots; they zigzagged around them, sticking to the center of the path, where it was driest. The ponds were as dark and irregular as ink stains. They pooled around the roots of the thorn trees, here and there, and glistened in the moonlight. How long had they been there? If it was really water, why hadn't it dried out?

Thea broke a long thorn off one of the vines. "Wait. I want to try something."

"Don't get too close," Nox warned.

"I'll be careful." She knelt and dipped the tip of the thorn into a puddle. Nox held his breath, but nothing happened. She pressed down, and the thorn went in easily, as if the puddle was much deeper than it appeared. The thorn was a solid five inches long, and Thea let it sink until most of it was submerged.

"Can you feel the bottom?" Noah asked.

She shook her head. "It's almost more like a well than a puddle. I think it just keeps going."

The thorn slid out much more slowly than it had gone in; she had to pull with both hands to get it out, and the liquid substance clung to it like sludge. It left a black residue on the thorn. Nox grabbed the top of Thea's backpack, paranoid that she would fall in. With a final hard wrench, she got the thorn free and fell back on her heels with a huff.

"I have no idea what this could be," she said in fascination as she turned the thorn over, holding it by the dry base as she studied the residue on the length of it.

"Experiment over. Can we keep going?" Nox said.

She dropped the thorn back into the puddle, where it sank away and vanished, creating no ripples and leaving behind no sign that the surface had ever been disturbed.

But as they kept walking, it became harder to avoid the inkblot puddles. Tendrils of it strayed into their path, so that they had to step carefully over them. This was a challenge for Noah especially, who winced every time he had to hop over a wide patch of ominously shining liquid. When he almost lost his footing and staggered back into a long stretch of black, Nox snagged him by the collar and tugged him forward into safety.

Noah smiled gratefully at him. "Nice save."

Over Noah's shoulder, Nox saw movement.

"Look out!" he said, dragging Noah out of the way just as something leapt at the place where he'd been standing. It sailed past and dove into the ground, melting away until only a splotch of black ink remained.

The things that Nox had mistaken for ponds were alive.

He looked back at the path that they'd walked down, passing about a dozen of the ponds. All of them were stirring—shifting position, sliding across the path, as if they were piles of fabric being blown along by the wind and not bottomless pools of darkness. In a few of them, something broke the surface, a pointed shape—and then one of them launched itself into the air. The tip of a snout emerged, followed by a sleek, curved body, and it leapt across the path in a graceful arc, trailing a banner of inky blackness behind it. When it landed between the roots of two thorn trees, it sank into the earth and left only a rippling black shadow behind.

"It's another trap," Noah said breathlessly.

"We're surrounded," Thea said. Beyond her, in the direction they'd been walking, the dark pools went on as far as Nox could see, up until the path disappeared into shadow. Another shape leapt across the path, and then another; when they were in the air, they had glossy skin and something that looked like fins. Fish, or—based on the way they jumped—dolphins. Moonlight flashed off a shiny dark hide as another one propelled itself from the earth and flew directly at them.

"Duck!" Nox said, and all three of them dropped to the ground.

Thea had her crossbow loaded in a flash. She shot at one of the dark spots creeping across the path. Her arrow disappeared into it—and then, a moment later, was shot back out, missing Thea's face by inches.

The swimming shadows circled them now, more like land sharks than dolphins, closing in with every second, so that the patch of earth they stood on was a diminishing island of safety. They could run for it—like the most messed-up game of dodgeball in history—but there were dozens, and Noah wasn't agile enough to swerve at the moment. Nox didn't know what would happen if they let the black substance touch them. He remembered the thorn Thea had used for her experiment. If one of them was caught, would they sink until they disappeared, too?

"Uh—hey!" Noah said, raising his voice as if speaking to a crowd. "I'm—I'm a Keeper of Night, and I . . . I order you to let us pass!" He hesitated. "Please?"

A flicker in the corner of Nox's eye; he leapt backward just in time to avoid another inkblot creature as it soared between them in a fluid jump. He caught a glimpse of sharp teeth in its long, rubbery snout as it streaked past. Once it made contact with the ground, it lost its form, spreading apart and becoming a pond-like thing again.

Thea was digging through her backpack. She produced her book of matches, struck one with trembling hands, and tossed it at one of the inkblot swimmers. Her target surfaced from its liquid form and caught the burning match in its fang-lined jaws as it sprang at Thea. She shrieked and rolled away. As she pushed herself back up, another shadow spread toward her hand like the edge of a rising flood. Noah threw himself at her, hauling her up by the shoulders and dragging her away—and he shouldn't have been fast enough, but the shadow receded, backing off like a scolded dog.

"Not fire," Thea said in a squeak, diving into her backpack again. "Come on, come on."

"They're giving you space," Nox realized.

"But not the two of you," Noah said. "Maybe if you stay close to me—"

A shrill, screeching noise made them both jump. Thea had a whistle in her hand, the kind hikers used as an emergency signal, and was blowing into it with all her might.

The shadows froze.

But the moment she stopped to take a breath, they started moving again, more restlessly than ever, circling and leaping and sending Nox to his knees as he ducked out of the way. They didn't go for Noah, but they had no problem going *around* him, or even sailing right over his head, and Noah couldn't shield them from every side.

Thea blew into the whistle again, three times.

The inkblot swimmers slowed their frantic orbit. Nothing jumped out at them.

"Keep going!" Nox said hoarsely.

They inched back down the path as Thea blew into the whistle again and again. The inkblots stayed still, so that they almost looked like ponds again, except that they were shivering faintly, as if from tremors deep within the earth. She alternated short notes with long ones, and Nox assumed she was using some kind of hiker distress signal or Morse code or the like— because it was Thea, after all—until, pausing to take a deep breath, she gasped: "Music. I think it's music."

Nox and Noah traded confused looks. But Thea was running out of breath; as she lost the rhythm she'd started with the whistle, the inkblots began to move again, slowly but surely, stalking them as they traveled down the path.

"Uh . . . *Pleeeaaaase don't hurt my frieeends!*" Noah sang. *"We don't want to die here! That would really suuuuck!"*

Noah was good at a lot of things. Singing wasn't one of them.

But supernatural aquatic creatures made out of darkness beyond mortal comprehension apparently had low musical standards, because they came to a complete stop, as if listening raptly. Encouraged, Noah continued warbling various pleas for mercy. Nox, who would have actually rather died than sing in this moment, took the whistle from Thea—she wheezed out a weak thank-you—and provided a stuttering accompaniment. Like this, they made their way back to the start of the path. A few eris moths drifted alongside them, their reflected blue glow traveling across the surface of the ponds. Noah kept his solo going after they passed the last inkblots. Two or three still trailed along in their wake, a few feet behind, but not as threateningly now—less like great whites that had smelled blood in the water and more like ducklings. By the time they reached the crossroads, even these last curious ones had dropped away. Tentatively, Nox lowered the whistle. Noah took a bow.

"Thank you!" he called back down the path. "You've been a great audience!"

Thea clapped obligingly. He beamed at her.

"I get the music," Nox said, "but was the dancing really necessary?"

"In theater, we call that being a triple threat," Noah said, with exaggerated haughtiness. "You wouldn't get it."

He and Thea dissolved into laughter. Even Nox couldn't quite suppress a smile.

"Thea, you're a genius," Noah said once he'd recovered. "How'd you figure that out?"

"It was an accident," she admitted. "I thought a loud noise might scare them away. And then I realized they stopped the longer I kept going."

"Music, huh?" Nox said lightly. "Not a very scientific approach, if you ask me."

She grinned. "I formed a hypothesis and tested it. That's as scientific as it gets."

Before Nox could respond, a noise interrupted him—metal striking metal, like the links in a chain banging together. It was coming from the path they'd avoided before, to their right, and this time, it was closer.

24

THEY ALL FELL SILENT, BUT WHATEVER WAS OUT
there didn't show itself.

"I guess we do have to go back to the river," Nox whispered.
The idea of backtracking didn't upset him as much this time as
it had before. They'd had close calls, but they were also figuring out how the maze worked, piece by piece—Noah and Thea
were figuring it out, anyway, and Nox was staying out of their
way.

"No." Noah had his left hand tucked under his other arm
and a stubborn gleam in his eyes. "Let's see what it is."

"You really want something else chasing us?" Nox said.
Pretty soon, Noah wouldn't be able to run anymore. They had
to avoid the maze's obstacles at all costs.

"Nox is right," Thea said, a sentence Nox would have trea-
sured in any other situation.

Noah's shoulders slumped. "I know. It's just . . . the maze
is probably going to get more dangerous the closer we get to
the center. Assuming that's where we're going. We have to start
figuring out how to get *through* the obstacles and not just avoid
them."

"I was thinking about what you said before," Thea said. "About how the Devil was trying to protect something. If that's true, then maybe this isn't the kind of maze that's a puzzle you're meant to solve. It's more like a fortress that's meant to keep you out."

And that would mean there might not be a way through at all. It was the most disheartening thought yet.

They didn't have much time to decide; whatever guarded the right path was coming closer, as if tired of waiting for them. As it emerged from the shadows, Nox made out a tall, broad silhouette, with parts that jutted out at harsh angles. It *clank*ed with each footstep.

"We need information," Noah said. "Otherwise, we'll wander around forever without getting anywhere."

"Fine." That was enough to earn him a startled glance from Noah. "But you have to hide. *I'll* see what it is."

"But—"

Nox cut him off. "Thea can back me up. Right?"

Thea nodded, already locking a fresh bolt into place.

"And I can run if I need to," Nox said. "I'll lead it away and then come back and find you. But I can't do this if I'm afraid you'll get hurt."

He jogged away before Noah could protest, throwing a final *"Hide! Now!"* over his shoulder.

Whatever was there in the dark, it was almost upon him. Trembling, he switched on the flashlight.

The beam landed on a pair of knees. They were, unquestionably, the biggest set of knees Nox had ever had the misfortune of encountering. And he had taken a lot of knees to the gut. He had to point the light up, and up, and up before he could wrap his mind around what he was seeing. It was a person, kind of. He was twice as tall as a normal man, arms bulging with veiny slabs of muscle, and wore armor that looked like something out of Nox's ancient history textbook: a bronze helmet and cuirass, a round wooden shield strapped to his arm. The helmet covered most of his face, with a vertical breathing slit and openings for his eyes, which were obscured by shadow. He held a club in a fist the size of a bowling ball. A sword swung from his jewel-studded belt.

"Uh. Hi?" Nox tried.

The warrior giant opened his mouth and released a sound like boulders grinding together. Like he wanted to talk but he didn't have the equipment for it.

Nox figured this was the part where he should probably run. Pretty soon he was going to get stomped on or worse. But he couldn't look away. It was the belt—that row of three bluish white gems kept drawing his eyes.

They were important somehow. They *meant* something. But what?

"Nox!"

That was Thea's voice. She was probably wondering why he hadn't retreated.

An arrow zipped over his head, narrowly missing the warrior's arm. Another arrow chased it; this one, he batted away with his shield. The moonlight washed out his bronze helmet, transmuting it into steel.

The warrior lunged, club raised over his head. It swung down on a collision course with Nox's skull. He heard the rush of wind and Thea's scream—

He jumped out of the way. The flashlight slipped from his hand. He didn't have a chance to pick it up again. The warrior was already following him, his armor rattling, puffs of steam from unnaturally hot breath escaping the helmet. More arrows bounced off his armor and shield; one sank into his shoulder and stuck there, but it did nothing to slow him down. But Nox didn't want to run yet. He was close to figuring something out—he could feel it.

Noah had wanted to stop running away from the maze's obstacles and start getting through them. Maybe this was Nox's chance to make that happen. Without putting anyone else in danger.

"Nox—"

That was Noah.

"I'm fine!" Nox shouted. He wheeled away backward while the warrior bore down on him. "I just— I'm trying to see something. Stay back!"

Another swing of the club. In his mind's eye, Nox saw the crumpled, empty skin floating atop the river where he'd almost drowned; he saw Nine's wings blowing up twice their size amid a hurricane of feathers. If he and Noah really did have powers, then maybe—

He dodged the club. It whistled past him, inches from his nose. Instead of backing away again, Nox caught hold of the warrior's arm, wrapping his hands around a tricep so muscular it felt like a baseball in a nylon sleeve.

Stop fighting me! Nox thought. He tried to summon the feeling he'd had when he—*maybe*—made the river monster release him. When he'd maybe gotten himself and Thea off the endless staircase at Zahna's watchtower. A spark of energy in his chest, fighting its way out.

Nothing happened.

The warrior lifted his arm, dragging Nox up—*way* up—to eye level. He opened his mouth, revealing crooked yellow teeth, and roared wordlessly in Nox's face.

With a motion like he was flinging a door open, he threw Nox off him. Nox's fingernails dug into the warrior's skin, clinging, but it was useless. He went flying and landed hard, slamming his head. Pain exploded through his skull. Groaning, he flopped over onto his back. The night sky sagged overhead like a tarp sinking under the weight of the stars. Then the warrior was standing over him, his belt shining in the beam of Nox's flashlight.

And Nox recognized him, finally. He knew why the belt with its three gems had caught his attention; he knew the warrior's *name*.

But it was too late. The edges of his vision went black. He passed out.

When he woke up, the warrior was gone.

How long was I out? he thought, sitting up. Then he winced and pressed his hand to the back of his head, which felt like it'd been smashed into a billion pieces and then hot-glued back together. His fingers ran over a crusty patch of dried blood.

"Nox! Are you okay?"

Thea shuffled over to him on her knees. Her crossbow lay at the foot of a tree, next to Noah, whose expression was oddly tense. What was wrong with him? Was he in pain? What had Nox missed?

"How long—" Nox croaked.

"Maybe ten minutes," Thea said. "We were starting to get really worried."

"Where did he go?"

"Nowhere," Noah said shortly. He nodded at something over Nox's shoulder. Nox followed his gaze and jerked back at the sight of the warrior. He stood to the side of the path, arms at his sides, as if awaiting orders. That ancient bronze face was menacing even when he wasn't in motion.

"He was going to kill you," Thea said in a low voice, as if she didn't want the warrior to overhear. "Noah ran up to him—"

"You *what*?" Nox said.

"Like you can talk!" Noah snapped. It finally dawned on him that Noah wasn't in pain, or even worried. He was *livid*. "You should've run away instead of— What were you thinking, anyway?"

Thea held up a hand before Nox could retort. "It's okay. As soon as he saw Noah, he stopped."

Noah glanced away uncomfortably.

"I—I was trying to see if . . . ," Nox said, feeling like it was about time he explained himself. "There was this thing in the river, and it tried to drown me, and then I touched it and—"

Noah's eyes lit up. "You have powers, too! I knew it!"

"Maybe not. I mean, nothing happened when I touched—"

He stopped himself from saying the name he instinctively wanted to call the warrior. He was still sorting things out in his head, trying to make sure all the pieces of his theory lined up.

"It probably didn't work because of something the Devil did to protect the things guarding the maze," Noah said.

"Maybe," Nox said slowly. Or maybe it hadn't worked because he hadn't been angry enough. Both times he'd gotten himself out of trouble using his . . . powers, or whatever they were . . . he'd been furious at what was happening to him. He looked up, about to ask Noah whether Nine had done something to piss him off, and stopped.

Noah was cradling his left hand to his chest. Or what *had* been his hand. Now it was a gnarled wooden claw, the fingers fused together, already dotted with tiny green sprouts.

He forgot what they were talking about. He forgot about the warrior, about their powers, about Adam. His mind went blank, except for a single question: "What did Zahna mean when she called you the *firstborn child*?"

"Is he . . . not?" Thea asked.

"No. I am," Nox said. "So what happened? Did Adam get it wrong?"

Noah's silence was as revealing as the guilty look on his face.

"What did you *do*?"

"I didn't do anything you wouldn't have done," Noah said, which was a strong contender for the last thing Nox wanted to hear from him.

Thea looked back and forth between them, eyes wide. "What happened?"

Noah's hand twitched up as if to run through his hair; then he grimaced and stopped.

"A few months ago," he said, when the silence grew unbearable, "I woke up in the middle of the night. There was all this dust floating in the air." He blinked rapidly, as if clearing a fog from his eyes. "It was gold. Some of it came in through the vent, and some of it slipped inside around the edge of the window glass. Then I realized it was gathering over your bed."

Nox had a horrible suspicion he knew where this was going.

"I was still half-asleep," Noah said. "I thought I was dreaming. I just remember thinking, *Well, Nox can't sleep there.* So I woke you up as much as I could—you were still pretty out of it—and moved you to my bed. I don't think you even noticed."

"I didn't," Nox managed. During their sleepwalking years, it hadn't been unusual for them to wake up in strange places. Mom would find one or both of them on the kitchen floor, or in the bathtub, or slumped against the front door. He didn't remember it happening recently, but then, he wouldn't notice the zombie apocalypse if it happened before eight in the morning. Let alone waking up in the wrong bed.

"Since you were in my bed, I took yours. I didn't think about leaving the room or getting Mom or anything. Dream logic, I guess. The last thing I remember from that night is the dust drifting closer to me," Noah said. "But it was kind of nice, like stars. Like I was floating through outer space. I started coughing the next day. But I didn't make the connection for a long time. After you saw the wolf for the first time, and then when I realized Aster and Weston's treatments weren't doing anything, that was when I got suspicious. Before that, I really thought it was just a dream."

"Wait, but then—why did the warrior stop attacking when he saw Noah?" Thea said. "If Noah's *not* the heir, then—"

Noah laughed so hard he started coughing and had to stifle it in his sleeve. "Don't you get it? Zahna said an heir could be born *or* chosen. She just assumed the firstborn would automatically become the heir. But what if she was wrong? What if it could have been *either* of us? We both got powers from our dad. Maybe the only difference between us is that he was going to choose you."

"How do you know he chose me?" Nox objected.

"Uh, I don't know, maybe your *name*?" Noah said, as if this was so obvious he couldn't believe he had to spell it out. "Isn't *nox* just Latin for *night*? He literally could not have made it any clearer. But Zahna said Adam attacked him the night we were born. Maybe he never got to see us. He didn't get to name you himself. Mom just called you by the name he was going to give you. So . . . he never chose his heir out of the two of us. You know who did? Adam." Noah grinned triumphantly. "He sent the moros seed to the Devil's firstborn, assuming you were the heir just like Zahna did. But we weren't different enough for the magic to tell us apart. Neither of us was the chosen heir yet. So when I switched with you and the magic infected me, that became the difference between us—suddenly I had all this extra night magic, Keeper magic, inside of me. Magic you don't have. That's what made me the heir. By poisoning me, Adam *made* me the Keeper."

"What's funny about that?" Nox said, stricken. "When you're—you're— And this whole time, it should've—"

It should've been me, he thought. Adam wanted them both dead, but Noah was never meant to be *first*. Noah had taken his place. He had put himself through the worst few months of his life; he had risked dying. For Nox. And he had never planned to tell him. He didn't want to be thanked. He hadn't even wanted an apology when Nox had snatched a cure away from him.

Nox's eyes burned. He looked down, willing the others not to notice until he pulled himself together.

"Because if Adam can make a mistake once, then he can do it again," Noah said. "We can beat him."

Thea's face scrunched up doubtfully. It wasn't exactly iron-clad logic.

But Noah had saved him; it was Nox's turn now.

He got to his feet. "Then we have to keep moving."

"We still don't have a plan," Noah said. "Look . . . maybe you'll go faster if I stay here."

"No splitting up!" Nox and Thea said in unison.

"Okay, okay," Noah grumbled. "Jeez."

"Anyway," Nox added, "I figured something out."

"What?" Thea said. She and Noah looked at him expectantly, waiting. Suddenly he wasn't so certain that the brilliant discovery he'd made in the moments between almost getting his skull cracked open and passing out hadn't just been a delusion, one that told him nothing except that he probably needed to be checked for a concussion. His eyes strayed to the silent, watchful warrior again. The belt, the club, the armor.

"I think that's supposed to be Orion," he said, blurting it out before he could reconsider.

"Orion?" Noah echoed, squinting in confusion. "Like, the hunter from the myths? You told me that story."

"Yeah," Nox said. "If the Devil made the maze, maybe he made the things inside it, too. I think he based the obstacles in the maze on the constellations."

"Are you sure?" Noah said.

"No, not really. But . . ." Nox broke a thorn off the greenbrier vines and used it to draw a circle in the dirt, with a point in the middle to represent the North Star. He was still piecing it together even now. "The bull, Taurus. The river, Eridanus." He hesitated a moment, remembering that Eridanus had contained salt water. It probably housed the sea monster, Cetus. What might have happened if they'd tried swimming across like he'd wanted before Thea had talked him out of it? The thought made a shiver of retroactive dread sweep through him. Shaking it off, he continued. "The giant dog we saw when we first got into the maze was Canis Major. The hare was Lepus. The dove was Columba." He marked the diagram with *X*s where the constellations lay in relation to each other in the night sky. "The hare and the dove weren't really obstacles—maybe more of an alarm system? But it all fits."

"So if the middle of the maze represents Polaris," Thea said, following his logic, "then you can use the obstacles to navigate. You'll be able to tell if we're getting close based on which constellations we run into."

"And you can help us avoid the most dangerous ones," Noah said. "I don't think any of them will hurt me—even Taurus. Thea shot it in the eye, so it probably couldn't see that well. It didn't recognize me. But neither of you are safe. And if I have to get between you and whatever's in here with us, I'd rather be dealing with doves than Hydras."

Nox bit back the instinctive objection he wanted to give to the idea of Noah volunteering himself as their human shield. He wouldn't be talked out of it. It was going to be Nox's job to make sure he wouldn't need to do anything drastic.

"I just don't understand Delphinus. That's what those . . . shadow dolphin things were, I think. In the myths, this poet who gets thrown overboard at sea is rescued by a dolphin because he sang a dirge. Which is . . . I guess . . . kind of what Noah did," Nox said wryly. Noah beamed as if this was high praise. "But Delphinus shouldn't be anywhere near Orion."

He sat back on his heels, thinking. If he got this wrong, they'd end up even more hopelessly lost than they already were.

"What about the clock trap?" Thea said. *Horologium*, he thought, his mind supplying the name of the constellation he was fairly certain the trap was based on. "There's more than one of it. Maybe Delphinus is like that, too—a trap that shows up more than once in the maze."

"So there are traps and obstacles," Nox said, following her line of thinking. "The traps repeat themselves, but the obstacles that guard the main paths don't."

"It's smart," Noah said. "The obstacles are bigger and more dangerous than the traps. But if you want to get through the maze, you have to use the obstacles to find the way out."

"Okay. I think . . ." Nox marked a few more spots on the map. "If we avoid going back to Taurus, then our route will take us past Gemini or Auriga. Those will probably be human. If we can find Perseus, we'll be really close. But if we see Lepus or Canis Major again, then we've gone the wrong way."

"Nerd," Noah whispered. Nox shoved him.

"Let's go, then," Thea said, standing.

Nox blinked up at her. "You don't think it's kind of a risky plan?"

"We don't have a better one. Anyway, you know what you're talking about. I trust you."

You do? He almost thought she was being sarcastic. But sarcasm wasn't really Thea's thing. He rewound the words in his head: *I trust you.* It made him feel something complicated—a little embarrassed, and kind of proud, in a weird way, because he didn't think anyone but Noah had ever trusted him with anything.

Most of all, though, it made him nervous. Nervous he'd screw it up.

I trust you.

Great. No pressure, though.

25

NOX DIDN'T KNOW HOW LONG IT TOOK THEM
to solve the maze. Toward the end, his body ached with exhaustion. Only Noah's slow deterioration marked the passage of time. His every unsteady footstep was a grain of sand falling through an hourglass; the moment he surreptitiously tugged his sleeve over his good hand to hide it was an alarm ringing in Nox's head.

They reached a stretch of the maze where a two-wheeled wooden cart rode back and forth, drawn by a pair of black goats with curved horns and steered by a scarlet-clad charioteer. Nox didn't get a good look at his face. They ducked into the shadows and hid while the cart passed by, the trundling of its ancient wheels dissolving until silence reigned once more. Then they hurried onward. Their options were forward or left; Nox led them forward, but they hit a dead end at a solid wall of thorns. Eris moths sailed over their heads and alighted on the barbs, like a ghostly imitation of fairy lights on a lethal Christmas tree. They doubled back, avoiding the charioteer again, and took the left fork after all.

When he caught on to the fact that there were no bats in this part of the maze, he knew something was wrong.

"Stop," he breathed, holding up a hand before Thea and Noah could go on. His eyes scanned the treetops. The moonlight cast deep shadows beneath the canopy, and the shiver of the leaves under the wind's combing fingers drew his eyes, tricking him into seeing things that weren't there.

A low growl came from directly above him. He looked up into a pair of flashing golden eyes under pointed, black-tipped ears—*just like Patch's*, he thought hysterically—and barely suppressed a shout. They fled, going back the way they'd come, but somehow they got turned around and ended up at the edge of a lake.

Nox frowned. None of the constellations near the Lynx involved a lake . . . unless . . .

A great darkness appeared in the moon-glossed surface of the water. Ripples at the center of the shadow ballooned outward, until small waves lapped at the shore where Nox and the others stood. A pincer the size of a skiff broke the surface, swiftly followed by another, and then a vast, barnacle-crusted hill that Nox belatedly identified as a shell.

"Back, we're going back," Nox hissed, and they retreated. "We have to get past the Lynx."

"There's no other way?" Thea said.

"If we're at Cancer, then we're going in the wrong direction. And I don't like how close we are to the Hydra and Leo," he said. "We'll just have to charge through and hope the Lynx doesn't catch us."

"I can't," Noah bit out. He looked away as if ashamed. As

if he'd done something wrong, when it was *Nox's* fault that he couldn't run from the Lynx.

Nox shook his head. "*We're* going to run. *You're* going to catch a ride."

And that was how Nox and Thea ended up sprinting through the Lynx's territory while it bounded after them with its teeth bared and its golden fur bristling. Noah followed in Auriga's chariot, squeezed into the back next to him. "Here, kitty, kitty!" Noah tried.

The Lynx did not dignify that with an answer.

When Nox's lungs were burning and his thighs were crying out for mercy, and he was sure he wouldn't last another ten seconds, the sound of the Lynx's huge paws striking the ground abated. It turned away with a dismissive flick of its tail, leaping over the thorned trunk of a tree and back up to its perch in the branches.

He and Thea nearly collapsed where they stood while Auriga zipped past with Noah.

"Um, you can drop me off here," Noah said, but Auriga was stopping before the words were fully out of his mouth. Like the Lynx, it seemed that he'd gone as far as he could.

"Are we close?" Thea said under her breath as Noah limped back to them.

"I think so."

And they were. Nox led them through another intersection, praying he didn't get them lost again—they had no more time for detours.

Then the path opened before them. The walls broke off as

abruptly as they had at the river, and they emerged into a tranquil clearing. The moon and stars shone as bright and clear above them as they had that first night in Evergreen, on the roof of the Day house. Gone was the dead black earth of the maze; the clearing was lush with lavender and mint and rosemary, their scents mingling in the air. In the center stood a perfect little fairy-tale cottage.

Yeah, right, Nox thought. *Like anyone's going to fall for that.*

He didn't care how innocent it looked on the outside. The Devil had lived there once, and they weren't going anywhere near—

"Let's go in!" Noah said, already hobbling toward the cottage. Nox jumped in front of him.

"We have to find the axe, and it's probably not in there," he said.

Noah looked at the cottage and then Nox, clearly torn. "Don't you want to see it?"

"Not until we find the axe."

Maybe not even after that, he thought. *Maybe never.*

"Where do we even start?" Thea murmured.

There were eight ways back into the maze—eight openings in the trees. Nox turned a slow circle, examining each of them, his mind racing. If it had been him in the Devil's place, knowing that Adam was coming, he would've gone to the constellation he considered the strongest for backup. That constellation probably guarded the axe now.

But which one would the Devil have chosen?

Nox's first pick would've been Orion, but they'd seen him

already. He didn't have the axe. What, then? The Hydra? Cetus? Hercules?

Maybe it wasn't any of the beasts or warriors. Maybe . . . if Nox and his supposed father were anything alike, then . . . maybe he had gone to the one he thought he could most rely on, not the one with the biggest teeth or the sharpest sword.

"Okay," he said. "I have a guess."

Noah and Thea watched in bemused silence as Nox made a circuit around the clearing, peering into each of the maze's entrances, until he saw movement. He inched closer. Sure enough, a small brown bear guarded one of the openings. Though he used the word *guarded* very loosely. It plopped at the foot of the path, chewing on a leafy plant.

Thea gasped and dashed over for a better look. "It's amazing!"

"Don't get any closer," he warned. If Ursa Minor was here, then Ursa Major wasn't far off. But now he knew which way to go. He led Thea and Noah to the other side of the clearing and back into the maze.

It didn't take long to find what he was looking for. She was, as ever, steady and constant and not far from the North Star.

Cassiopeia waited for them in a straight-backed throne that shone like solid sunlight. In all that dark and gloom, she was so bright it was painful to look at her. More details came into focus as they haltingly approached: the flowing gown, the coppery red-gold hair piled atop her head, the way her skin glistened faintly as if brushed with moondust. Shackles on her wrists and ankles bound her to her throne; the links of her chains pooled around the base like iron blossoms. Propped against the side of the throne was a silver mirror. A handful of eris moths fluttered around her, as if daring each other to approach.

"I don't see the axe," Noah whispered.

"Ask her."

"*Me?*"

"Yeah, you," he hissed back. "If she doesn't have it, maybe she knows where it is."

Cassiopeia shifted in her seat, her chains clinking faintly. Her head turned. She had no eyes, just two round cavities where they should have been.

"What happened to her?" Thea said under her breath.

"She was punished for vanity," Nox said, even more quietly.

Thea shot him an affronted look.

He raised his hands placatingly. "Take it up with Poseidon."

They stopped and let Noah take the final steps, Nox making a *go ahead* gesture when he hesitated.

"Um, hi," Noah said, standing before the throne. Even sitting, she dwarfed him; it was like being in the presence of a goddess. "I'm looking for an axe."

"*You shouldn't,*" said Cassiopeia, in a voice that chimed like crystal. "*You should leave it alone.*"

"Right, I wish I could." Noah's voice was high and strained. He avoided her hollow eyes. "But I really, really need the axe. Can you tell me where it is?"

Cassiopeia reached down, picked up the silver mirror, and propped it on her knees. She gazed into it. Noah gave him a sideways glance, like, *What am I supposed to do now?*

Nox shrugged helplessly. Before he could come up with a plan B, Cassiopeia moved again. She lifted one glittering hand and touched the mirror's surface.

Her fingers disappeared.

She reached inside the mirror with all the fanfare of a mechanic digging into a car's guts, her arm vanishing to the shoulder as she rummaged around. When she withdrew at last, it was with some difficulty. Noah jumped forward to prop up the back of the mirror as she pulled out her hand. She held a thick ebony shaft. As Noah supported the mirror, she used both hands and leaned back to extract the rest of it. The handle connected to a blade marked with intricate carvings; it exuded a dark energy. Even Cassiopeia's light seemed to dim in its presence.

It was just like Zahna had said: Nox knew it when he saw it. This was *the* axe.

Noah lowered the mirror and leaned it against the throne again. Cassiopeia held up the axe, presenting it to him handle-first. She had hidden it for the Devil; now she returned it to his heir. Before Nox could move to help, Noah was accepting it with apparent ease, even though it was almost as large as he was and had to weigh a ton.

"Thanks," Noah said dazedly, blinking down at the weapon and then up at Cassiopeia again. She sat back in her throne and did not reply.

"You okay?" Nox asked.

Noah limped back to them, axe propped on his shoulder. "It's a lot lighter than it looks."

"Let's go back to the center and find our way out of the maze from there," Thea said. "We'll stick to the route we took before, and . . . Shouldn't you be more careful with that?"

Noah was bouncing the axe in his good hand, a quick catch and release.

"Nah, it's—" His stiff fingers slipped on the next toss, and the axe landed on the ground with a *thunk*, blade embedded in the dirt. Hastily, he yanked it free, casting a sheepish look back at Cassiopeia. "Oops. Okay, I'm ready. Let's head back."

Up in the trees, the bats roused and took flight all at once.

"What was that?" Noah whispered.

"I think something scared them," Thea said.

"The moths," Nox said suddenly. "There's more of them."

He'd gotten so used to seeing the moths everywhere that he'd thought nothing of it when they'd infiltrated the maze. They were just part of the scenery.

Which was why they made the perfect spies.

Something flashed through the air—an arrow, whizzing past Nox's head. *That was close,* he thought. His relief was short-lived, because then:

Thea screamed.

26

THE ARROW HAD CAUGHT THEA'S SLEEVE, PIN-
ning it—and her—to one of the trees. She held her body at an
awkward angle to keep from being speared by the thorns.

Nox started toward her, but she made a slashing motion with
her free hand, the universal signal for *stay back*. "Run!"

"I can't leave you here!"

"No," someone said, in a deep, gruff voice that had gone so
silky and smug that it was almost unrecognizable. "No, you
really can't."

Adam strolled up the path, followed by Zahna, who was
already nocking another arrow. Her wound was bandaged up,
but she gritted her teeth as if every step pained her, and her
armor was still bloodstained. Adam, on the other hand, had
never looked better. He carried himself like a king in his court.
The moths alighted on his broad shoulders and arms, as if in
welcome.

"Zahna?" Thea said, in a tone of betrayal, like they couldn't
have seen this coming from a mile away. Yeah, Nox didn't feel
betrayed. He felt like a chump.

"I'm sorry," Zahna said, sincerely enough that Nox almost

believed her. "I had to make a deal with Adam so that he would save Umbra. Otherwise, she would have died. This was the only way."

"Nox, just *go*!" Thea said.

She tried to reach the arrows in her backpack, but with the way she was twisted around, she couldn't. Noah stood frozen in place with the axe clutched between his good hand and the useless wooden stump where his other had been. If Adam got his hands on the axe, Noah was dead. They all were.

But Thea—

"Nox," Thea said coldly. "*You owe me.*"

He remembered the pact they'd made after she'd pulled him out of the river. And he knew why she was bringing it up now. When she said, *you owe me*, she didn't mean *save me*.

She meant *trust me*.

Nox took off, snagging Noah's sleeve on the way.

"Think you can outrun me, boys?" Adam said, amused. But they didn't have to outrun him. As Nox and Noah dashed past Cassiopeia's throne, she rose. She was taller even than Adam. When she stood in the middle of the path, facing him, her chains glowed with an ominous inner light. She'd defended the Devil many years before. She was going to defend Noah now.

And she'd probably lose, just like last time. They had to get away before that happened.

Zahna sent a volley of arrows at them, but they kept running, shoes pounding over the dirt, until they found another intersection and skidded around the corner to safety. They kept running until they couldn't hear the sounds of Adam's fight with Cassiopeia anymore. Until they were too far away to hear if Thea changed her mind and called for help.

I can't believe I just left her, Nox thought numbly. After everything they'd been through, he'd abandoned her there with Adam and Zahna. How could he have done that?

Noah held the axe propped over one shoulder; as soon as they were out of immediate danger, he slowed, hissing with pain. Blood trickled out from under the hem of his jeans and dripped down from his sleeve. He made it only another few steps before stopping with a gasp—a horrible, winded sound like he'd been punched in the stomach.

"C'mon," Nox panted. "Just . . . just a little farther."

Noah tried to lower the axe to the ground, froze with a pained groan, and dropped it. He held his arms out to the side, elbows bent at awkward angles.

"I don't think I can," he croaked.

"You *can!*" Nox said. "I'll carry you if I have to!"

"Too late for that."

"What are you . . . ?"

He looked down. Noah's sneakers were busted open, completely shredded, and where his feet should've been, tree roots were slithering into the soil.

"Take the axe," Noah said. Bark had consumed his hands, twisting them into crooked branches. Twigs sprang from them, budding with leaves. His sleeves strained as his arms thickened into boughs.

"I can't—" Nox's voice broke. "I can't do this alone."

Where his roots had plunged into the ground, new ones

sprouted nearby, sliding over his body, wrapping him in heart-wood and new bark. It slowly climbed up his chest, encasing him.

"If anyone can," Noah said, "it's you."

His voice was thin, wet, like his airways were flooded and he was drowning on dry land.

"What, because of some freaky powers we don't even know how to use—"

"No, 'cause you always fight. No one ever scared you or made you back down, no matter how many times you got your butt kicked." He wasn't resisting his transformation anymore, Nox could tell. He was just trying to hold on long enough to get the words out. "You used to have to fight for both of us because I couldn't stand up for myself, and . . . I should've helped you. But I couldn't then. And I guess I can't now."

Nox's heart rate was skyrocketing. He could barely under-stand what Noah was saying—he could barely even think. "It wasn't like that!"

"I know you don't think of it that way, but you've always been the stronger one."

"That's not—"

"Don't let him win," Noah said. The skin on his face was turning gray, his eyes going dull. Sap welled up in the cracks in his dry lips. "You have to save Thea. *Promise me.*"

"Noah—"

"*Please.*" It came out raspy and breathless, as if the last bit of air in his lungs had abandoned him.

"I promise!"

What else could he say?

The outermost layer of bark crept over Noah's face, which froze like a carved wooden mask. He didn't look like the moros trees around Adam's cabin yet, but it was all too easy to see how it would happen, how in a few years, Noah would be unrecognizable, his features stretching and morphing and disappearing into the grain of the wood . . . how the moths would soon find him and burrow inside—

Nox didn't know where he found the will to do it, but he picked up the axe, and he ran. Tears blurred his vision. He'd failed. He'd lost Noah.

And Adam was still coming for him.

The axe felt perfectly weighted in his hands, like it was made especially for him. It had to be some kind of magic, because nothing that size and made of iron could possibly be that light. He clutched the handle tighter and adjusted it on his shoulder as he ran, palms growing slippery with sweat. Bursting into the clearing again, he found the cottage resting before him like some hibernating beast.

Do I just go in?

No—he didn't know if there was a back door or not. He'd be trapped. He had to lead Adam to another obstacle—something strong.

He knew just the thing.

He skirted around Ursa Minor. As he started to turn right, movement down the path to the left drew his eye. It was another bear, observing him from the shadows, this one so large it could've lifted its paw and smacked one of the trees to the ground. He froze. But it only cocked its head at him, amber eyes glistening, before it lumbered away.

It had recognized him as Keeper. That meant Noah was really gone.

Angrily, he swiped at his eyes and kept going. The ally he was searching for would be close by.

"Ah, ah. Not so fast, boy."

Adam was suddenly right behind him. Nox didn't have time to react. Adam hooked the back of his collar with one hand and plucked the axe neatly from his grasp with the other. Then he was shoved to the ground. He landed hard, face bashing into the dirt. His teeth cut his lip; he spat out blood as he pushed himself back up.

Adam stood over him, staring at the axe in his hands with a savage grin.

"You know," he said, his terrible black eyes finding Nox's, "I only had enough power to infect one of you at a time. I knew it was a risk. I thought I'd have to wait years before I could gather enough magic to make a new moros seed and send it to you. So imagine how amazed I was—how *ecstatic*— when you, the next and last in the line of succession, showed up at my doorstep."

He raised the axe high over his head. The iron gleamed, the curved edge of its blade bright as a crescent moon.

"Time for me to finish the job."

The axe swung down with a powerful *whoosh* of air—Nox rolled out of the way, barely in time, and the blade sliced deep into the ground. Adam tugged it free and raised it again. Nox crawled away, tried to get up and stumbled—

An earsplitting roar filled the air. His heart leapt as something flashed out of the darkness—something with wings and fangs, flames licking out of its maw—

It crashed into Adam, burying him in a cascade of claws and scales and teeth.

Nox didn't wait around. He got to his feet and fled, leaving Adam to deal with Draco alone. The clearing was almost a welcome sight at this point. He threw himself at the cottage door, flung it open, and locked himself in.

Not that he really thought a locked door was enough to hold Adam back. But he didn't have any other options. He needed to breathe—needed to stop and *think*—

A darkness and silence that had gone undisturbed for twelve years settled over his shoulders like a pair of skeletal hands. He pressed his back against the door. So this was it, huh? The Devil's house.

Nox's birthplace.

27

HE SNEEZED.

The place smelled musty and stale. Layers of dust coated every surface: the floor, the doorknob, the table by the window. The glass was caked with grime, so only the dimmest strains of moonlight made it into the room.

God. What was he doing here? What was the point?

He had no axe. No brother. No plan.

No way out.

To his shame, his eyes stung with tears. He'd really thought he could save Noah. Up until the very end, he had been convinced they'd find a way, because the alternative had been unfathomable. He had never let himself imagine what he would do if he failed. Now he realized it was because his imagination couldn't stretch to accommodate something as outrageous as the idea of Nox without Noah. Deep down, part of him believed, irrationally, that if Noah was gone, then Nox would cease to exist, too—in the same way that, when you turned off the lights, the shadows also vanished.

A scratching sound at the door made him flinch—something was trying to get in.

Great, he thought. *That's exactly what I need right now. More monsters.*

The scratching came again, patient and inquisitive, almost like a dog begging to be let back inside after a walk. Nox frowned to himself. Monsters didn't knock. Adam sure wouldn't.

Since he'd established that he had nothing to lose, he flung the door open.

It was the Devil himself. His puppet, anyway. The twitching wings and gnarled limbs were as sinister as ever. But Nox couldn't summon any fear. He was too tired.

"What do *you* want?" he asked. It didn't respond except to hop once. A leaf from its stuffed rib cage slipped loose and fluttered to the ground.

He stepped aside and let it in.

It bounced like an ugly pogo stick, the clack of its footsteps softened by all the dust. Its wings swept a clean trail over the floor. Nox shut the door and turned on the flashlight. It revealed a simple room not too different from Adam's cabin: there was a kitchen, a fireplace, some books. But there were also heaps of art supplies. Sketchbooks on the table. An easel in the corner. Tins of paint and colored pencils.

Nox's throat closed up. That was Mom's stuff.

She'd really lived here, with the Devil, or whatever his real name had been. This had been her home. Maybe she'd even planned to raise them here. Nox imagined it for an instant: growing up in the Nightwood, surrounded by magic, with a living dad, with a happier version of Mom who had time for her artwork because she didn't have to worry about holding down two jobs, maybe even with the settlement and Violet and her friends as a kind of surrogate extended family. Maybe the Nox from that alternate universe would've been smarter and stronger, and not just angry all the time. Maybe that Nox would've known how to deal with Adam.

How are you going to tell her about Noah?

It was such an awful thought he went lightheaded and had to press a palm flat against the filthy wall for balance. Suddenly, packing up and moving to Camp Chickenshit forever didn't sound like such a bad idea.

He followed the Devil down a hallway to the bedroom. The door was ajar. Inside, the Devil stood in the corner, facing the wall and hopping in place.

"What's wrong with you?" Nox said.

It hopped again. He scanned the rest of the room. The bed was spotted with dark brown bloodstains.

His stomach turned over. *Is that where we were born?*

Then it hit him. Mom had been here that night, when Adam had killed the Devil. But she'd gotten away with Nox and Noah. That meant . . . she'd had an escape route. One that Adam didn't know about. Otherwise, she would've had to navigate the maze after giving birth, bleeding and carrying two screaming newborns, without getting found by Adam or killed by one of the constellations. And yeah, Mom was pretty tough, but no one was *that* tough.

On a hunch, he went around the bed, to the corner where the Devil stood. He pressed his hand to the wall.

The wood flared with warmth and a faint inner glow, and

a polished ebony door materialized in the wall. Nox opened it and aimed his flashlight down what turned out to be a wide, tranquil forest path. Cool air wafted inside.

It was Myte's shortcut. Nox remembered what he'd said about one of the doors: that it led *to the heavens themselves and a hell like no other.*

The Devil went through the door and hopped away.

"You're welcome," he said to its back. Soon it had gone outside the range of Nox's flashlight.

So that was how Mom had gotten away.

Nox could leave, too. He could survive this. Maybe he could come back with help and . . .

But he couldn't bring himself to walk out of here without Thea. Not even to get help. It was out of the question. Anyway, no one out there *could* help him. Nox was the Evergreen Devil's heir. That made him the only person with any hope of fixing this. Maybe he'd die in the process, but as long as he bought Thea time to get out . . . then did that even matter?

He shut the door, and it vanished again. Somehow, just having a choice made a difference. He wasn't trapped. He *could* have left. But now that he'd decided not to, he had to follow that choice to the end, wherever it led him.

He had no brother and no weapon, but he did have allies.

Probably.

A plan formed in his mind while he pried the window open—no easy feat, as years of neglect had left it practically glued shut. It faced an opening in the thorn trees, far away from where Adam was *hopefully* still fending off Draco. He climbed out the window and dashed across the clearing as silently as he could, into the relative safety of the maze.

Adam wouldn't look for him there. Not anymore. Why bother? He had the axe and he had Thea. If Adam was smart—and he was smarter than Nox, that was obvious by now—then he wouldn't kill her. He had no reason to, not when he could use her to get what he really wanted: Nox. He'd take Thea and wait for Nox to come after her, back in his own territory, the cabin at the edge of the woods.

So that was where Nox had to go, too.

There was just one thing he had to do first. He found Perseus and led him back to where he'd left the tree formerly known as Noah Winters. Nox was probably wasting time—time he couldn't really afford to lose. But he couldn't leave Noah alone there.

"This is your new job," he said, looking up into Perseus's shadowed face. His armor was similar to Orion's, except his helmet was attached to his belt. In one hand, he carried the head of Medusa, from which Nox carefully averted his gaze. In his other, he wielded a diamond-bright sword. "Stay right here and guard this . . . tree. Don't let anyone near it. If you see any of those blue moths, kill them. Got it?"

Perseus nodded silently and shifted into a battle stance, his back to the moros tree, sword raised. Nox eyed it. Could he take a weapon from one of the constellations . . . ?

You kidding? he thought. *Who do you think you are?*

He grimaced to himself. Yeah, no. Nox was no warrior. If he tried waving a sword around, he was more likely to decapitate himself than do any damage to Adam. And there was no way the constellations' weapons did the whole "changing weight to match the person wielding it" trick like the axe. He'd be lucky if he could even lift it.

But then he glanced up again at Perseus, and the helmet swinging at his hip. In the myths, Hades loaned Perseus his Helm of Darkness to prepare him for his battle with Medusa.

It was supposed to turn its wearer invisible.

"Hey, Perce." He pointed at the helmet. "Think I could borrow that?"

28

DECIDING TO CONFRONT ADAM WASN'T THE
hard part.

Nothing Adam could do now would be worse than what
he'd already done. Losing to him meant death. But winning
just meant going home to a place that would never really be
home again. It meant figuring out how to live in a world without Noah. He'd never walk past Noah sitting crisscross on the
living room floor, painting a prop for the drama club. He'd
never have to kick Noah's gross track jersey at the hamper
because Noah left it lying around again. He'd never wake up
at the same time as Noah, make a mad dash for the bathroom,
and slam the door on him so he could brush his teeth first. He'd
never stay up past midnight with him watching horror movies
with the volume turned all the way down so they wouldn't wake
Mom up, or climb onto the roof together to look at the stars.
He'd have to go to high school without Noah, choose a college
without Noah, have dinner every single day with Mom and this
gaping absence between them. Tell people he *used to have* a
brother. In ten years, Noah would just be a fading memory. A
relic from his childhood, left behind, the way other people left

behind trick-or-treating on Halloween and Saturday-morning cartoons. The future yawned over his head like a black hole. Nox had nothing to lose. It was freeing, in a horrible sort of way.

No, the hard part would be convincing Violet to help.

The gap in the thorn wall didn't seal itself up when Nox left the Web. Now that the heir had returned, the Devil's territory was open again for good. Nox crept through the woods as quickly and quietly as he could manage. He didn't bother with the flashlight or the map—he remembered the way back to the settlement, and the Nightwood's perpetual darkness didn't hinder him the way it once had. He sensed the path without seeing it, knew just when to turn off toward camp, wove around the trees and stepped over tangles of bracken and poison ivy without having to look down. He could tell when he walked above a foxhole or rabbit warren, and that the things that lived there were aware of him, too. The Nightwood had its roots in him. No wonder Noah had asked if they'd been here before. He must have felt this, too.

Soon enough, he could make out the light from the settlement filtering through the woods. Shadow must have backed off, and much more quickly than Nox had expected him to, especially after what Violet had said a few hours ago. But the air smelled off. Rotten somehow. As he got closer, he heard shouts mingled with shrill, inhuman calls.

Something was wrong.

Nox broke into a run, quickly reaching the gate with the sentry tower.

"Hey!" he called up. "Let me through!"

But no one appeared. He put his shoulder to the gate and tried shoving; it wasn't locked, and he managed to push it open just enough for him to squeeze inside. He quickly passed under the outermost tree houses and suspension bridges and skidded to a halt somewhere in the middle of the campsite. The scene was pure havoc. The pungent smell of fish mixed with campfire smoke almost made him gag. Scaly, wriggly, terrier-sized creatures swarmed the place, tearing tents open with their sharp claws, knocking over the lanterns, tangling between people's feet and tripping them. One scurried between Nox's legs; he wheeled around to get a better look at it before it vanished. It had a sinuous, serpentine body with a long neck, and a face like a moray eel, all beady eyes and needle-sharp teeth. Its purple-blue scales reminded him vividly of the discarded skin from the river monster that had almost gotten him. No way these things got that big, though . . . did they?

What looked like every single resident of Camp Chickenshit had abandoned their usual duties in favor of dealing with the infestation. They chased the little eel-dragons with nets, pried them off the ladders to the tree houses, swore colorfully when they were bitten.

Did Adam do this? Nox thought, stunned.

A flash of purple caught his eye.

"Violet!" he shouted.

Startled, she dropped the writhing bundle of cloth and scales she'd been holding. An eel-dragon freed itself from its blanket prison and zipped away.

"Nox?" Her eyes traveled over his shoulder, noting the fact

that he was alone, lingering on the helmet he carried. "You lost the others."

"Look, I—I need your help," he said. "I should've asked before. *Please.*"

"I'm kind of busy!" she said, waving a hand at . . . everything.

"Hey, Nox! What happened to the other two musketeers?" They looked up. Nine hovered about ten feet over their heads, his powerful new wings flapping idly, clutching a handful of eel-dragons by the tail. They twisted and snapped at each other and made high, scratchy noises of complaint.

"Hi, Nine," Nox said.

"Wait there." Nine flew to the river and dropped off his hostages. They kept biting at each other the whole way down, until they disappeared into the water with a *plunk.* Then he landed beside them, his wings sending up eddies of dirt and dust.

"What's this?" He swiped the Helm of Darkness from Nox and tossed it up and down like a basketball. "Looks like you dug it out of a crypt."

"Forget about that. What are . . . those things everywhere?" Nox said.

Nine gave the helm another toss and then volleyed it back to Nox, who caught it against his chest—*ow*—and scowled at him.

"They're gastfers," Violet said.

"Caspers?" Nox said, mishearing.

"*Gastfers.* Rats with scales," she said darkly. "They live in the river and almost never come ashore, so I don't know what . . ."

"The birds are terrified." Nine pushed his goggles up to his hairline and tucked his hands in his pockets. "I heard their

301

warning calls earlier. You think something happened to Zahna?"

"Something did," Nox said. Bitter fury coursed through him at the sound of her name. "What does she have to do with this?"

"The three Keepers are linked to the Nightwood's magic," Nine said. "Zahna rules over the animals, and I *think* she's got some kind of freaky psychic connection to them—"

"She does not!" Violet interjected.

"If something's wrong with her," Nine said, ignoring her, "that would explain why the gastfers are acting up. I bet it won't be long before we're dealing with something even worse."

"Then there's no point putting them back in the river." Violet's eyes scanned the destruction of the settlement. Nox could practically feel the misery radiating off her. "They'll just come back. Echo would know what to do, but her team hasn't come back from the boglands, and Mom took a party to see Lord Wick. I have to go get one of them."

"No!" Nox said. "This is happening because of Adam. If you want this to be over, we need to deal with him."

"Deal with him how?" Nine glanced over Nox's shoulder, at the empty spaces behind him, like Violet had. And Nox knew what he was thinking: *Haven't you learned your lesson yet?*

"There's no *dealing* with Adam," Violet said. "He's inhuman. He's . . ."

A monster. Like Nox's father. Like Nox, too.

"*I* can deal with him," Nox said, doing his best to sound like he believed it. "But not alone. You said the boglands move around, and I'm guessing Lord Wick isn't a quick stroll away, either. It could take ages to find Echo or Radar. The longer you wait, the worse shape the settlement will be in."

Violet hesitated.

"We can't decide without everyone," Nine reminded her.

Nox wanted to argue—to demand they drop everything and leave *right now*. But he knew that demands wouldn't get him anywhere with Violet. Grudgingly, he followed her back to the lookouts' tree house while Nine fetched the others.

The lantern was already lit. Patch cowered in the corner; Betty sat opposite him, holding a gastfer in her lap. It gurgled happily as she stroked its neck.

"*Violet!*" Patch whined. "Make her get rid of it!"

Betty covered the gastfer with her arms and shot Violet a mulish look.

It was only minutes before Nine returned. He alighted on the edge of the doorway and squeezed inside, his wings tucked tight against his body. Deadlock climbed in after him. His sleeve was torn, and he had three neat cuts on his jaw that looked like they'd been made by a set of miniature claws.

"Great," he said when his eyes landed on Nox. "You again."

Nox would've apologized for what had happened the last time they'd seen each other, except, well, he wasn't sorry.

"Thea's in trouble," he said instead, looking around at the others.

And then he told them everything. Even the part about who—*what*—he was. They didn't interrupt, didn't even look that surprised. Until he explained his plan to get Thea out.

Deadlock's brow furrowed. "That's it?"

"Do you have a better idea?" Nox said, a little irritated.

"It's not that bad," Nine said. "If it works, Zahna and Adam won't even see us. It's a rescue mission, not a battle."

"If Thea and I can just get out of the Nightwood, Adam won't follow us," Nox said, pressing his advantage. "He loses most of his powers in the daytime, and I can hide from him the way my mom did. He'll have to give up on killing me until he can make another moros seed. And Zahna can go back to doing . . . whatever she does to keep the Nightwood under control."

"I'm in," Nine said. He shook out his wings.

"Show-off," Deadlock muttered. Then, louder: "Sorry, no. We're not in. Not even Nine."

"Hey! I'll go by myself if you don't—" Nine said.

"*No.* I'm the oldest, so I have to watch out for you guys. You're not picking a fight with the Nightwood's Keepers, especially not for a couple of outsiders."

"Thea didn't do anything wrong," Nox said. He knew he sounded desperate. He knew he'd crossed the line from persuading to pleading. A few days ago, he would've died before he begged anyone for help. But everything was different now. "If it wasn't for me, she'd never have gone anywhere near the Nightwood in the first place. I have to fix this."

"Count me out," Patch said, shrinking back into the corner. He tugged his hood down, as if to hide. "Zahna's scary. Never met Adam, but he s-sounds scary, too."

"But we need you!" Nine objected.

"We're *not* doing it," said Deadlock.

"You don't need me. Anyway, someone has to stay with Betty, right? Won't you be lonely if we all go and you don't?" Patch said hopefully.

Betty shook her head.

"Ha! See? Betty thinks you should help us," Nine crowed.

"Everyone shut up for a second." Violet glared into the middle distance, deep in thought. "I don't want to leave Thea there. If it was Nox, that's one thing, but . . ."

"Thanks a lot," Nox said, but there was no heat to the words. His spirits lifted. When Violet spoke, the atmosphere of the whole room changed.

"You know what I mean. It's like you said. Thea's not really part of this. But you . . . us . . . we *are* part of the Nightwood, like it or not. So . . ."

"No!" Deadlock said. "This is *not* happening."

"Patch, you can stay back if you want," Violet said. "No one's going to make you do anything."

"But . . . you're really going? All of you?" Patch said in a small voice. The others nodded, except Deadlock, who just sighed in a defeated sort of way.

Patch pressed his forehead against his knees. "F-fine. Guess I'm coming, too."

"Okay, so let's go, already," Nox said. Adam wasn't going to keep Thea around forever.

"Wait," Deadlock said. Nox braced himself for another argument, but Deadlock held out his hand. "Do what Noah did for Nine."

"Huh?"

"If something goes wrong," Deadlock said evenly, "I bet a power-up would come in handy."

"Are you sure?" Nox said. "We don't know what'll happen to you. And I don't know if I can undo it."

"Deadlock, *no*," Violet said.

Nox had to give him credit—Deadlock didn't waver. "There's no point in going if I can't help. Just try."

Nox didn't even know where to start. Or did he? He'd guessed that being angry was the trick. The thing that triggered whatever . . . abilities . . . he had now. Maybe this was a chance to test that theory out.

Fine. Get mad. Easy enough for him.

"Uh. Why are you glaring at me like that?" Deadlock asked.

"Give me a sec. I'm trying to focus."

His fingertips brushed Deadlock's. He held his breath; everyone did. And . . .

Nothing happened. He just sat there holding Deadlock's hand and feeling increasingly ridiculous. Nox pulled away.

"I can't get it to work," he said, scowling at his clenched fist, frustrated and ashamed all at once. "I've never done it on purpose before."

"Nox. It's okay." Deadlock sounded so patient it startled him. "Let's try it one more time. If it doesn't work, we can forget about it."

He held out his hand again.

Nox took a second to collect himself. What was he doing wrong? Did he need to be in mortal peril to make it happen? Noah had done it by accident, too. And it hadn't happened because his life was in danger. For Noah, it had been . . . natural. But it didn't seem to work like that for Nox. Maybe he needed a stronger trigger—he needed *more* anger.

He had been trying so hard to stay calm. To focus on his mission. To just—keep it together long enough to rescue Thea. So he'd tried to hold back the rage he felt toward Adam. There was so much of it he almost frightened himself. He was used to his anger coming in quick, short flares. *This* was different. This was a killing rage bubbling under his skin, ready to consume every other thought and feeling if he just let it. His blood pounded in his ears. His vision went dark at the edges. His hands shook.

Adam had taken Noah from his family—had taken *so many people* from all their families—and Nox was going to make him pay. No matter what it took.

Deadlock's eyes widened, and he flinched back, his hand beginning to drop. Acting purely on instinct, Nox grabbed his wrist. There was a sting like static electricity, a horrible shocked noise from Deadlock's throat, a dark flare as if light was being sucked out of the world—and Nox realized, suddenly, what a *terrible* idea this had been. He ripped his hand away. Deadlock wrenched back from him at the same time, banged into the wall, and then froze there, shaking, both hands clutched over his chest. The muscles in his shoulders rippled unnaturally, in a way that reminded Nox of Zahna's transformation.

Nox watched in guilty horror, praying to every deity he'd ever heard of, including Shadow, that Deadlock was going to be okay. Patch covered his eyes. The feathers on Nine's wings stood up, making them look about twice their actual size. Violet was the only one who moved, scooting over to Deadlock on her knees and propping him up when it looked like he might collapse.

"I'm fine—" Deadlock gasped. "Just feels weird— I think it's—"

Gingerly, he pulled away from Violet and rested against the wall.

"It's over." His breath escaped him in a *whoosh* of relief. His shirt didn't fit him quite right anymore; it stretched tight across his chest and shoulders, as if it'd shrunk. He tugged the neck down. Just under his collar was the edge of what looked like a brown shell, covering his chest like armor. "God. Wasn't expecting that."

He grabbed at the window frame to pull himself upright. The sill broke in his hand.

"Wow," Nine said. He reached over and rapped his knuckles on Deadlock's new and improved exoskeleton. "I bet this is bulletproof."

"Let's not test that theory out," Deadlock said weakly. He glanced up at Nox. "Thanks."

Nox wasn't sure if Deadlock should be thanking him, but he nodded.

They gathered what they needed and prepared to leave. Betty sat with the gastfer in her lap, soothed and sleepy now, its reptilian yellow eyes slitted shut. When she met Nox's gaze, there was a knowing glint in hers.

"Aren't you going to tell them?" Nox said suddenly.

Everyone looked at him, but he didn't take his eyes off Betty.

"*What gave me away?*" she said. The others jumped. They'd all heard the voice as if it was coming from inside their heads.

"B-Betty?" Patch said, eyes huge.

She looked at him dolefully. "*Don't tell me you're frightened of me now. I'm the same as I've always been. We all have our secrets, don't we?*"

"She's a Keeper, too," Nox told them, putting it together for the first time even as he spoke. "Not like me, though. Her powers come from the dimension of time."

He explained what Zahna had said, about how she and Adam had made a deal with a Keeper of Time to help them stabilize the Nightwood after the Devil's death had thrown it out of balance. Nox hadn't thought about who or where that Keeper of Time might be, and if he'd stopped to consider it, his first guess would've been someone like Echo. But a Keeper probably wouldn't have needed a rifle to deal with the bog witch—and it was Betty, and the people closest to her, who bore the marks of night magic on them.

"But your help came with a price, didn't it?" he said.

Betty pulled down her mask, revealing the spots that started at her cheeks and ran down her neck. One by one, they opened: not spots at all, but *eyes*, every last one of them aimed at Nox.

"*They gave a small part of the Nightwood over to my rule,*" Betty said. "*That's why they allow the settlement to exist. Because it's mine.*"

"And that's why no one ages here," he added.

"*Because I don't want them to,*" Betty said. "*Out there, I can't stretch your tiny life-spans. The other Keepers are so strict about* that kind of thing. Here, I can do what I want. I gave you eternal youth. I forbade Adam from harvesting anyone in the settlement for his moros trees. And I gave you gifts, too."

Betty glanced up at Patch's ears. Their mutations. That was what she meant by *gifts*.

"You did this to us?" Violet said, aghast, hand flying to her wrist, where her snake scales began under her jacket sleeve.

"*I didn't know it would upset you,*" Betty said defensively. All of her eyes swiveled around, blinking out of sync. "*I borrowed a little bit of night magic to do it. I am no true wielder of night magic, but what power lies in the land that Adam and Zahna gave me is mine to do with as I please, within reason; I took just a drop of it from the woods and gave it to you. It's because you're my favorites. It was supposed to be a good thing.*"

"That's why Noah and I could make their mutations stronger," Nox guessed. "We were just manipulating the night magic that you put inside them."

The others were staring at her in horrified silence.

"*You like your gift, don't you?*" she said plaintively, turning to Nine.

"I mean, yeah," Nine said, laughing awkwardly. "But you could've asked me first, you know?"

Her many eyes welled up with tears. "*Do you hate me now?*" she asked, sounding as young as she looked.

To Nox's surprise, it was Patch who answered.

"Of—of course not," he said. He shuffled over, gingerly lifting the gastfer's tail to make room, and put a tentative arm around her shoulders. "You're still our friend, right?"

"*Uh-huh,*" she said. But she was looking at Violet.

Violet inhaled shakily. "Patch is right. I wish you'd told us sooner, but I guess . . . we're your first human friends, huh?"

Betty nodded.

"And you're probably the reason Shadow gave us our lights back, right?" Nine chimed in.

"*The lord of ephemeral things has close ties with the dimension of time,*" Betty said. "*He listens to me. He has no choice. I could strip him of his godhood.*"

She sounded downright terrifying. Patch's ears went flat for a second, but he didn't take his arm from around her shoulders.

"Any chance you can help us with Adam?" Nox asked with little hope.

"*I made a deal with them to keep the Nightwood's magic stabilized,*" Betty said. "*To involve myself in a conflict between its Keepers would do the very opposite. I am bound by my word.*"

"What about the moros trees?" he asked. "Couldn't you . . . turn back time to undo the transformation, or . . . ?"

It wasn't until he had spoken that he even realized this hope had materialized within him, and as soon as he was aware of it, he wished that he wasn't. All of her eyes closed again, except the two normal ones, which were the deepest brown and looked suddenly much older than the rest of her.

"*Reversing time to bring someone back from the dead is not an option, for many reasons,*" Betty said. "*But you need not worry. They are not suffering, or aware of what has happened to them. Those moros trees are not people anymore. They are only trees, the same as any other in the forest.*"

That word, *dead*, sank inside him like an anchor. He kept having to re-remember that this word, which had always been *just* a word to him, was now something immense, something concrete and inescapable that encompassed Noah. A place where Noah was and Nox could not yet go. He had been thinking of Noah as *gone* or *lost* as if Nox had just misplaced him. But Noah was dead. Noah was dead. Noah was dead, and if Nox kept thinking about it, he wouldn't have the willpower to stand up and do what needed to be done.

"I understand," he told Betty distantly. It was the kind of lie you told when there was nothing left to say.

He left with the lookouts, Betty's dark eyes watching them climb out of the tree house and creep into the woods. As he'd suspected—and Violet quickly confirmed—there was a short-cut they could take to return to Adam's cabin. A pine tree stood alone in a small clearing on the edge of the settlement, where the moonlight lent its needles a frosted, wintry quality. Set into its trunk was a door with a brass knob. They all slipped through it one by one, chased off by the chittering cries of the gastfers.

29

GRIEF WASN'T A FEELING.

It was a metamorphosis. It rearranged Nox on a molecular level. He felt like his heartbeat had lost its rhythm, like his brain was twisting itself into pretzel shapes trying to assimilate this new reality.

More than anything, it was this grief that made him feel ready to take on Adam. The idea of being the Devil's heir and becoming one of the Nightwood's Keepers was so obscure to him—he barely had any idea what it really meant, other than that he didn't trip in the dark anymore. But he knew he was changed. He *felt* changed.

It was because of Noah that he could do this. Through him, Noah was still fighting.

As soon as the first moros tree burst into flame, Adam's back door opened. A shining carpet of light unfurled over the garden; black shadow seeped from the doorway, where a silhouette stood limned in gold. Zahna emerged, slamming the door shut.

She raised a hand and swept it down, and the flames abated.

Instantly, another moros tree caught fire.

"I don't know what you think you're doing, Nox Winters,"

Zahna said, "but it won't work."

She made her way to the burning tree, where the flames had spread rapidly, consuming its branches. Again, she snuffed out the blaze. She inspected the charred remains and examined the ground as if searching for tracks.

But Nox wasn't the one starting the fires. And Zahna shouldn't have been looking *down* for the culprit. She should've been looking up.

Another tree lit up like a torch, this one nearer to the side of the cabin than the back. With each new blaze, Patch—climbing through the canopy with a lighter and an oil canister borrowed from the settlement—was slowly leading Zahna away from the cabin.

The way to get good at winning fights was to lose a lot of them first. That was Nox's only advantage over Zahna and Adam: they didn't know how to lose. They didn't expect it. It hadn't crossed their minds that Nox could ever be anything resembling a threat.

And in their vast, lonely existences, it hadn't occurred to them that Nox had anyone to ask for help.

Once Zahna was out of sight, Violet darted from her hiding place to pound on the door. Then she stuck a hand up into the air. Nine swooped down to pick her up. Except he was wearing the Helm of Darkness, which made him invisible—so from Nox's vantage point, it was like she launched herself onto the roof by springing off a trampoline.

The door swung open a second time.

"I knew you'd come back," Adam said, with a wide smile. It

was as if he'd somehow gotten bigger since the last time Nox had seen him; his shoulders barely fit through the door. The flickering light from the fireplace inside was a subdued imitation of what the lookouts had started in the grove of moros trees.

He stepped outside, the axe propped comfortably against his shoulder. "I'll give you a quicker death than the one your brother suffered. Come, now. Don't draw this out."

Nox wasn't paying attention to him. He listened for Thea's voice—a scream for help, anything to let him know she was all right. But there was nothing.

That didn't mean anything, though, he told himself. She'd been quiet when Violet had captured them, too. She was probably too busy thinking of a way to save herself to do something as irrational as screaming.

Adam took a step into the garden.

And then the axe slid out of his hands.

Fury transformed his features into something ghastly and wicked. It was almost impossible to believe that this was the same man who'd sat Nox and Thea at his table with steaming mugs of tea and told them about jackalopes.

He spun around to find the axe hovering over his head. It swung down at his skull, forcing him to duck. But he recovered fast—too fast. He tried to snatch it from the air. His fingers brushed the handle. The axe jerked out of reach just in time.

Come on, Nine, Nox thought. *Quit messing around.*

"How are you doing this, boy?" Adam said quietly, like he was thinking aloud.

Nox tensed. Was Adam onto them already?

Nine carried the axe away from the cabin and the hiding place where Nox waited with Deadlock for their opening. Adam cast one last contemplative look into the woods. For a heart-stopping second, his eyes drifted over them, and Nox was certain they'd been spotted. But then he went after the axe, just like Nox had planned. The door hung open behind him, leaking its golden light into a sea of shadows.

Another twinge of worry tugged at Nox's mind. Who left a door open when they had a prisoner? Unless Thea wasn't there after all.

Or unless he wanted Nox to go in.

He and Deadlock crept closer to the cabin. Distantly, he heard the gasp of trees bursting into flame. Patch had led Zahna all the way around to the front of the cabin by then. In the other direction, there was a crashing, like Nine was swinging the axe around wildly. Which he probably was.

Nox and Deadlock would have to make a break for it across the open stretch of the garden and hope Zahna didn't see them through the window when they snuck into the cabin.

"Ready?" he whispered to Deadlock.

A shrill scream came from the front yard. Patch.

Deadlock inhaled sharply, a stricken look on his face.

"Was that—"

"I think so."

"I have to—"

"It's okay. Go!" Nox said.

Deadlock dashed through the woods, circling the cabin,

and quickly vanished. Nox didn't wait any longer. He bolted to the door, staying low. It took a second for his eyes to adjust to the firelight inside, and it was so quiet that at first he was sure he was alone. His heart sank.

Then he heard Thea's voice. "Nox?"

There weren't words for the relief he felt then—a relief that said even if everything else went wrong tonight, it wouldn't matter in the slightest. Because at least he'd gotten this one thing right.

30

THEA WAS PROPPED UP AGAINST THE FIRE-
place, where it was the brightest, which was why Nox hadn't
seen her right away. Her wrists and ankles were tied up. She was
dirt-streaked, scratched, and bruised, but he was pretty sure
she'd gotten most of those injuries before Adam and Zahna had
grabbed her. The crossbow she'd stolen from Zahna lay abandoned in the corner.

He grabbed a knife from the kitchen and hurried to her side.
"You okay?"

"Yeah. What's going on?" she asked. "Where did they go?"

"Um, well . . ." He sawed through the cords around her
ankles. They were so tight they left purple welts on her skin.
Shouts filtered in from outside.

Thea craned her neck so she could see out the window. "Oh
my god."

Automatically, Nox looked up—just in time to see Deadlock
pick Zahna up around the waist like a wrestler and throw her
into one of the singed moros trees. The blow would've snapped
a normal person's neck. Cinders rained down like black snow.

With a feral shriek that raised goose bumps up Nox's skin,

Zahna transformed into the half-wolf monster from before. It wasn't any easier to watch this time around, as her muscles swelled grotesquely, as she sprouted fur and fangs, as a row of bony spikes grew down her spine. Blood seeped through the bandages on her side; she'd reopened her wound, not that it seemed to slow her down any.

Like this, she was nearly twice Deadlock's size. She leapt at him, knocking them both to the ground; he pushed at her neck, holding her back, as her jaws snapped at his face.

Violet jumped off the roof. No, not *jumped*—she had one hand raised, clutching Nine's invisible one. She let go some five feet off the ground, landed in a crouch, and tackled Zahna, knocking her off Deadlock. Zahna flung her away with ease, rolling to her feet. But then the iron axe, suspended in the air, was swinging at her head. She ducked the blow and swiped blindly with her claws. They must have connected, because blood rained to the ground, and the axe trembled as if about to fall. Then Deadlock leapt at her again—

Nox forced himself to look away and focus on getting Thea free. If Nine was out there fighting Zahna, then Adam was probably returning to the cabin at that very moment. He had to get them all out of here, fast.

"Did you know," Thea said excitedly, "that a horned dung beetle can lift over a thousand times its own body weight?"

"Cool. Can you stop moving before I cut your hand off by accident? Also, maybe don't call him a dung beetle to his face."

He managed to slice through the last of the cords. Thea

rubbed at her wrist, where she had more of those crisscrossing welts. They ran for the back door.

But then Adam surfaced from the darkness beyond the threshold. His arms were crossed over his chest. As they froze in terror, he laughed, a booming sound like war drums.

"Nice try," he said. "But I don't need an axe to kill an arrogant little boy."

He closed the door, locked it.

"Thea, run," Nox said. He pushed her toward the other exit.

Adam was across the room in three huge strides. His hand wrapped around Nox's throat, lifting him off the ground. Nox stared into his empty black eyes while the fingers on his neck squeezed tighter, and tighter, and tighter. He couldn't breathe. Rainbow spots bloomed in his vision.

"You're still human, you see," Adam said. "I wanted the axe, yes. I'll need it, eventually, when the Keepers of the other realms try to interfere with my plans. But for you . . . well, anything will do."

Nox used his last mouthful of air to spit in Adam's face. It was worth it. As the edges of his vision began to darken, as his world narrowed down to Adam's twisted look of rage, his last thought was, *At least Thea got away.*

And then Adam bellowed like a wounded bull. His grip must have loosened, because Nox fell to the ground, gasping for air.

"*Witch,*" Adam hissed, turning. His hand covered a bleeding wound in his side. Thea stood before him, brandishing a poker from the fireplace.

"Get away from him!" She stabbed at him again. He caught the poker, tore it from her hand, and cracked her around the face with it. She toppled, a red mark slashed across her cheek.

"Thea!" Nox shouted. Thea tried to get up, but she was too dazed. She shook her head once, as if to clear it, but her elbow slipped and she ended up flat on the ground again. Adam stalked toward her, poker in hand.

Nox got to his feet. He lunged at Adam, grabbing the arm that held the poker. Adam's skin was feverishly hot, and his elbow bashed against Nox's chest. Nox held on, scratching blindly at Adam's arm and neck and collar, using all his weight to drag him down.

But it was like wrestling a slab of concrete. Adam was unbendable. With his free hand, he pried Nox off him and threw him to the side. Nox's world was a kaleidoscope of sensation—the hellish heat of Adam's skin disappearing, the rush of air around him, and then the slam of his back against a hard surface. His head bounced off the wall. He slid to the ground, pain radiating through his body. A metallic taste flooded his mouth—he'd bitten his tongue. He saw everything in threes; when he raised his hand to the back of his head and then brought it down to examine, there were fifteen bloodstained fingers wobbling before his eyes.

Someone was calling his name over and over. He heard it just faintly through the ringing in his ears. A dark shape swam in his vision.

Nox blinked, and the shape turned into Adam. He wore a vindictive smile. His shadow fell over Nox. His hand reached down. Nox couldn't move, and he couldn't have said if it was because of the pain or because he was still stunned from the blow to the head or if, really, he just couldn't think of a good enough *reason* to move.

If Adam didn't kill Nox now, he'd get him later with another moros seed. Noah was already gone. Thea would run once it was clear Nox was past saving. His half-baked plan was in shambles; his last hope was that he hadn't gotten Deadlock or Patch killed, too.

What was he holding on for?

He took a ragged breath. The musty reek of decay filled his lungs. Adam's hand snagged his collar and pulled him up.

A *bang* pierced the air like a gunshot; the front door bowed inward, splintering in the middle. Another *bang* and the iron axe's blade pushed through the hole. Another *bang*, and then a crash as the door flew off its hinges and fell to the floor in pieces.

The axe hovered in the threshold.

Adam dropped Nox and lunged for it.

31

THE AXE MADE A SWOOPING ARC IN THE AIR.
But Nine wasn't trying to hit Adam this time. He flipped the
shaft horizontal and shoved it against Adam's throat. Adam
choked and sputtered, hands reaching up to pry it away.

Then Violet flung herself through the door and collided
with him. Nox honestly had to admire her dedication to being
a human bowling ball. Adam was probably stronger than both
her and Nine combined, but they'd managed to unbalance
him—they pushed, and he staggered back, wobbling like a
Jenga tower as he tried to regain his footing.

Thea caught on to what they were doing before Nox did.
She grabbed the back of Adam's collar, unbalancing him even
more, and dragged him with the others to the fireplace. As they
heaved him over, she ducked out of the way.

Adam fell into the fire.

He let out an anguished roar that reverberated through
Nox's aching head. The flames engulfed Adam instantly. His
clothes and hair and beard caught fire. His skin blistered and
blackened. He clawed at the mantel, but his fingers slipped off,
unable to get a grip.

Thea pulled Nox to his feet.

"Come on!" she said.

The axe floated back outside. Violet and Nox followed; Thea was right behind them after she retrieved her crossbow and backpack full of arrows from the corner.

"Nine, you okay?" Nox called, remembering how Zahna had clawed at him earlier.

"It's fine. Just a scratch."

Zahna was pinned to the ground by a moros tree that had been messily chopped down at the base—Nine's work, probably. Deadlock and Patch held it down while she bucked and frothed at the mouth and tried to flip them off her. Even with their combined strength, they were barely holding on.

Nox jumped up between the two of them, adding his weight. He looked down into Zahna's eyes, her snout inches from his nose, her lips pulled back from her fangs in a ceaseless growl.

Traitor, he thought, baring his teeth in return. *You should've stayed out of this.*

"Nine!" Deadlock yelled. "Do something!"

"You can't kill her!" Violet was near hysterics. "The settlement— Oh my god we're all *dead*—"

Without Zahna, the settlement would be overrun with the Nightwood's many terrors.

"If we let her up, we won't make it out of here alive!" Deadlock fired back as Zahna roared wordlessly. Patch was pretty much just clinging to the tree for dear life at this point. His eyes were closed, and every now and then he let out a little whimper, like a kitten having a bad dream.

"I could just cut off one of her legs maybe?" Nine said in a reasonable tone of voice, the axe hovering over Zahna's clawed feet.

"*Don't you dare!*" Violet shrieked.

"Um," Thea said. "I think Zahna called in backup."

The predators of the Nightwood had come to their Keeper's aid. Wolves and panthers prowled through the woods, alongside other things that Nox couldn't so easily identify—a bearlike creature with a shaggy coat, a fox-ish animal with pricked ears and oversized paws, a long-necked reptile with teeth like a gator. Beings that were the distant relations of lynxes and hyenas and snakes. Like the jackalope and the gastfers, they loosely resembled animals from the outside world—except they had the wrong number of eyes, or a horn where there shouldn't have been one, and more fangs and claws than he could count.

They were surrounded.

With one last shove, Zahna flung the moros tree up and off, sending Nox, Deadlock, and Patch flying. The trunk landed inches from their heads and splintered with a deafening crash. Zahna got to her feet, shoulders heaving, blood and spit dripping from her teeth. Something that wasn't quite a coyote sidled up to her, and she rested one of her hands on its head.

"Give me the axe," she growled, her voice barely recognizable. "And perhaps I will let you go."

"What do I do, Nox?" Nine called from somewhere above him.

Nox pushed himself to his knees and took stock of his allies. Patch was curled up in a ball on the ground. He didn't look hurt. Just paralyzed with fear. Deadlock was clutching his head, bleeding from a cut in his temple. Thea and Violet stood back to back, Violet holding her puny stone knife and Thea aiming her crossbow at a big cat—a very big cat—that was eyeing her like she was made of tuna. She was almost out of arrows, though.

Zahna had won.

Maybe if Nox stopped fighting, she'd at least leave the others alone. He could take the punishment for all of them; it was only fair. As he opened his mouth to surrender, something moved overhead.

Eris moths streamed into the cabin, ribbons of them rising from the moros trees and braiding together as they flooded through the doorway. They converged on the fireplace. From the flames, Adam's charred hand reached up and thrust into the cloud of blue wings. He snatched a fistful and stuffed them into his mouth.

Zahna took their moment of distraction as an opportunity to make a grab for the axe, which hovered about ten feet in the air in Nine's invisible hands. She cleared the distance in one huge bound. Her pack took that as their cue to swarm the clearing, all of them baying and yowling and hissing with aggression. Nine swerved and just managed to avoid Zahna.

"Over here!" Violet shouted. He flew to her and dropped the axe.

Violet caught it and swung it wildly around, warding off the beasts. They stayed barely an inch out of its reach, teeth bared and snarling viciously. While Violet covered them, Thea shot three arrows at Adam in quick succession, bracing the crossbow against the ground to load each new bolt and then smoothly lifting it to her shoulder again and taking aim.

Deadlock had been cornered by a trio of mountain lions. He shuffled backward as they advanced—but then Nine swooped down and picked him up by the wrist. There was a horrible pop as his shoulder dislocated, and he gave a strangled cry of pain. But he was clear off the ground before they could leap at him. They collided as they landed in the space he'd been occupying, and a tussle broke out; they hissed and slashed at each other.

Zahna went for Violet—but Nox threw himself in front of her.

"Move, boy," she ordered.

"Make me."

He braced himself for the inevitable pain. But then a final silvery white shape streaked out of the woods, leapt straight over Nox's head, and pounced on Zahna.

It was Umbra.

She'd recovered, and now she was here, knocking Zahna to the ground, her paws on Zahna's shoulders and a growl rumbling deep in her chest. Zahna shifted back into her human form.

"Umbra, what . . . ?"

A noise from the cabin caught Nox's attention again. Adam hauled himself out of the fireplace. This time, when he grabbed on to the mantel for leverage, his ruined hand found purchase— had it gotten bigger? It must have; the brick cracked from his strength. He stood up, and his shoulders were so wide they scraped against the walls of the fireplace.

The top of the mantel broke as he pushed off it, crumbling away in a shower of coppery grit. A stack of books on top fell into the fire and then slipped out onto the ground, burning. But Adam didn't seem to notice. He helped himself to another fistful of moths, shoving them in his mouth.

Thea fired another arrow. It sank into Adam's gut, vanishing almost all the way to the fletching at the end. Adam plucked it from his belly like it was nothing more than a splinter and tossed it into the fire. Blood gushed from the wound. But it was nothing compared to the rest of his injuries. Half his beard had burned off, and the skin underneath was red and peeling. His clothes were in tatters, and his arms were scorched so badly in some places that white bone showed where the flesh had melted off. If he could still feel the pain, it did nothing to slow him down.

Zahna's pack had retreated; the ones who weren't taking out their aggression on each other had their eyes trained on Umbra and Zahna, like they weren't sure which one to obey.

"Stand down, Umbra," Zahna said. She'd managed to get to her feet again, but Umbra stood between her and Nox, tail fluffed up and ears flattened. It seemed she didn't approve of Zahna's alliance with Adam, and she'd decided to intervene.

But it didn't make any difference, because Adam was stalking toward him now. Some of the moths alighted on his shoulders and what was left of his hair; the rest flooded the clearing, thick as a fog. The animals scampered away before the moths could land on them, some of them making distressed, fearful noises and high-pitched yowls of warning.

The sound of wingbeats and a scattering of the moths overhead signaled Nine's return. He swooped around Nox, plucked the axe neatly out of Violet's outstretched hands, dropped down behind Adam, and gave it a mighty swing.

Adam turned with remarkable speed and caught the blade. It sliced his palm open. He ripped it from Nine's grasp and then, with his other hand, snatched at the air. Nine yelped—he'd been caught. Adam swung him down and tossed him away, and Nine crashed into a moros tree, its branches shuddering from the force of the blow.

"Nine!" Nox yelled. With Nine wearing the helmet, he couldn't tell if he was hurt.

Behind Adam, the flames from the burned books were spreading through the cabin. The walls had caught fire; the chimney coughed out sparks; the inferno swallowed the debris from the broken door and licked its way out the entrance. But Adam only had eyes for Nox. He was at least ten feet tall now, his features warped almost beyond recognition.

Between him and Zahna, Nox was cornered.

32

"IF YOU WERE SMART," ADAM SAID, HIS VOICE A broken rasp, his lips stained with soot, "you would have given up instead of dragging the other brats into this. But you're not. You're stubborn, like your father."

Do something, he told himself.

Violet had rushed to Nine's aid. Patch was missing in action. Thea had only a few arrows left. Umbra and Zahna were behind him; he didn't dare look at them. He didn't want to see the moment when Umbra finally yielded to her master.

If I really was anything like my dad, Nox thought, *I'd be able to fight back.*

Nox had inherited a quantity of magic that Adam thought was worth killing him for, and he had no idea how to use it. What a joke.

But he had to try—he hadn't come this far and brought everyone with him just to not try—so he summoned the memory of Perseus in the maze. The Devil had made the maze and everything in it, hadn't he? So couldn't Nox do the same? If rage was really all it took . . .

He concentrated, and something materialized before him—

But he couldn't make it solidify. It was nothing but a hazy

image, a mirage, and when Adam slashed the axe through it, it vanished.

"Pathetic," Adam said. His next swings were aimed at Nox's head, the blade whistling through the air. Nox backed away. Tripped over the wreckage of the moros tree. Fell.

And Adam was standing over him, the axe drawn back over his shoulder at the apex of his swing, so high in the air the cloud of moths fluttered around it like blue lightning sparking off a metal rod. Nox's breath came quick and shallow. His palms stung from landing on them, and his eyes stung from all the smoke.

It hadn't worked. And of course it hadn't. A lack of anger wasn't the problem this time; it was a lack of *skill*. He wasn't his father. But there was one thing he *knew* he could do. It could backfire on him, but it was all he had.

The axe came down, and Nox rolled out of the way. Its blade sank into the earth inches from Nox's cheek. In the time it took Adam to wrench it free, Nox lunged and grabbed hold of his burned, bloodied arm. Adam's face was inches from his, brows drawn together in confusion over bloodshot tar-black eyes.

This is for Noah, he thought.

The Nightwood's magic *wanted* to transform Adam. It wanted to transform anything it touched. And so it needed only the slightest suggestion from Nox.

By the time Adam realized what was happening to him, it was already too late.

"Impudent little wretch," he gasped in a voice shredded with pain. He grappled with Nox, prying at his hands, but Nox held on for all he was worth. At least until Adam's fist slammed into his side. Nox's strength left him; he instinctively curled into a protective ball.

Adam stood, the axe clasped loosely in one hand. Between the glare of the flames and the sweat dripping into Nox's eyes—the heat of the burning cabin was becoming unbearable—it was impossible to see him clearly. He had to get up, retreat, before the next blow came—

But Adam backed away first: one step, and then another, with jerky puppetlike movements. Nox blinked to clear his vision, until Adam swam into focus again. There was something . . . wrong with him.

His muscles grew again until his skin began to tear and bleed. Dark brown wings unfurled from his back. They dangled limp and weak. He staggered, his free hand clawing at his chest, as if he was on fire again.

The clearing was getting very, very hot. In his peripheral vision, there was movement, running—fighting? But Nox didn't dare take his attention off Adam, not for a second.

A broken, agonized noise escaped him. He dropped the axe.

Nox scrambled forward on his hands and knees and seized the handle. Adam lunged for him, but his new body was unwieldy, unbalanced. The firelight was reflected a thousandfold in his eyes, which had blown up to the size of baseballs and were covered in lenses like an insect's. He toppled over while Nox climbed to his feet.

A moth fluttered past his face and landed in Adam's outstretched hand. He devoured it.

No way was Nox letting him get another power-up. He

swung the axe. There was no time to think, no time to hesitate. Adam lifted himself out of the way, and the axe sliced into one of those flimsy wings. He let out an awful scream. The wing tore off as he pulled away—all he had left were a few ragged strips of it hanging from his back.

Another moth landed in his hand. This time, instead of bringing it up to his face, his mouth dropped open and a long, dark tube lolled out. A proboscis. It sucked the moth in— Adam's throat moved as he swallowed—and then withdrew, Adam's teeth clamping shut after it.

"What's . . . what's happening to you?" Nox said, revolted.

Then Adam was on his feet again, swiping at Nox's throat, so much bigger and stronger than Nox it hardly seemed to matter that Nox had the axe. There was so much smoke in the air. He was going to suffocate if this lasted much longer. Could he risk another swing? If Adam caught it again—

But Adam wasn't looking at Nox or the axe anymore.

"No!" he roared, his voice high and warped like the scream of wind flaying the eaves of an old house, his one remaining wing spasming weakly.

Only then did Nox realize that the cabin wasn't the only thing burning. Around them, the moros trees were bursting into flame. Not one, but three, five, ten of them were ablaze. The roar of the fire was so deafening it seemed impossible Nox hadn't noticed it sooner. Flames leapt at the sky, and the branches shook, as if writhing in pain.

As the moros trees died, the moths began to die, too. Their bodies rained down on the clearing. Nox shielded himself with his arms, looking around for the culprit.

His eyes found Thea first: she shot flaming arrows into the woods like Artemis herself, one by one, barely pausing. Patch, beside her, must have collected them when she'd run out. He doused her remaining bolts in oil, lit them up, and passed them to her. In the opposite direction, a branch with the end lit up like a torch hovered in the air, seemingly by itself, setting a trail of moros trees on fire. *Violet.* Nine must have given her the helm so she could sneak away from Zahna's pack, who abandoned the clearing as the fire spread. The trees nearest the cabin finally caught, too. The fire pressed in on three sides. And Nine? He and Deadlock—Deadlock, with his dislocated arm dangling useless by his side, who'd had a chance to get to safety but had come back anyway—grappled with Zahna. Deadlock held her off while Nine kept Umbra away from them, clutching the scruff of her neck with both hands, his wings beating hard as she struggled against him.

It was endless chaos and violence. People Nox had never done anything for, standing up for him like he deserved it. This had gone so much further than it ever should have.

As dead moths carpeted the ground, Adam's wings disintegrated like wet napkins, falling away from him in clumps. Either the damage to the moros trees or the dying moths had weakened him. He sank to his knees, picked up the moths in handfuls and stared at them uncomprehendingly.

Trembling, Nox hefted the axe over one shoulder and approached. This was it. He had to end this now, when Adam was helpless.

Then another voice said, "Enough!"

Zahna.

He inhaled sharply, looking around for Nine and Deadlock. But they were okay, mostly. Deadlock had finally collapsed, and Nine knelt by his side, tugging his good arm around his shoulders and shifting as if to carry him away from the battlefield, for good this time. The wound on Zahna's side bled heavily; the bandages were completely soaked through, useless. She bore bruises, knife cuts, thin gashes as if from catlike claws.

But her shout hadn't been directed at Nox. She went straight for Violet, wrestled the flaming branch from her, threw it to the ground, and stamped it out. Umbra knocked the crossbow from Thea's hands.

Shakily, Zahna tried the same sweeping gesture that had made the flames abate before, but her movements were sluggish. She had lost too much blood. And every time she put out one of the trees, another caught fire. The blaze was spreading fast despite her efforts. The smell of the burning moros trees was putrid and overpowering, like sewage mixed with smoke.

"Adam!" Zahna said, whirling around to them. "We *must* put this fire out."

But Adam didn't move. He was bloody, burned, and his face—half-insect, half-human—was slack and dazed.

"Listen to me!" Zahna shouted, still fighting the fire with her faltering magic. "If this spreads any farther into the Nightwood, we won't be able to contain it."

Nine had dropped Patch off somewhere with Deadlock and returned. He picked up Violet next; only Thea remained, but

Nine would be coming back for her, too.

"Come with us!" Thea called to Nox, holding out her hand.

"Just go! I have to finish this," he said, and turned to Adam.

Nox had never wanted to kill anyone before. He wasn't sure he wanted to now. But he'd also never hated anyone or anything more than he hated—

"*Adam!*" Zahna's voice rose with the din of the fire.

The desperation in her voice made Nox look up again. Zahna was barely visible through the flames. The air shimmered from the sweltering heat; Nox had sweat through his shirt. Smoke poured into the night.

If Zahna failed, the fire would keep spreading unchecked.

And then what would happen? To Myte, and to Umbra, and to Shadow? To the Devil's Web and all the constellations, to Perseus and the moros tree he guarded, to the modest little home Mom had lived in once?

Nox had seen terrible things in the Nightwood. But he'd seen a lot of amazing things, too. And he'd never give Thea the satisfaction of hearing him say it out loud, but it was—kind of beautiful. It wasn't the Nightwood's fault Adam had done what he'd done.

But Noah was still gone. And Nox wanted revenge. He wanted it more than he could remember ever wanting anything else in his life. He hadn't really believed he could survive his encounter with Adam, but here he was, with the power to end him once and for all. As he stood over Adam's broken form, as he drew the axe back over his shoulder to swing, that power coursed like electricity through his blood.

Adam curled up on the ground, hands over his face, twitching like a dying roach. A single blow would be enough.

There was a long, dangerous creak somewhere close by, and Nox couldn't tell if it was louder than the fire—or if he'd *sensed* more than heard it. It had come from one of the moros trees near Zahna.

She didn't notice. Didn't move. Didn't even look around.

It tilted, poised to collapse on top of her.

33

THE AXE SLIPPED FROM NOX'S HANDS.

"Zahna! Look out!" Faster than he could have consciously made the decision to do it, he was running toward her, weaving around burning moros trees—but he was too far away to help.

She moved just in time. The tree crashed to the ground, red-hot splinters flying in every direction. Sparks puffed out of the smoldering wreckage.

He could've stopped then. Gone back and picked up where he'd left off with Adam. But he kept going and came to a precarious halt beside her, almost slipping on ash. She peered down at him in shock, her silver-white hair damp with sweat and blood, sticking to her face.

"Let me help," he said. He wasn't letting himself think about what he'd done.

Or what he *hadn't* done.

"My magic is almost completely drained," she said grimly. "You will have to take on the brunt of the work. But I will guide you."

"What do I do?" His throat felt ragged from the smoke,

and from where Adam had grabbed him earlier. Scrapes he hadn't even noticed he'd gotten stung as sweat ran into them. Everything hurt, even breathing hurt, and part of him was still certain that he was making a mistake.

"Tap into the core of your magic. You carry it here," she said, placing her palm over her abdomen, below her sternum. In the firelight, her skin took on a sick yellow tinge. A pink burn streaked across her cheekbone. "That's the root of your connection to the Nightwood."

Nox pressed a hand over his ribs and tried to feel the power that he'd used to tamper with Adam's transformation. Instantly, the fires surged up, higher than ever. They were two or three stories tall, solid walls of flame and fury on the verge of engulfing them both.

Zahna grasped his shoulder. "Calm down! Your anger is making the fire stronger."

"How can I not be angry?" Nox yelled. He was dizzy from the heat; he felt like the skin was going to melt off his bones. There wasn't an inch of him that wasn't soaked with sweat. And Noah was *still gone*, and Adam was alive, and he was supposed to somehow calm down?

"You must find a way!" Zahna snapped in return.

"It only works when I'm mad!"

A peculiar expression crossed her face, like he'd surprised her. Her grip tightened on his shoulder for an instant, and then gentled.

"If rage is what you give it, then rage is what you'll get in return," Zahna said.

But what if he let go of the anger and there was nothing else left in him? Not even fear or grief. Just nothing.

"I'll help," she said, in a strained tone of voice that might have been an attempt at reassurance. "Everything that's left of my power, I'll use it to prop you up. Two of us will be enough for this task. I promise."

Fine. It wasn't like he had another choice.

He forced himself to take long, even breaths, to slow his heart rate like he meant to fall asleep. He shut his eyes. The light bled through his eyelids, and the heat wrapped around him like a quilt on a summer night, oppressive and thick. He remembered the way Noah had studied Nine's wings with such awe. Despite everything that had happened to him, he'd thought the Nightwood's magic was amazing. Miraculous, even. Maybe that was the key. Maybe it was all about accepting the power and everything that came with it. The good and the bad.

The part of Nox that could navigate in the dark and map out animal burrows by intuition alone also knew all the places where the Nightwood burned. Once he was aware of it, he couldn't *stop* being aware. It overwhelmed him. What he felt wasn't pain—because pain was not exactly how wood experienced flame—but he felt something, and it was agony, an inhuman agony.

Any fire that burned the Nightwood became part of the Nightwood, and so it was part of Nox, too. He reined it in like his own anger. As he did, more memories surfaced: the river, the staircase, Deadlock's power-up, Adam's transformation . . . they all had something in common. Every time he'd used his powers successfully, he had been thinking of Noah.

Anger wasn't what had given him the strength to survive. It was something else, all along.

The fire dwindled. Its roar quieted, and the suffocating heat lifted incrementally. But after all outward signs of it were gone, it was still inside him, burning, and somehow he was certain it always would be.

When he opened his eyes—stinging, he told himself, because of the smoke and nothing else—Adam's cabin and the grove of moros trees were blackened ruins. The axe was where Nox had left it, an island of gleaming iron in a sea of dead moths.

But Adam was long gone.

Thea and the others were waiting for him at the crossroads where the path from Adam's garden split toward Myte's short-cut. It seemed like ages since Nox had been there, though he knew it had been less than a day. He carried the axe. Zahna accompanied him in silence, and Umbra limped along at her side.

Violet stepped back warily at the sight of her. Patch went so far as to hide behind Deadlock, who clutched his injured arm with a pained grimace. Only Nine looked comfortable. He sat crisscross on the ground, combing the ash out of his wings.

They'd risked so much for Nox. And for each other and, maybe most of all, for their home. They could've hated the Nightwood for what its magic had done to them. But they didn't. What the Nightwood had given to them was worth what it had taken. Like how having Noah as a brother had been worth how much it hurt to lose him. And how the hope of being able to save him had been worth everything Nox had gone through the last few days. Even worth how terrible it felt to have failed.

Maybe that was what love was. Accepting the bad that came with the good. Knowing the cost and making the same choice anyway.

Thea threw her arms around Nox the moment he was in reach.

"I'm so glad you're okay!"

He only just got the axe out of the way in time, holding it down at his side. His other arm went around Thea and squeezed back lightly. Just for a second.

"Ugh," he said with mock disgust, after the second had passed. "Get off me."

"Jerk." She pulled away with a weak smile.

He grinned tiredly back at her and then glanced up at Zahna. "Are her parents going to be okay?"

"Yes," she said stiffly, as if she, too, was wondering what she was still doing there. "Adam poured much of his magic into the moros trees. Now that they're gone and he is weakened, the spell he cast on your elders will have worn off. It will take him a long time to regenerate his powers."

"Not all of the moros trees are gone," Nox said. "There's still—"

He couldn't finish the sentence. Beating Adam and saving the Nightwood had seemed so very important in the moment. Now that it was all over, though, he wasn't sure any of it had mattered. Probably nothing would matter ever again.

"Your brother?" Zahna finished for him. "So he completed his transformation."

"Yeah," he said blankly. "He's in the maze."

"And have the eris moths claimed him yet?"

"No," Nox said, certain that Perseus hadn't failed him. He put the axe down and wiped his sooty hands on his jeans, looking at no one.

"The eris moths and the moros trees represent a cycle of life and death. When the eris moths infest a moros tree, they sap the life force from the transformed victim, and thus new eris moths can be born. After that stage, the victim is well and truly gone," Zahna said. "But as long as the eris moths have kept away, the transformation can be undone."

It took a second for those words to penetrate. When they did, he spun around, heart hammering. "By Umbra?"

At the sound of her name, Umbra gave a plaintive little whine and lay down, resting her head on her two front paws. Her coat was more gray than white now and lacked its usual shine.

"Umbra is still unwell, and my magic is entirely depleted. But you are the Nightwood's Keeper now, too. You can perform the extraction yourself," Zahna said. "A self-extraction is not possible. If there hadn't been another heir to take his place, then he would have needed me or Adam. But *you* can save him now."

Nox was too stunned to respond.

Nine got to his feet and shook out his wings. "Sounds like you'll need a lift."

He left the axe with Thea, got waved off by Violet and the others when he tried to thank them, and finally took Nine's

343

outstretched hand. Nine launched into the air, towing Nox with apparent ease. They'd barely touched down in the maze before Nox was running to the moros tree, inspecting it from every angle. Perseus was right where he'd left him. No moths in sight.

"Um, here," Nine said, passing the Helm of Darkness back to Perseus.

Nox could make out Noah's features all too clearly in the deeply grooved bark. Was saving him really as simple as Zahna said? What if he did something wrong, and made it all worse? *Again?*

But Noah needed him to try.

Nox reached out. His fingertips brushed the trunk of the moros tree. Then they kept going, sinking into the bark with only the lightest push. He could kind of feel it—a faint tickle, like powder settling over his skin. Then a warmth that felt, incongruously, like daylight. He reached for it until his fingers closed around something solid, and then he withdrew his hand. The moros seed's brilliant light showed through the cracks between his fingers. When he uncurled them, it shone like a palm-sized sun.

Bark gave way to skin. Roots unburied themselves. Leaves and branches dissolved into dust. And then Noah was there, himself again, collapsing. Nox barely caught him before he slammed into the ground.

He was real. Solid.

His closed eyes and slack expression terrified Nox for an instant, until he heard the rasp of his breathing and remembered what Zahna had said before: Noah was in a healing sleep.

He'd wake up on his own. This time, Nox didn't have to do anything but wait.

For all that Nox had struggled to accept the thought of moving on without Noah, it was almost as difficult to believe that he no longer had to. He stood perfectly still, propping up Noah's slumped body, terrified that if he so much as breathed, Noah would dissolve into nothing like the moros tree had, and this illusion of victory would be shattered.

"So . . . are we standing around for a reason or . . . ?" Nine said.

Nox looked up, having forgotten he was there. Nine ambled over to them, his sleek new wings tucked against his back. Perseus stood to the side, head tilted toward Nox. In the Web, the only sound was the gentle swaying of the thorn trees, the occasional fall of their leaves.

"Just one more thing I need to do," Nox said.

He dropped the moros seed and stomped on it until it turned to golden dust under his shoe. At last, the first cautious traces of relief grew within him, like dawn on the horizon. Nine took half of Noah's weight. Flying was out of the question—Nine wasn't strong enough to manage two passengers. But Nox had once promised that if Noah couldn't walk, he would carry him. He could finally keep his promise.

Together, they walked Noah out of the maze.

34

IT WASN'T EASY GETTING NOAH TO THE DAY house. The trip took them twice as long as it should've, but between him and Thea, they managed. The sun beamed down on them, a white-gold medallion in a pale blue cape of clear sky. The front door hung open. He and Thea traded uneasy looks.

Sounds floated out of the kitchen—footsteps, a woman's voice.

Nox deposited Noah on the couch in the living room, and then he and Thea crept up the hall.

The first thing he saw was the Devil puppet: it stood in the corner, hopping serenely in place. In the unforgiving light of day, it wasn't scary at all. Just sad and run-down.

Thea's parents were still sealed in their cocoons. Someone with wavy red hair, her back to the doorway, was carefully cutting them free.

Nox was just about convinced he was seeing things.

"Mom?"

She turned. The knife slipped from her grasp and landed on the floor with a clatter.

"Nox," she said, voice breaking with relief. Nox didn't remember crossing the room, but then her arms were around him, and his face was pressed into the collar of her blazer, and he could faintly smell her lavender perfume, and if he closed his eyes, he could almost pretend he was home again.

When they'd all stopped answering their phones, Mom had gotten in her car and driven straight to Evergreen. She found:

The Day house in the middle of being digested by the Nightwood.

Her best friend and his wife, unconscious and slowly turning into bugs.

Two empty bedrooms and three missing children.

And a clay-and-wood rag doll that had her dead boyfriend's wings pinned to it.

From there, she'd pieced together most of what had happened.

Nox had so many questions for her they all ran together in his mind, mixing into a nonsensical jumble, like loose Scrabble tiles. He decided to save them for later, after they'd all cleaned up the house—pulled the weeds from the floorboards, released the toads safely into a nearby pond, opened the windows so the bats could pour out at dusk. And after Noah woke up. Because he deserved those answers just as much as Nox did, or maybe more.

Once he emerged from his "healing sleep"—which turned out to be a week later—Noah got to quit his online classes and go back to a real school with Nox. If you could call Grayville Middle that. Nox still thought it was more like purgatory. But since he'd just transferred in, Mom wanted him to finish the semester there. Anyway, in the chaos of their return, she had forgotten to let anyone know she wouldn't be in the office the next day, and now she was out of a job. They needed time to regroup, and Weston insisted they do it there in Evergreen.

"Besides, I owe you," he said over breakfast.

Mom set her mug down too fast, so a bit of coffee spilled over the rim. "For what?"

It was Noah's first Sunday morning awake and healed, and Aster had commemorated the occasion with a feast: heaps of eggs, pancakes, and bacon, a plate of sliced apples and berries, two pitchers of iced tea. Nox was so busy stuffing his face he almost missed the turn the conversation had taken.

"It's really my fault Nox and Thea took matters into their own hands," Weston said, tugging his hat down in a fidgety, embarrassed gesture. "He told me he saw Umbra, and instead of explaining, I, well, I tried to make him think he'd imagined it. I was afraid he'd panic if he knew the truth. I didn't want to scare him. And I knew it would lead to questions about—about his father, and—"

"And *I* made you swear not to tell him about that," Mom finished. "So if anyone is to blame, it's me."

"No one is to blame but Adam," Aster said firmly.

Nox had frozen with his fork halfway to his mouth. He'd thought it was a given that everyone blamed *him*. Yeah, and Adam. But Adam was evil. So he didn't really count.

Maybe no one expected any better from Nox. But Nox expected better from himself.

Thea studied him across the table like his thoughts were scrawled over his forehead. Avoiding her eyes, he slammed his fork down and grabbed a pitcher of tea instead, nearly spilling it as he refilled his glass.

"Why didn't you want to tell us about Dad?" Noah said through a mouthful of bacon.

"I didn't want you to have to worry about sprouting horns, or—"

Noah swallowed. "We . . . won't, right?"

"I'm—I'm pretty sure," Mom said.

"Okay." Noah prodded at an egg yolk with his fork, brow furrowed in thought. "Did he really have horns?"

"I kind of liked them," she said wistfully.

Noah looked like he wished he hadn't asked.

But Nox suspected that was the other reason Mom was suddenly fine with staying in Evergreen: the puppet.

The Day house had been her safe haven as a teenager. Whatever fraction of the Devil remained inside the puppet still knew that much. That was why it used to fly around the house at night. Why it used to scratch at the window of the bedroom she'd once occupied. And why it was so determined to get back to the cottage, with the hidden passage that she had used to escape the Nightwood. All this time, the Devil had been looking for her. Now it followed Mom around the house like a duckling. She swore she was going to take it back to the Nightwood soon, but she also got misty-eyed when she talked about it. So Nox stopped asking. He had enough to worry about. Like whether he'd made the right choice in leaving Adam alive.

Knowing that Adam was still out there kept him up at night. But at least he had the axe. It rested against the wardrobe with Noah's jacket dangling off the handle, enjoying a new life as a coat rack. If Adam tried anything, Nox would be ready.

Soon, winter sauntered up the driveway and peeked inside through the windows. Most nights, Thea joined him and Noah on the roof, all of them bundled up in scarves and sweaters. They shared packets of chips and played games on their phones and told each other scary stories featuring the sort of monsters that—they were fairly certain—didn't actually exist. But sometimes Nox caught her resting her chin on her knee and gazing off to the north with a look on her face he couldn't read.

He nudged her shoulder. "What's up?"

She shook her head and leaned back on her hands. "Nothing. It's just—I thought I knew everything about Evergreen," she said. "But there's this whole other side of it that I never knew existed."

"We're better off pretending it doesn't," Nox said. Thea was silent. "*Right?*"

"What? Yeah! I mean, obviously," Thea said, not meeting his eyes.

"You think they'll be okay without you?" Noah asked quietly.

"*Who?* The constellations? Taurus won't care if I never show my face in the Nightwood again, I promise."

"Not them. I mean, like, everything. The Nightwood. All of it," Noah said. "It's supposed to have three Keepers. Now it's only got one."

He was lying back, black hair fanned out against the shingles.

The light from the attic diffused into the air and put a yellow glow in his eyes. Nox wondered if Myte was looking at that attic light right now. Then he forced himself to stop wondering. He didn't care. *Really.*

"They'll figure it out," he said, and the words were unconvincing even to him.

Okay. So maybe he cared. He had reached into the Nightwood's magic with his own—the magic that lived within him still, which he felt most acutely when the stars came out. He had snuffed out a wildfire, and sometimes he still woke up drenched in sweat, convinced he was surrounded by flames. He thought a lot about Camp Chickenshit—fine, *the settlement.* Had they gotten the gastfer infestation under control? He hoped so.

He lay back next to Noah, letting his head thunk against the roof. Thea's shoe tapped lightly against his, and he held his breath, expecting her to say something ridiculous—something like, *Maybe we should go back*—an idea he'd have to shut down right away, of course—

"Yeah," she said reassuringly. "They'll be fine."

He breathed out. Right now, he was exactly where he was supposed to be, with the people he was supposed to be with. The woods murmured sleepily of secrets it did not care to share with him. The stars made their predictable rotations. Tomorrow, he would find them again, just where he expected them to be.

For Nox, that was enough.

ACKNOWLEDGMENTS

I am immeasurably thrilled and grateful every time I near the end of a new project and have the opportunity to look back on the journey that led here. I have many people to thank for making this possible, chief among them being my editor, Megan Ilnitzki, whose input drew so much more magic and adventure out of this story, and made it better than I'd even imagined it could be. Thank you as well to my agent, Erica Bauman, who has supported both me and *Nox* every step of the way.

Next, thank you to the Harper team for their hard work on this book throughout the publishing process: Caitlin Lonning, Lana Barnes, Alexandra Rakaczki, Jacqueline Hornberger, Mimi Rankin, Nicole Wills, Christina Bryza, and Abby Dommert. And I am grateful beyond words to designer Molly Fehr and illustrator Xiao Tong Kong for creating the cover of my dreams and bringing Nox, Thea, and Umbra to life so beautifully.

My fellow wolf-loving author Meg Long was *Nox*'s first reader and biggest cheerleader. Thank you, Meg, for your support, advice, and friendship, and also for telling me that I should let Nox hug Thea back, even if it was only for one moment. Additionally, a huge thanks to Katie Zhao, M. K. England,

Anne Ursu, Lisa Stringfellow, Lora Senf, and Tracy Badua for the kind words they shared about *Nox* when it was just starting to head out into the world. To my friends in the industry, both near and far—especially Rachel, Chelsea, Kamilah, Ysa, and Gina—thank you for countless hours of drafting together (or at least pretending to draft) over cups of coffee, for swapping memes and Sephiroth fan art, and for reminding me that even in the pursuit of a craft as solitary as novel-writing, you're never really alone. Finally, I am always grateful to my family for their love and support.

Thank you to the booksellers, librarians, reviewers, and educators who help books like this one find their readers—and thank *you*, reader, for spending a little of your time with this story. *Nox Winters* kept me company through many long days and even more nights, and I hope that you, too, find something in its pages worth staying up for.